BLOOD AND TREASON

There was silence for a moment as the naval officer stared off into space. When he answered, his face was devoid of all expression. "Everything has a price, Sam. . . . Including peace. Bridger's out there somewhere right now. He's a highly trained naval officer, a combat veteran, an expert in strategy and tactics, and quite knowledgeable about our current defensive capabilities." Swanson-Pierce met McCade's eyes. "Think about it, Sam. . . . What if he offered that experience and knowledge to the Il Ronn, in return for their assistance in destroying the pirates?"

"What you're saying," McCade said thoughtfully, "is that the Il Ronn might allow themselves to be used . . . and in doing so, learn enough from Bridger to give them an edge in a war with the Empire."

"Exactly," Swanson-Pierce replied.

GALACTIC BOUNTY

WILLIAM C. DIETZ

ACE BOOKS, NEW YORK

This book is an Ace original edition.
It was previously published under the title *War World*.

GALACTIC BOUNTY

An Ace Book / published by arrangement with
the author

PRINTING HISTORY
Ace edition / November 1986

The Penguin Putnam Inc. World Wide Web site address is
http://www.penguinputnam.com

ISBN: 0-441-87346-4

ACE®
Ace Books are published by
The Berkley Publishing Group, a member of Penguin Putnam Inc.,
375 Hudson Street, New York, New York 10014.
ACE and the "A" design
are trademarks belonging to Charter Communications, Inc.

PRINTED IN THE UNITED STATES OF AMERICA

10 9 8 7 6 5 4

To Grace Dietz who taught me to love books,
To Marjorie Dietz who believed I could write one,
To F. M. Busby for his advice and support,
And to Sue Stone, who found this story, read it,
and improved it.

One

FROM HIS VANTAGE point at the bar, McCade could watch the entire room. It was saturated with smoke and noise and filled to overflowing with people. Cadien was there somewhere. McCade could feel it. An evil presence. A hunted animal gone to earth. But where? All sorts of people mixed and mingled in a swirl of movement and color. There were miners just in from the asteroids eager to live out fantasies devised a million lights away. There were long-haul freighters, the stink of their sweat still on them, celebrating the end of a three-month run. Navy men drank and laughed, trying to forget the fear and boredom of patrol along the frontier. And yes, there were also those like McCade himself. Hunters of men, watching and waiting for one of the many faces they'd memorized, hoping that tonight they'd make the big score. Among them moved drug vendors, thieves and prostitutes, all plying their various trades. All were welcome in Floyd's Pink Asteroid Bar and Grill. All helped make Imperial Earth possible. None were welcome among its more refined pleasures.

McCade slid off his stool. His stained leathers creaked slightly as he stood. Alien suns had darkened his skin and etched deep lines around his gray eyes. Under thick black hair, his features were strong and even. A muscle twitched in his left cheek. He moved with the smooth confidence of a man well aware of his own ability. His right hand brushed the grip of the slug gun worn low on his right thigh.

He felt the familiar flutter of fear low in his gut as he began to circle the room. Cadien scared hell out of him. Psychopath. Professional assassin. Butcher. Cadien was all these and more. On New Britain he'd fulfilled an illegal assassination by blowing up a yacht along with its owner. In the past he'd committed many lesser crimes and gotten away.

But this time Cadien'd gone too far. Among those who died on the yacht was the Emperor's favorite niece. A price was placed on Cadien's head. One million Imperial credits, dead or alive. Every hand was turned against him, so Cadien ran. From planet to planet and from system to system. Bounty hunters followed—men like Sam McCade.

Since the cost of creating and operating an Imperial police force was considered prohibitive, interplanetary law enforcement was carried out by bounty hunters. They were a strange breed. Both hated and feared, loners mostly, they were forever excluded from the society they served. Planetary law enforcement officers resented them, and placed them on a par with those they hunted. Citizens often romanticized them, imagining their lives to be both glamorous and exciting. But no one wanted them around for longer than it took them to do their job. So bounty hunters were constantly on the move.

For a few credits at any public terminal, they could punch up a current list of Imperial fugitives, including their names, known histories, habitual weapons, and most important of all, the reward offered for their capture or termination. Occasionally the reward would be conditional, specifying that the fugitive must be brought in alive, but most often dead or even proof of death was just fine. Having picked a fugitive, the bounty hunter could request and receive a hunting license for that particular person. Capturing or killing a fugitive without a license was considered fortuitous, which meant no reward.

A record number of bounty hunters had requested licenses on Cadien, including Sam McCade. One million credits was an unusually high reward. But time passed and Cadien had proved to be both cunning and elusive, so most of his pursuers gave up, turning their attention to other less difficult prey. But McCade was tenacious, and a million credits was a lot of money—enough to buy a ship of his own.

For a bounty hunter a ship was both a status symbol and a tool, a means of catching more fugitives. But at times that goal seemed distant indeed. Expenses had consumed most of his money, and the trail was growing cold. But finally, just when McCade was about to give up, a paid informer led him to Cadien's mistress. It took time, and the rest of McCade's money, but the information she provided had led him to the Pink Asteroid. He was broke, and liners were notoriously expensive, so to get there he'd been forced to ship out as third mate on an ore freighter. It had touched down on Imperial Earth three days before. Each night he'd waited for Cadien to show. Maybe tonight would be the night.

As he moved, McCade's eyes continually scanned the crowd, comparing each face with the memprinted image of Cadien burned into his mind. Some eyes met his in open challenge. Those he ignored. Others slid away. Those he followed, checking and comparing. Toward the center of the room he noticed a miner who looked a lot like Cadien. Casually he moved between the tightly packed tables to get a better look.

He had just decided it wasn't Cadien when something tugged at his arm, and the miner's head exploded. He turned, dropping to one knee. His gun roared three times. The heavy slugs tore Cadien's chest apart. A woman screamed. Suddenly everyone wanted to be somewhere else. The crowd pushed toward the doors and streamed outside.

McCade's left arm hurt. Cadien's slug had passed right through it before hitting the miner. He clutched it as he walked over and looked down at the miner's crumpled body, dully wondering who he'd been, why he'd died, and whether anyone else would care. A trail of red dots followed him over to Cadien. He'd seemed larger than life, almost superhuman, as McCade had tracked him across the stars, but dead, he looked small and empty. McCade would have preferred to bring him in alive. But sometimes they didn't give you any choice.

His arm hurt more now and was covered with blood. The bastard had nicked a vein or something. His vision was fading. He was falling. He heard distant voices. They didn't seem to make any sense. "Tourniquet . . . under arrest for . . ." Rough hands grabbed and lifted. There was an explosion of pain and then nothing.

He struggled to clear his vision. Gray ceilings and walls swam into focus. Wherever he looked he saw surveillance sensors. Made obvious to intimidate? McCade smiled wryly. If so it was working. His left arm was numb. Turning his head he tried to see it, but couldn't. From the shoulder down it disappeared into an automedic. The machine hummed softly as it speeded the healing process along. It was a standard, navy model. As was the bed, the room's single chair, and everything else in sight. No doubt about it, somehow he'd wound up in a navy brig. The Pink Asteroid was located in Santa Fe. So they'd probably taken him to Earth Fleet Base, which sprawled across most of New Mexico. But why? McCade didn't know . . . but somehow he felt sure that he wouldn't like the answer. He felt very tired, or was it just that the automedic was pumping a sedative into his system? He decided it made very little difference and fell asleep.

When he awoke he felt better. The automedic was gone. His left arm was bandaged and sore but seemed able to move normally.

Silently a section of wall slid back. A man stepped into the cell. "Hello, Sam. It's been a long time."

He was strongly backlit, and it took McCade a moment to recognize him. Walter Swanson-Pierce. A little older, hair dusted with gray, but still trim and fit. Never a friend, but not exactly an enemy either. More like a friendly adversary. But that was a long time ago. While time had passed, it had done nothing to change the smile that rang slightly false, the eyes that reflected vain arrogance, or the face still a shade too pretty for a man. Still, some things had changed. The gold rings on Swanson-Pierce's immaculate, space-black sleeve were those of a full captain. Lieutenant to captain in ten years. Not bad. Good old Walt had done well for himself. McCade felt sorry for those who'd been in the way.

Squinting into the light, McCade replied, "Hello, Walt. Since you're in, I might as well ask you to sit down. You will anyway."

The other man crossed the room with a smile. "It's nice to see you've retained your sense of humor." He lowered himself gracefully into the skeletal form of the chair. "Yes, it's been a long time. Those were the days, weren't they, Sam? The old *Imperial* wasn't much compared to today's battleships. Still we showed the pirates a thing or two, didn't we? By god we were bright-eyed and bushy-tailed back then!"

"Cut the crap, Walt," McCade replied. "The *Imperial* was a stinking old tub that could barely lift off-planet and you know it. And we weren't bright-eyed and bushy-tailed. More like hungry, tired and scared shitless. Let's get on with it. . . . What're you doing here? Or, more to the point, what am I doing here?"

"Why, Sam," Swanson-Pierce said. "I see your charming directness hasn't changed a bit! In answer to your question, you're the guest of the Imperial Navy, recovering from wounds suffered while ridding the empire of a dangerous criminal. Or so it says in this morning's news. By the way, the Emperor sends his thanks." Swanson-Pierce leaned back, the hint of a smile touching his lips.

McCade grimaced. "Walt, you know where you and the Emperor can shove it. I don't want your hospitality. I just want out. Now."

Swanson-Pierce frowned in mock concern. "Sam, you really must be more circumspect. Imagine! Telling the Emperor to shove it. Why some would call that treason. Fortunately I know you jest." His look hardened. "As for leaving, wherever would you go?"

McCade sighed. Swanson-Pierce clearly enjoyed toying with him, and for the moment there wasn't much he could do about it. It reminded him of junior officer's mess when they'd both been aboard the *Imperial*. As the most senior lieutenant—his commission had predated McCade's by a week—Swanson-Pierce had always enjoyed playing games with those junior to him. Not so much with McCade, who refused to be intimidated, but especially sub-lieutenants and midshipmen.

McCade forced a smile and said, "I'll tell you what, Walt, you let me out of here, I'll toddle off, collect the reward for killing that dangerous criminal you mentioned, and then I'll check into a nice hotel." McCade smiled hopefully.

"Well I'd like to Sam, I really would," Swanson-Pierce replied gravely. "But there is the matter of the Imperial Claims Board."

"The Imperial Claims Board?" McCade asked, dreading the answer.

"Why yes," the naval officer replied innocently. "All claims for reward stemming from the death of a fugitive from Imperial justice must be dully considered and approved by the Imperial Claims Board," he recited. Swanson-Pierce watched to see if McCade would take the bait—just as he had taken it so long ago.

"Since when?" McCade asked through clenched teeth, unable to resist.

"Since yesterday," Swanson-Pierce answered happily, the game won.

For a moment the two men stared at each other. Swanson-Pierce with barely disguised glee, and McCade with disgust verging on hatred. Now he remembered why they'd never been friends. Straining for control, McCade asked, "How long will it take for my claim to be approved?"

"That's really hard to say," the other man replied thoughtfully. "The Board's just getting organized, and of course they'll want to agree on some rules and what not, why I suppose it could take months!"

"In that case," McCade said grimly, "I'll just leave and wait for my claim to clear." He sat up and swung his feet over the side of the bed. A wave of dizziness and nausea swept over him.

Swanson-Pierce summoned up a look of fatherly concern. "I really couldn't allow it, Sam. You're obviously not up to snuff." He paused judiciously, regarding McCade through steepled fingers. "I hesitate to bring this up, considering your health and so on, but there is one other small difficulty. It seems you're under arrest. Something about discharging firearms within the city limits."

McCade allowed himself to fall back against the pillow. Obviously Swanson-Pierce still wanted something, and he'd have to provide it before he could go. "All right, Walt,"

McCade said wearily. "You've had your fun. Now cut the bull. Exactly what do you want?"

The other man smiled as he rose from his chair. Walking toward the door he shook his head in pretended amazement. "Sam, you'll never change." He turned in the doorway. "Get some rest, Sam. We'll talk again soon." He stepped out of the cell and the door slid silently closed behind him.

For some time McCade lay there, rigid with frustration. He'd done it. He'd tracked Cadien halfway across the empire, damn near got his ass blown off, and earned a million Imperials in the process. Right now he should have been getting drunk, getting laid, and getting ready to pick out his ship. Roughly in that order. Instead, a naval officer with a sadistic sense of humor had gone to a great deal of trouble to lock him up. Why? Nothing came. One by one he ordered his muscles to relax. Gradually they obeyed and finally he sank into the oblivion of sleep.

He awoke with the sun in his eyes. The wall in front of him had become transparent. Outside, the huge naval base sprawled to the horizon. In a way, it symbolized the entire planet. As the center of a vast empire, Terra was almost entirely dedicated to the various branches of government, the military, scientific research, and of course the pleasures of those so engaged. He sat up and swung his feet over the side of the bed. He felt better. His arm was still a little stiff but the pain had almost disappeared. There were clothes draped over the chair. Moving gingerly he stood and shuffled over to them. His worn leathers had disappeared and been replaced by a new set in navy black, without insignia of course. Everything fit perfectly. Except the memories. Those belonged to someone else, someone younger. Someone who'd believed what they taught him.

The door slid open. McCade accepted its unspoken invitation and stepped outside. Two Imperial marines stood waiting in the corridor. Both snapped to attention. McCade smiled. The hand of steel within the velvet glove. Just Walt's way of letting him know where he stood.

The larger of the two marines wore the chevrons of a section leader and the confidence of a professional. Bright brown eyes looked straight ahead from under bushy brows. When he spoke, his lips barely moved. "Will you accompany us, sir?"

McCade almost laughed. As if he had a choice. He nodded, and together they moved off. One marine fell in ahead and the other behind. Down corridors, through halls, along autowalks and, on one occasion, two hundred feet straight up a vertical shaft using some kind of new anti-grav belts. He was impressed. He hadn't been to Terra for years and had forgotten what it was like. Everywhere, he saw purposeful activity and new technology—little things, many of them, but still new.

In spite of the empire's vast size, Terra was still the principal source of new technology. That fact had helped her remain at the center of human endeavor instead of being relegated to its past. In 3,112 years of recorded history, man had inhabited hundreds of worlds. Many had never seen Terra and never would. But for the most part all still thought of Terra as home.

By the time they arrived in front of huge, ornate doors, McCade was tired. They'd come a long way and his arm had started to ache. As they approached, two more marines snapped to attention. They seemed to come in pairs, like bookends. To McCade's surprise they opened the heavy doors by hand to let him pass. Their deference indicated the status of whoever he was about to meet. Or the ego, he reflected sourly.

As he entered, he noticed that the room was simply but elegantly furnished. A long walk across plush carpet carried him to a large desk. The chair behind it stood empty. The top of the desk was bare. But deep in its black surface a star map could be seen, accurate in every detail. He recognized many systems and planets. Imperial stars were colored silver, and, in spite of the empire's size, they were few against the immense backdrop of space. Between them tiny red sparks flew, which McCade supposed were navy ships, continually striving to bind the empire together.

"Impressive isn't it?" Surprised, McCade looked up into amused blue eyes. The sound of the man's entry had evidently been lost in the thick carpet. His white hair suggested age, but his movements retained the quick precision of youth. His face was round and unlined, yet there was a profound weariness in his eyes. His simple white robe bore no mark of rank. He needed none. The feeling of power surrounding the man was almost palpable. His smile seemed genuine and McCade found himself responding in kind. "Please be seated, Citizen McCade," the man continued. "I'm Admiral Keaton."

The floor behind McCade extruded a formless-looking chair. As McCade sat down, the chair quickly molded itself to the shape of his body. He'd never seen one like it. He was amazed.

Admiral Keaton! The man was a legend. He'd helped build the Imperial Navy under the first emperor. Then he'd shaped it, molded it, and used it to further expand the empire. Later he'd commanded the fleet that defeated the pirates near the planet Hell. McCade knew because he'd been there, aboard the *Imperial*.

"First allow me to apologize for the considerable inconvenience we've put you to, though, as you'll see, this is a matter of grave concern to the Empire." The Admiral's tone was that of one equal addressing another on a problem of mutual concern. In spite of his distaste for the military, McCade couldn't help feeling complimented. "I'm aware, of course," Keaton continued smoothly, "that your separation from the navy wasn't entirely voluntary."

"A court martial rarely is. . . . Voluntary, I mean," McCade replied dryly. He remembered the cold empty feeling as he entered the enormous wardroom of the *Imperial*. Facing him from behind the semicircular table were nine senior naval officers. One for each planet in Terra's system. Each had commanded a ship in the Battle of Hell. Their verdict was unanimous. Guilty. McCade could still see the grim satisfaction deep in the eyes of his commanding officer, Captain Bridger. He felt the familiar surge of anger and hatred sweep over him and pushed it back as he'd done a thousand times before.

Admiral Keaton nodded knowingly. "For what it's worth . . . I would have favored a less severe punishment than dishonorable discharge. I think we both realize that Captain Bridger's personal feelings may have colored his judgment. However you did choose to disobey a direct order. As I recall, you admitted that. And once Captain Bridger brought formal charges, the Court had little choice." Keaton paused, regarding McCade with a thoughtful expression before going on.

"Of course, no one but the Emperor can change such a verdict after the fact."

McCade's thoughts churned. Had he just heard a veiled hint? If so, at what? His commission reinstated for services rendered? If so, why the heavy-handed approach from good old Walt? Surely the Admiral must be aware of the kind of leverage Walt had used to get him here. Of course he was. The carrot and the stick. He was being expertly conned. He didn't know what was coming—but he felt sure it would be a real lulu.

"I'll get to the point," Keaton said. "There's an important service you could render. Though I realize you may feel little loyalty to the Empire . . . I think you know it's necessary. The alternative is anarchy."

McCade didn't know if he believed that or not, but he certainly knew the theory. The Academy instructors had hammered it home day after day. It was the basic tenent underlying the Emperor's rule. There had been a confederation once. But there were too many stars, too many systems. Each had a point of view, special needs and special problems. Each saw itself as the center of the human universe. An entire planet had been set aside as a capital. It was populated with millions of representatives sent to vote on behalf of thousands of worlds. But the democratic process constantly broke down into endless bickering and squabbling. Nothing effective was accomplished because decisions always called for sacrifice by one or more special interest groups. Eventually a coalition of systems seceded from the Confederation. A bloody civil war followed. Finally after years of conflict a strong and brilliant leader emerged. He amassed a great armada and used it to conquer all the planets then held by man. His supporters proclaimed him emperor . . . and the Empire was born. His rule proved reasonable and consistent, preferable to the profitless anarchy of war. Eventually, most became willing subjects. However a stubborn few fled to the Empire's frontiers. There they eked out a marginal existence on uncharted worlds, or raided the Empire's commerce as pirates. Now the first emperor's son ruled, and little had changed.

Admiral Keaton paused as though gathering his thoughts. "We can also offer what we think is generous compensation for your services."

McCade would've sworn there was a glint of humor deep in the Admiral's eyes. "In addition to helping you resolve your legal difficulties, we are prepared to offer you a first-class ship. I believe such a vessel is central to your future plans." Admiral Keaton allowed himself an amused smile.

Blast them! McCade thought. They were leading him around like a child. He knew it, they knew it, and right now there wasn't a damn thing he could do about it. Forcing an even tone and sardonic grin, McCade said, "You're too generous, Admiral. You offer to pay me what's already mine, and throw in the ship I could have bought with it to boot. Terrific. It's a great deal. But before I agree . . . I'd like to know what's involved. So let's skip the bull and get on with it. What do you want? And why me?"

For a second McCade saw anger flicker in the other man's eyes and wondered if he'd pushed Keaton too far. But then the anger vanished to be replaced by a grim smile.

"All right, maybe I deserved that, McCade. . . . So, as you put it, I'll skip the bull. As for what we want, well, you did the Empire a service when you tracked Cadien down. We want you to find another fugitive for us and bring him back." The Admiral paused for a moment and said, "Failing that, we want you to kill him."

McCade experienced a sinking feeling. Whatever the game was, it obviously involved high stakes.

Keaton looked at him appraisingly. "As for why we picked you, well, you have quite a reputation in your, ah, chosen profession. I'm told your peers hold you in very high esteem. What's more important, however, is that you know the fugitive, how he thinks, what makes him tick. And that may well give you an edge in finding him. And last but not least . . . you just happened to be in the right place at the right time."

"Or the wrong place at the wrong time," McCade replied sourly. "Who am I supposed to find?"

"Captain Ian Bridger," Keaton replied grimly. "Ironic, isn't it?"

Totally insane is more like it, McCade thought. Find Bridger and bring him back dead or alive. Deep down he knew a part of him would enjoy tracking Bridger down. And they knew it, and were counting on it. But what had Bridger done? Whatever it was must be big.

"I'm already starting to feel underpaid," McCade said. "I want the bounty for Cadien, plus the ship, plus let's say, half a million for Bridger." He was as much interested in Keaton's reaction as in getting what he'd asked for.

The Admiral smiled crookedly. "The offer stands as is. If you succeed, we'll consider a bonus. Otherwise, I suggest you prepare for a long stay while the Claims Board gets organized and then considers your case."

For a moment McCade just sat there, wishing he could see some way out, but finding each possible door closed to him. With a sigh he said, "All right, you've got a deal. What exactly did Bridger do?"

"Swanson-Pierce will fill you in," Keaton replied, his face remote now, already considering the next item on his agenda for the day. "Good hunting, McCade." And with that, the Admiral shimmered and disappeared, leaving only an empty chair.

Suddenly McCade realized Keaton had never been there at all. Some kind of holo? If so, it was the best he'd ever seen. Thoughtfully he got up and made his way across the plush carpet to the massive double doors. They opened on silent hinges, and as he stepped out of the room, the four marines snapped to attention.

"Ready sir?" asked the section leader who'd brought him.

McCade nodded. "Yes, thanks, Section."

Together the three men started down the corridor. McCade noticed it was busier now. Glancing at his wrist term, he saw it was almost noon. People were heading for lunch. Moments later, as McCade and the marines rounded a corner into a crowded hallway, the assassins made their move.

Two

THERE WERE THREE assassins, one ahead, one to each side. They were positioned to place McCade and his two escorts in a deadly cross fire. In keeping with Imperial law, they threw off their cloaks to reveal bright red jump suits. The word "assassin" flashed on and off in lights across each man's chest. The one in the middle delivered the formal warning.

"Attention! A level-three, licensed assassination will be carried out on Citizen Sam McCade five seconds from now." His amplified voice boomed down the corridor. People scattered and dived for cover in every direction. The lead assassin drew his blaster.

McCade dived for the floor and rolled right. Blaster fire splashed the floor where he'd just been. A wave of heat rolled over him, filling his nostrils with the stench of burned plastic. He looked up to see the lead assassin hurled backward by a blast from the section leader's energy weapon. Then McCade was hit from the side as the body of the second marine fell on him. There was a hole the size of a dinner plate burned through the man's chest. McCade rolled out from under the body, grabbing the marine's energy weapon as he did so. He fired as soon as his finger found the stud. Swinging left he punched a line of incandescent holes into the far wall before coming to bear on the lefthand assassin. As soon as the assassin filled his sights, McCade held the stud down. Pieces of the man flew in every direction.

McCade swung his weapon right, searching for another target. None remained. The assassins were dead. The section leader had killed two before being hit himself. McCade moved quickly to the marine's side. To his relief he saw the man was still alive. A blaster beam had grazed his right thigh. Fortunately it had cauterized the wound on its way by, so there wasn't any bleeding. McCade was something of an expert on wounds and had the scars to prove it. It looked like a stint in an automedic would make the leg as good as new.

The marine grinned at McCade through gritted teeth. "Glad you made it, sir. . . . For a moment there I thought we were all goners. Level three, for god's sake. . . . They must want you awful bad. . . . Woulda' been my ass if they'd got you though. . . . How's Reynolds?"

Slowly McCade became aware of the pandemonium around them. People caught in the cross fire screaming, others yelling commands, the smell of burned flesh, and the distant sound of approaching sirens. Good, someone had called the medics. McCade glanced at the other marine's crumpled form and then back to the section leader. "I'm afraid he didn't make it, Section."

The marine nodded unhappily.

"I'm sorry," McCade said, knowing it wouldn't help.

"Not your fault, sir," the section leader said. "You did your part." With a motion of his head he indicated the assassin McCade had killed.

"So did you, Section," McCade replied soberly. "I owe you one."

The marine shook his head. "No sir, that's what they pay me for. . . . But damn . . . level three . . . I can't believe it."

The marine's words still echoed in McCade's ears as he moved among the other wounded, doing what he could to help. A few minutes later he was brushed aside as the medics arrived, followed closely by a ground car loaded with marines.

"Level three . . ." McCade said to himself. Level three

meant assassins could kill not only their intended target, but any bystanders who happened to get in the way as well, all without fear of official reprisal. It was legal, of course. Legal but expensive. First you bought a license from the government. A nice source of revenue for the empire, by the way. Then you hired a member of the Assassin's Guild. Both were expensive. A level-three license, plus three Guild assassins would cost a small fortune. To have the hit carried out on a naval base would cost several more small fortunes. He'd never even heard of such an attempt before. But chances were, it was all legal and aboveboard. Otherwise, Guild assassins would never have gotten involved.

Of course every now and then there was someone stupid enough, or greedy enough, to try and cut both the government and the Guild out. Cadien was a good example. But for every Cadien there was a McCade. A bounty hunter willing to track a man across the empire for a fraction of what an effective Imperial police force would cost. And if McCade hadn't caught up with Cadien, the Guild eventually would have. They took illegal assassinations very seriously indeed. Particularly ones which offended the Emperor personally. Not only did such acts rob them of revenue, they gave assassins a bad name, and the Guild was already quite aware of its negative public image. The public rated assassins even below bounty hunters. What if assassination was made illegal? The very thought must send their blood pressure soaring, McCade thought sourly. Assuming, of course, they had blood in their veins.

Anyway, the section leader was right. . . . Someone did want him awfully bad. It wasn't a pleasant thought. McCade returned the section leader's wave as the marine was loaded into a ground vehicle that promptly disappeared in the direction of the base hospital.

"Citizen McCade?" The voice belonged to a tall, serious-looking marine captain.

"That depends," McCade replied. "Who are you?"

"My name is Captain Rhodes," the officer replied levelly. "My men and I are here to protect you." There was something superior about his expression and condescending in his tone. He put out an open hand for the energy weapon still tucked under McCade's arm.

McCade ignored the hand by taking a long slow look

around. The marine was forced to do likewise. The wounded were still being loaded into ambulances. Reynolds was being zipped into a black body bag, and robot repair units were starting to arrive. McCade turned back to the captain without saying a word. He didn't have to. The message was clear. In spite of a valiant effort to protect him, his previous body-guards had nearly failed. The marine flushed a dark red. McCade handed him the weapon and allowed himself to be ushered aboard an open ground car. He noticed they weren't taking any chances now. The marines surrounding him were heavily armed and the car mounted twin automatic weapons.

As the car eased into motion, McCade said, "Do I get to know where we're going?"

"Captain Swanson-Pierce has requested your presence," Captain Rhodes answered stiffly, as though unable to under-stand why anyone would request McCade for anything.

McCade turned away from the resentful marine and looked out the side of the speeding vehicle. The faces that passed by merged into a blur, along with his thoughts. He remembered the screams of those caught in the cross fire. Strangers had been hurt or killed because of him. Why? It made no sense. Of course he'd made enemies as a bounty hunter. But most of them were dead, or sentenced to a prison planet for life, if you could call that life. Friends or relatives were always a possibil-ity. But why now? And why in the middle of an Imperial Navy base? It didn't make sense . . . unless of course it was some-how connected with the Bridger thing.

McCade put those thoughts aside as the vehicle left the confinement of the building and emerged into bright sunshine. Lush green grass, still slightly moist from the rain pro-grammed to fall at exactly 0500 every morning, reached out to touch a bright blue sky. The air smelled fresh and clean. Pol-lution and crowding were things of the past. At least on Terra they were. For hundreds of years, Earth had exported her problems, including both heavy industry and excess popula-tion. As a result, much of Terra's surface was dedicated to vast forests and parks. Cities were designed for beauty as well as function. Even naval bases had been made easy on the eye, so that visitors from off-planet couldn't imagine the crowded, polluted misery of a thousand years before. In the distance, the neat symmetry of a spaceport could be seen shimmering in the early heat, surrounded by concentric rings of navy ships. Thunder rolled as the slender needle shape of a destroyer rose toward the sky.

The ground car stopped in front of a black building which soared a thousand feet upward. The building bore no sign announcing its purpose. There was a momentary wait as Captain Rhodes issued orders to his men. McCade used it to read a small gold plaque set into the permacrete at his feet. It read:

> *The first to see,*
> *The first to hear,*
> *The first to know,*
> *The first to die.*

The motto of Naval Intelligence. Those who worked within were the Emperor's eyes and ears. From here they wove an invisible web between the stars. A network of information that touched every planet held by man . . . and quite a few that weren't.

As McCade and Rhodes approached the building its black surface grew blacker. Evidently the entire building was protected by a force field. The area directly in front of them shimmered and disappeared, leaving an opening just large enough for them to pass through.

Inside, both men were invisibly but thoroughly scanned by hidden security sensors as they waited by a lift tube. The captain's sidearm was detected immediately, its serial number checked against the one issued to him, his entire personnel file quickly reviewed, all in a fraction of a second. McCade was identified by his retinal patterns and also checked. A moment later computer approval flashed back, allowing the lift tube doors to open. They stepped aboard the waiting platform and it moved smoothly upward. McCade followed the marine off at level eighty-six. They went a few steps down a gleaming corridor and into a roomy reception area, where they were greeted by a very attractive lieutenant, who looked stunning in navy black and, from her slightly amused expression, knew it.

"Citizen McCade reporting as ordered," Captain Rhodes said.

McCade winked at the lieutenant, and to his surprise she winked back. She nodded to the marine and murmured into a wrist mic before turning away to tap something into the terminal on her desk.

"Sam, you've been at it again. You really must stop shooting people in public places. . . . It's so messy." Swanson-Pierce had appeared in a doorway. He also wore an amused expression and another perfectly tailored uniform. "Come on in," he said, turning and disappearing back into his office.

As McCade entered he noticed the office was quite luxurious, resembling more the working quarters of a successful businessman than the spartan day cabin of a naval officer. After dropping into a chair facing Swanson-Pierce's highly polished rosewood desk, McCade reached to pluck a cigar from an open humidor, and settled back. Puffing it alight, he watched Swanson-Pierce through the smoke. "Speaking of shooting people in public places, Walt . . . you wouldn't happen to know why I'm suddenly so unpopular, would you?" McCade allowed some white ash to drift down toward the plush carpet.

Swanson-Pierce laughed. "Why Sam, considering your vast wealth of personal charm, I must admit I'm surprised. Old, ah, clients perhaps?"

McCade regarded the naval officer soberly and shook his head. "I don't think so. It takes a big bankroll to swing a level three . . . especially in the middle of a naval base. If I'd offended somebody with that kind of clout, I'd remember. No, I think it's something else, maybe connected to this Bridger thing."

Swanson-Pierce nodded in agreement. "Our people are looking into that possibility at this very moment. It's too bad all three assassins were killed. It would have been interesting to talk with one of them." He frowned at McCade disapprovingly.

"Yeah, that was too bad. I'll keep it in mind next time," McCade replied dryly.

Swanson-Pierce shook his head in mock concern. "Sam, what'll I do with you?"

"Let me go?" McCade asked hopefully.

"That hardly seems wise right now, does it, Sam?" the other man said, his brow furrowed in apparent concern. "What with all those nasty types looking for you? Not to mention your regrettable financial situation. No, I think not. And besides . . . you did agree to undertake this little chore for Admiral Keaton."

"Yeah," McCade said. "Let's talk about that little chore." He tapped his cigar, sending an avalanche of ash toward the expensive carpet. "First, I didn't 'agree' to take this Bridger thing on. I was forced, as you very well know. Second, I think it's about time you told me what this is all about. Since when does the navy need a bounty hunter to find their officers? Especially dead or alive. Come to think of it . . . why bother? Is there a shortage of war heroes or something?"

Swanson-Pierce frowned as he watched the last of the cigar ash on its journey toward the carpet. "For one thing, Captain Bridger is AWOL, but you're right, if that were the only concern, we wouldn't need you. Needless to say we don't normally send bounty hunters after errant naval officers. But this is a special case." Swanson-Pierce touched a series of buttons in the armrest of his chair. The room lights dimmed as a section of wall to McCade's right slid aside to reveal a holo tank. Color swirled and coalesced into the face and upper torso of Captain Ian Bridger.

As the sound came up it was apparent Bridger was lecturing a class at the Naval Academy. He was every inch the naval officer. He stood ramrod straight. His rugged features radiated confidence. The Imperial Battle Star hung gleaming at his throat. Rows of decorations crossed his barrel chest. And when he spoke, his voice carried the authority born of years in command, and the confidence of a man who has lived what he's teaching. In spite of himself, McCade had to admit the lecture was good. Bridger's thoughts were well organized, and delivered in a clear, distinct manner. He gave frequent examples, and skillfully extracted an occasional laugh from his audience.

As he described the Battle of Hell, however, his commentary became increasingly heated. He grew more and more agitated. His pupils dilated. His eyes took on a strange look. A vein in his neck began to throb. He called the pirates "vermin and filth in the eyes of God." He described in gruesome detail how a pirate cruiser had blasted an Imperial lifeboat out of existence. A reaction shot of the audience showed hundreds of shining eyes. They believed every word.

Picture and sound dissolved together as the room lights

came up. Swanson-Pierce swiveled his chair toward McCade, and regarded him through steepled fingers. "What you just saw was a routine audit taken a few days before Bridger disappeared . . . about six weeks ago."

"Practically yesterday," McCade said, blowing a perfect smoke ring.

"Bridger gave himself a four-week head start by taking a month's leave," the other man replied defensively. "And unfortunately it was a week after that before his disappearance was taken seriously."

McCade raised an eyebrow quizzically. Swanson-Pierce responded angrily.

"Damn it man . . . we don't check captains in and out like children at a boarding school."

"What makes you so sure he took off of his own volition?" McCade asked. "How do you know he wasn't abducted or murdered?"

"We don't," Swanson-Pierce answered, frowning down at the surface of his desk. "But we've received no ransom demand and his body hasn't turned up anywhere." His eyes came up to meet McCade's. "So we're forced to assume he's disappeared voluntarily . . . and we've got to act on that assumption." McCade nodded and the other man continued. "As you saw in the holo, Bridger still feels a pathological hatred for pirates, which is hardly surprising. What happened to his wife and daughter is common knowledge. The liner *Mars* found drifting, its drive sabotaged by the crew, stripped of cargo, lifeboats still in place, but no crew or passengers aboard, except for the bodies, of course."

Swanson-Pierce fell silent for a moment, possibly thinking about the fate of those passengers and crew who had survived. It was said the pirates were always short of women. And then there was slavery. And Bridger's daughter had been very pretty, even beautiful. Both Swanson-Pierce and McCade had admired her from afar during her frequent visits to the *Imperial*.

Swanson-Pierce resumed his narrative. "And there's Bridger's career. It didn't prosper after the Battle of Hell, and I imagine that too fed his hatred of the pirates."

The naval officer stood and began to pace back and forth.

"After you, ah, left the *Imperial*, we, along with the rest of Keaton's fleet, chased the pirates as far as the frontier. Then they split up and took off in all directions. Rather than divide his forces, Keaton decided discretion was the better part of valor, and we returned to base. Chances are the Il Ronn got quite a few of the pirates in any case."

McCade knew the other man was right. Of all the alien species Man had encountered, the Il Ronn were the most dangerous. Not because they were the most intelligent or advanced. There were many alien races more advanced than either Man or the Il Ronn. But because the Il Ronn were the most like Man, they were a constant threat. They too had built a stellar empire at the expense of less aggressive races. They too had almost unlimited ambitions. Now only a thinning band of unexplored frontier worlds provided a buffer between the two empires. Fortunately the races had physiological differences which were expressed in a desire for radically different kinds of real estate.

The Il Ronn preferred the hot dry planets avoided by Man and shunned the wet worlds humans liked, in spite of the fact that water held tremendous religious significance for them. Occasionally, however, both would desire a single planet regardless of climate, usually due to its unique mineral wealth. When that happened, conflict usually followed. But so far one or the other had always backed down short of all-out war. Nonetheless the Il Ronn considered any ships straying into their sector fair game, and both Imperial and pirate craft alike frequently disappeared along the frontier.

Swanson-Pierce continued. "As you can imagine, we returned to a hero's welcome. There were medals and promotions all around."

"I trust you weren't left out," McCade said dryly.

"No I wasn't," the other man replied evenly. "However, Bridger was. Oh, he received the Imperial Star all right. It isn't every day a commander personally leads a boarding party, and then wounded, returns to command his ship for the rest of the battle. Usually such a man could expect automatic promotion to admiral. But not Bridger. Nothing was ever said officially of course, but it was whispered that Bridger was too unstable, too fixated on pirates, for promotion." Swanson-

Pierce stopped pacing long enough to remove an invisible piece of lint from the left sleeve of his immaculate uniform before dropping into his chair.

"About the same time, Bridger became more and more outspoken about his religious beliefs. Apparently he told anyone who would listen that the pirates were the 'spawn of the devil.' A view which became increasingly unpopular as it became obvious that killing pirates was counterproductive. So Bridger was appointed to the Academy, there to serve out his days in academic obscurity. And that's what he did . . . until six weeks ago . . . when he disappeared."

McCade stubbed out his cigar in a small porcelain candy dish which sat just inches from an ashtray. Swanson-Pierce winced. "Since when does the navy consider killing pirates to be counterproductive?" McCade asked.

Swanson-Pierce allowed himself an amused smile. "Sam, you never cease to amaze me. In some ways you're incredibly naive. Haven't you ever wondered why we didn't just wipe them out? We could, you know, or at least we think we could. Anyway, in the period right after the Battle of Hell, we tried to patrol the frontier worlds. Our ships were constantly ambushed by both pirate and Il Ronn raiders. So we sent more ships. But it didn't do any good. In that kind of conflict a fleet simply makes a bigger target." Swanson-Pierce paused dramatically. "Then Admiral Keaton had a brilliant idea."

"I'm surprised his staff was able to recognize one," McCade said innocently.

Frowning, Swanson-Pierce continued. "Keaton's idea was to pull all our ships out, except for occasional scouts, and let the pirates and Il Ronn go to it. Hopefully they'd keep each other in check. That's exactly what we did and it works very well. So now we try not to kill too many pirates. We just keep them confined to the frontier. Someday we might even have to step in and save them . . . if it ever looks like the Il Ronn are getting the upper hand. In the meantime the pirates are holding their own quite nicely. So as you can see, it wouldn't do to have someone like Bridger running around killing pirates."

McCade shook his head in disgust. "And the settlers, and merchant ships the pirates take just inside the frontier . . . what about them?"

There was silence for a moment as the naval officer stared

off into space. When he answered his face was devoid of all expression. "Everything has a price, Sam. . . . Including peace. Imagine the cost of a navy large enough to do the job alone. Taxes would be astronomical. . . ." He left the thought unfinished as his eyes slid away to the star map decorating one wall.

"Bridger's out there somewhere right now. Among other things he's a highly trained naval officer, a combat veteran, an expert in strategy and tactics, and quite knowledgeable about our current defensive capabilities." Swanson-Pierce met McCade's eyes. "Think about it, Sam. . . . What if he offered that experience and knowledge to the Il Ronn, in return for their assistance in destroying the pirates, something they've got to do anyway in order to defeat us?"

"I don't believe it," McCade replied. "Bridger may be a few planets short of a full system, and god knows he's a total bastard, but he's no traitor."

"Basically I agree," Swanson-Pierce said. "But try to see it from his point of view. The Empire has two enemies. The pirates and the Il Ronn. Of the two he believes the pirates are the worse. So if he can use the Il Ronn to destroy them . . . he's halved the enemy . . . performed a great service for the Empire . . . and satisfied his own desire for revenge."

"What you're saying," McCade said thoughtfully, "is that the Il Ronn might allow themselves to be used . . . and in doing so . . . learn enough from Bridger to give them an edge in a war with the Empire."

"Exactly," Swanson-Pierce replied. He paused for a moment as though considering his next words carefully. "And there's one other small item to consider."

"Uh-oh," McCade said. "I've got a feeling I'm not going to like this."

Swanson-Pierce shook his head. "It's nothing really, but I suppose it could have a bearing, so I'll mention it just in case. Since Bridger's disappearance our people have gone through his personal affairs with a fine-tooth comb."

"God knows they've had plenty of time to do it," McCade interjected sweetly.

"And," the naval officer continued, pointedly ignoring McCade's jibe, "they inform me Bridger may have stumbled onto something. He was forever poking around the artifact

planets while on leave, publishing articles on his pet archeo-
logical theories, and boring everybody to death at the officers'
club. Anyway there's the possibility that he's come up with
something of military value . . . and is planning to hand it over
to the Il Ronn in order to gain their cooperation."

"Is that possible?" McCade asked, one eyebrow raised.

The other man shrugged. "Anything's possible, I guess.
But people have been messing about with those planets for
years and never discovered anything useful in the military
sense. It's probably a good idea to remember the man's a bit
eccentric, to say the least. Anyway, I'll get you access to what
information we've got, and you can decide for yourself if it
means something."

Both men were silent for a moment. McCade tried to sort
out his feelings. On the one side was the Empire's cynical
balancing of forces and the ruthless sacrifice of innocent lives.
On the other was a single renegade officer whose desire for
revenge might touch off an interstellar conflict that would destroy billions of lives. The whole thing was sick.

McCade's thoughts were interrupted as an autocart rolled
into the room on silent treads. "I took the liberty of ordering a
late lunch for both of us," Swanson-Pierce said.

As the cart rolled up to the naval officer's desk and began
disgorging dishes of food, McCade said, "All right, I'm convinced. But how am I supposed to succeed where your spooks
and gumshoes haven't?"

"Well," the other man replied mildly, helping himself to a
cup of fragrant New Indian tea, "it's true we haven't found
Bridger yet, but I remain confident we will. You are by way
of, ah, insurance. A weapon, if you will, that happened to be
in the right place at the right time. Besides, from what I hear,
you're reasonably good at what you do." Swanson-Pierce
blew steam off the surface of the dark blue tea with evident
satisfaction. Looking up, he said, "Actually our people have
learned quite a bit. It occurred to Admiral Keaton that their
knowledge, combined with your rather gruesome talents,
might very well lead to success. Quite frankly your, ah, profession should provide a perfect cover, allowing you to pursue
paths of investigation not open to our personnel." Swanson-
Pierce sipped his tea delicately, gazing at McCade with an
innocent expression.

"And of course if I happen to get killed, it's no great loss ... and nobody's likely to complain," McCade said, selecting three of the four sandwiches on the autocart.

"Well, yes, there is that of course," Swanson-Pierce replied serenely. "Though I suspect any number of creditors would grieve your passing." He picked up the remaining sandwich and examined it critically prior to taking a tentative bite. The Lor Beast had been cooked rare the way he liked it, and had traveled well from Asta II.

With his free hand he punched a button in the armrest of his chair, and once again the holo tank swirled into life. This time it displayed the likeness of a young woman dressed in the uniform of a cadet squadron leader. She was cute, rather than pretty. Short black hair cut in the style approved by the Academy framed an elfin face. Brown eyes regarded the camera with indifference.

"I give up. . . . Who is she?" McCade asked, his mouth full of the second sandwich.

"Cadet Squadron Leader Marsha Votava," Swanson-Pierce answered. "When Bridger left, he evidently took her with him."

"She left of her own accord?" McCade asked, studying the face that stared back at him from the holo.

Swanson-Pierce nodded. "It would seem so. There's no sign of violence in her quarters. Six weeks haven't turned up her body, or for that matter, any information about her whereabouts."

McCade finished the last sandwich and washed it down with coffee. "A love affair then?" he asked.

"Perhaps . . .," the other man replied, placing his empty dishes on the cart, "but we're not sure. It could also be hero worship."

Swanson-Pierce touched the "dismiss" button on the autocart. As it trundled toward the door, it blew up with a deafening roar.

Three

THE FORCE OF the explosion hurled both men to the floor. McCade found himself sprawled across the wreckage of an antique oriental table. He staggered to his feet. His ears were ringing and he was bleeding from numerous small cuts. Otherwise he seemed to be in one piece. Across the office Swanson-Pierce pushed some fallen ceiling panels off his legs and, using his scarred rosewood desk for support, stood up. His right arm hung limply by his side.

The office was a smoking ruin. McCade noticed that the areas nearest the cart had suffered the most damage, especially the ceiling. Apparently the top of the cart had blown off first, directing the blast upward and probably saving their lives.

A squad of marines burst in through the blackened doorway, weapons at the ready. Finding no current threat, the squad leader motioned, and men dressed in fire-fighting gear entered to spray foam over the smouldering debris.

A muscle in McCade's left cheek began to twitch as he made his way over to Swanson-Pierce. The naval officer was bent over, sorting through the rubble at his feet. He straightened up with a smile on his face and a fistful of cigars in his left hand.

"Might as well salvage something," he said, clenching a cigar between his teeth. "Here, Sam, help yourself."

"Don't mind if I do," McCade replied, taking most of the cigars, and puffing one alight. "How's your arm?"

Swanson-Pierce glanced down ruefully. "It doesn't hurt yet . . . but I suppose it's going to." He looked thoughtfully at the blackened autocart. "It wasn't assassins this time."

"Nope," McCade agreed, adding a stream of cigar smoke to the already polluted atmosphere. "This one was unlicensed all the way. No official warning of any kind."

"How fortunate you ate our lunch so quickly," Swanson-Pierce said dryly. "Otherwise it would have blown up right next to us."

"A good point, Walt. You should have a word with the chef. His idea of dessert leaves something to be desired," McCade replied.

Just then a doctor and two medics appeared and took charge. McCade's cuts were quickly disinfected and covered with nuskin. Swanson-Pierce was helped onto a power stretcher. The pretty lieutenant McCade had met earlier materialized at the naval officer's side, and they spoke in low tones. McCade did his best to eavesdrop but couldn't make out more than a word or two. As the medics began to guide the stretcher through the door, Swanson-Pierce said, "Lieutenant Lowe here will take care of everything, Sam. Don't give her too hard a time, and good hunting!"

Lieutenant Lowe was very efficient. Swanson-Pierce was barely out of sight when she went to work. Questions were asked and answered. Forms prepared and signed. Calls were made, demanding or pleading, whichever would get the fastest results, so that by evening McCade found himself standing on the blast-proof surface of the spaceport looking up at the long, graceful lines of his ship. She was beautiful.

He resisted the temptation to call up her registry on his wrist term. He knew it by heart. Her name was *Pegasus*. Three hundred and fifty feet long, she'd begun her career as a navy scout. Decommissioned during the budget cutbacks a few years ago, she'd been purchased by a wealthy businessman for use as a yacht. He'd lavished considerable love and money on her. Unfortunately during a routine customs inspection, officials had found a small quantity of yirl hidden aboard. Rumor had it the illegal substance was planted there by rival merchants, but whatever the truth of the matter, the businessman was sent to a prison planet, and *Pegasus* was returned to the navy. Now she was McCade's. According to official records, he'd made a down payment of five hundred thousand credits for her. Money supposedly paid him for killing Cadien. The same records indicated that a final payment of twenty-five thousand credits was due in six Terran months. Just Walt's little way of keeping a handle on him.

McCade smiled crookedly as he walked up the ramp and palmed the panel next to the entry port. The lock cycled open and then closed behind him. Inside he paused for a moment as the inner hatch opened, allowing him to enter the ship.

An hour later he sat relaxing in the small lounge just aft of the ship's four cabins. He'd toured her from bow to stern and liked what he'd found. She was strong, fast, and well armed. Thanks to her previous owner, she was also quite comfortable. Just the kind of ship a successful bounty hunter would choose. Plus, he'd requested additional equipment from Lieutenant Lowe, and was pleased to see she'd granted about half of it. He'd been kidding about the swimming pool anyway. He reached over and punched a request into the ship's well-stocked bar. As he settled back with a drink in one hand and a cigar in the other, McCade asked the ship's computer for an update on the first assassination attempt.

After considerable effort, he'd convinced Lieutenant Lowe to grant him direct access to the Naval Intelligence computer. She'd finally agreed—but restricted his access to those matters directly related to Bridger's disappearance. He wondered idly if the computer would consider her personnel file to be directly related or not. A soft tone chimed as information flashed onto the screen opposite him. For some reason the ship's previous owner had preferred text, and programmed the ship's computer to use voice only in emergencies. McCade saw no reason to change that policy.

He wasn't surprised to find the report contained little more than a garbled account of the action. However, he was relieved to learn that, in spite of his fears, all the bystanders had survived, though some would be hospitalized for some time. The section leader's name was Amos Van Doren, and he was doing well. Judging from the nurse's notes, McCade guessed he'd be released soon. He got the feeling the nurses couldn't wait. Van Doren was evidently a difficult patient. As McCade read on, he learned that routine autopsies hadn't revealed anything useful about the three assassins. Each bore prints, retinal patterns, dentition and vocal cords they hadn't been born with. All standard for assassins. Inquiries to the Assassin's Guild had been met with the usual refusals on grounds of Guild-client confidentiality.

A request for the most recent report on the bombing in Swanson-Pierce's office was met with a notice reading "Investigation in Progress." With a snort of derision he asked for the intelligence summary on Bridger's disappearance. It wasn't very helpful either. They didn't know why Bridger went, where he went, or how he got there. They thought Cadet Votava was with him . . . but they couldn't prove it. The only thing they seemed sure of was where Bridger wasn't. According to "reliable sources," which McCade doubted, Bridger wasn't on any Imperial planet enjoying regular inter-stellar commerce. All arrivals and departures from such worlds had been carefully screened since Bridger's disappearance. They'd even checked the records of arrivals and departures for the last standard month. Nothing. Of course that didn't mean much, McCade reflected as he ordered another drink. He'd arrived on and departed from more than one planet without bothering to notify customs. Plus there were all the frontier worlds to consider. And to top it all off, Bridger had a six-week head start. But still . . .

He requested Bridger's service file and sipped his drink as it came up on the screen. Most of it was boring and routine. "Lieutenant Bridger was transferred to such and such a vessel on a particular date. Commander Bridger completed a Head-quarters course on logistics with honors." And much later, "Captain Bridger will go aboard the ship *Imperial*, there to take command of said ship, and all personnel aboard, conducting himself with honor and in accordance with Imperial naval regulations." It was all there. The thousands of entries which mark off the predictable path of a military career.

Just out of curiosity he ran the file forward to where the

first annual psych profile after the Battle of Hell should have been. It wasn't there. The screen lit up with "For Imperial Eyes Only. Enter access code." McCade leaned back, an amused smile tugging at the corners of his mouth. So they didn't want him reading what the shrinks had to say. No sweat. It didn't take a bulkhead full of degrees to know Bridger had been operating on about half-power. And at least he knew what they weren't telling him. But what if they'd simply deleted information? He'd have no way to know it was missing. And it would be Walt's style. The old "just tell 'em what they need to know" routine. Grimly he turned his attention back to the screen. He'd have to assume some things were missing.

The next regular entry recorded Bridger's assignment to the Academy as an instructor. He taught mostly naval history. And the regular evaluations by the head of the history department suggested Bridger was good at it. His interest in history even extended to his own time. This was the part Swanson-Pierce had mentioned. McCade read the subsequent information with interest. After the loss of his family, Bridger often used his leaves to make one-man expeditions to the artifact worlds.

Many of the artifact worlds were discovered during the early days of space exploration. They were empty of intelligent life, except in a few cases where other life forms native to that particular planet had gained sentience after the disappearance of the original builders. The fact that they'd had time to do so suggested the Builders had been gone a very long time indeed. In any case, the fantastic ruins and artifacts the Builders had left behind gave mute testimony to an advanced civilization whose people had occupied and ruled many systems. The similarities between artifacts found on different worlds left no doubt as to their mutual membership in the same empire.

But archeologists discovered little more than that. Oh, they had plenty of theories, but very little to base them on. For one thing, the evidence was so ancient that the ravages of time had reduced most of it to little more than enigmatic hints at what must have been a magnificent race and culture. But, every now and then, some lucky person or group would stumble onto a hidden cache of artifacts protected, by luck or happenstance, from the elements. Over time all sorts of things had been discovered in this manner, including a variety of machinery, art works, precious stones, written documents, and a great deal of thus far unidentifiable, but nonetheless interesting junk.

So each year countless academic and private expeditions were launched in an effort to find a hidden chamber deep inside the ruins of some artifact planet which would reveal the nature of those who preceded both man and Il Ronn into space. Some sought knowledge, and others sought the riches knowledge can bring, but so far no one had really succeeded. But while none had yet managed to strip bare the secrets of the Builders, quite a few did find something for their trouble, and McCade was intrigued to learn that Bridger was among the lucky few.

At the time, the press made quite a fuss over it, probably because Bridger was a war hero more than anything else. Then too Bridger's find turned out to be quite controversial, or at least the centerpiece of it was.

What made Bridger's find special was a large metal plate. Its composition was similar to durasteel. Inscribed on its surface was writing in what was clearly two different languages. One was the language of the Builders, examples of which had been found in many locations, but the other was a complete mystery. No one had yet managed to decipher the language of the Builders, though many had tried, so attention quite naturally centered on the new, and heretofore unknown second language. Bridger swore it was a form of ancient Il Ronn, so old that even the Il Ronnians had lost track of it. To support his thesis he pointed to various similarities between its characters and modern Il Ronnian script. Some experts supported Bridger, especially those who believed the Il Ronn preceded man into space by thousands of years. Others scoffed at his claims, pointing out that the characters were also similar to the pictographs used by ancient Chinese, and did he think the Chinese had somehow left Earth to meet with the Builders?

In spite of such criticism Bridger continued to claim that the plate could be the modern equivalent of the Rosetta Stone, which offered the first clue to understanding ancient Egyptian hieroglyphics more than a thousand years before. He argued that the layout of the metal document suggested a list of some kind, the decoding of which might provide an understanding of the Builders' language, or provide insights into what they were like. He even referred to it as the "Directory."

Had they chosen to, Il Ronnian scholars might have been able to confirm or deny Bridger's thesis. However, the on-again, off-again state of hostilities between the human and Il Ronnian empires made such cooperation impossible.

Nonetheless, Bridger continued to search the artifact worlds as his time and funds allowed, looking for evidence which would prove his theory. To that end, he also used a great deal of Academy computer time, running programs he hoped would unlock the secrets of the metal plate.

And there it seemed to end. McCade pulled out and lit a cigar. It was interesting stuff. Partly because it offered new insights into Bridger's personality, and partly because the naval officer's theory involved the Il Ronn, thus creating still another link between Bridger and that alien race. Walt had played down the importance of Bridger's hobby... but McCade wasn't so sure. Curious, he asked for the date of the last computer run prior to Bridger's disappearance. What he got surprised him. Bridger's last run occurred more than a month before he vanished. A long time for someone who made use of the computer almost every day. A quick check revealed Bridger had also wiped all memory assigned to him. Why do that unless you've got something to hide? Positive he was on to something, McCade asked for the last date on which someone else had requested the data he'd just received. When it flashed onto the screen he saw it coincided with the start of Swanson-Pierce's investigation. So they knew, but either felt it wasn't important, or didn't want him to think it was. The possibilities made his head spin.

So what did it all mean, if anything? McCade inhaled deeply as ashes from his cigar tumbled unseen down across the arm of his chair. It could mean any number of things. But his favorite theory by far was that Bridger cracked the mystery of the metal tablet on that last run. Somehow he'd found the key that eluded everyone else. He'd figured out the language of the Builders and learned something. Something valuable. Something he could use for his own purposes. Something Swanson-Pierce was trying to play down. So Bridger had re-corded or memorized whatever it was, and then wiped the memory. Then he'd taken some time to plan his next move.

It all made sense and fit together logically. Of course that didn't make it true. But it would explain something that had bothered McCade all along. Why now? After all these years, why take off now? The answer might be that Bridger's discovery had provided him with leverage. Enough leverage to convince the Il Ronn to do his bidding? If so it would have to be something military, as Swanson-Pierce had suggested. Nothing else would interest the Il Ronn sufficiently to enlist them in Bridger's cause. A hidden cache of Builder-designed superweapons perhaps? There was no way to know, but the theory felt good, and McCade had learned long before that a successful hunter often relies on intuition.

Putting Bridger mentally aside for the moment, McCade turned his attention to Cadet Votava. Where did she fit in? When her Academy file came up on the screen, he wasn't surprised to see she'd taken leave at the same time as Bridger. What was surprising was the routine personality profile the Academy shrinks had prepared on her the year before. For some reason McCade imagined her to be insecure, emotional and dependent. Hungry for an authority figure to worship and follow. Nothing could have been further from the truth. It seemed she was intelligent, confident, and extremely independent. So much so her life seemed to lack significant personal relationships of any kind. She had no close friends, lovers or enemies among her classmates. They described her as "smart but distant." Out of curiosity he scrolled back to her pre-enrollment personality profile. His eyebrows rose with surprise. It sounded like a different girl. Her instructors on Mars had described her as "warm, sociable, and expressive." Of course people change as they grow older . . . but it still seemed strange. He shrugged and read on.

It soon became apparent there was a notable exception to Votava's self-imposed isolation. Captain Ian Bridger. Her transcript and personal calendar indicated either a close personal relationship with Bridger, or a fixation on him. She'd taken every class Bridger taught—many of which weren't even required for her sequence. She wrote him notes. She sought his advice. She met with him for counseling. She attended his church. A quick check of Bridger's daily schedule confirmed that the two were in daily contact. And because their meetings all took place within the framework of an appropriate instructor-student relationship, no one had noticed or objected. It all seemed to point toward an impressionable young woman pathetically in love with an older authority figure. Except according to her most recent profile she was neither impressionable nor dependent.

McCade scanned the reports and research papers she'd written searching for something, anything, that might hint at where she and Bridger had gone, or what they planned to do. They all seemed routine except for two. Those he read with great care. The first dealt with the Empire's strategy regarding the pirates and the Il Ronn. Votava did an excellent job of demonstrating the Empire's use of the pirates to counter the aliens. In fact, she made it seem so obvious that McCade squirmed in his chair. She went on to suggest that with each passing year both the Il Ronn and the pirates became stronger, while the Empire grew weaker and more complacent. It all sounded very familiar, McCade thought, and he wasn't surprised to see that Bridger had given her a very high grade for it. Here then was something both of them had in common.

In fact, the more he read, the more Cadet Votava sounded like Bridger. Or did he sound like her? There's an interesting thought.... Which came first, the chicken or the egg? In any case she was quite persuasive. McCade began to wonder if she and Bridger were right ... maybe the pirates were too strong ... not that it made much difference to him.

The second document to attract McCade's attention was a research paper on methods used to transfer bulk cargo over interstellar distances. He read the paper with great interest, taking particular note of the marginal comments added by Bridger. Why would Votava's history instructor comment at all? The paper was for another class. Long after he'd finished reading, McCade continued to stare at the screen, lost in thought.

The computer chimed softly and the image before him changed to reveal the head and shoulders of Lieutenant Lowe at the main entry port. She looked very pretty. Dark brown hair cascaded down to surround a heart-shaped face. Her eyes looked tired. To McCade's annoyance the ship's computer let her in as she palmed the lock. He wondered what other liberties she'd granted herself. Moments later she arrived in the lounge and tossed a navy-style duffle bag in his direction.

"Your stuff's in there," she said, wrinkling her nose in distaste.

"Hello to you too," he replied as he opened the bag and rummaged through it. Inside were the things he'd taken along as he chased Cadien from one system to another. He'd last seen them in a cheap hotel near the Pink Asteroid. It was mostly dirty laundry now. At the bottom, his hand encountered the familiar feel of his slug gun. As he pulled it out, he saw someone had cleaned and oiled it. "Thanks, Lieutenant. By the way, did the navy issue you a first name?"

When she laughed it was warm and open. "My friends call me Laurie . . . although it's actually Lauren. May I call you Sam?"

"I wish you would," McCade replied. "Drink?" He motioned toward the autobar.

She shook her head. "No thanks. Not just now. Is everything squared away?" She glanced around the lounge.

"I think so . . . ," McCade answered, taking another sip.

"So what happens now?" she inquired.

"I try to bring Bridger in," McCade replied with a slight smile.

"Just like that? You just go out and pick him up?"

"No . . . I think a squad of marines might come in handy," McCade answered dryly.

"You're serious, aren't you," she said, leaning forward eagerly. "You know where he is."

"Correction," he replied. "I *think* I know where he is."

Laurie frowned thoughtfully, drumming her fingers on the armrest of her chair. "Obviously you think he's close. . . ." Suddenly her face registered surprise. "You think he's right here—on Earth!"

McCade smiled as he shook his head. "No you don't. We're doing this my way. Your people had their chance. Besides, if I'm right we don't have much time. Certainly not enough to waste trying to convince your superiors to get off their butts. Now here's what I need—"

"What *we* need," she interrupted. "Where you go, I go. Besides, if it's like you say, you'll need some help, and I was top of my class in hand-to-hand combat." Her features were set in hard, determined lines.

"I'll bet you were," McCade said reflectively as he pretended to think it over.

Six hours later McCade sat next to Laurie as she expertly nudged their small troop carrier out of Earth's atmosphere and into high orbit. She'd insisted on piloting the craft herself, pointing out that without her, he wouldn't be able to get either the ship or the marines. Unless of course he wanted to go through regular channels. He had reluctantly agreed. Going through channels would take forever, plus he'd probably end up with Walt looking over his shoulder, and that would be even worse. Whether he liked it or not, he needed help, and allowing her to run this part of the show was a price that had to be paid.

He glanced back, and received an answering grin from Section Leader Amos Van Doren. McCade had approached the marine, looking for some volunteer help. Van Doren quickly agreed to round up some "off duty" buddies. They all turned out to be friends of Reynolds, the marine the assassins had killed. They were eager to even the score. Van Doren himself had refused to remain behind, in spite of his wound. When McCade started to insist, the marine gently suggested that if he didn't go, the others wouldn't either. McCade knew when he was beat. Maybe they weren't doing it his way, but at least they were doing it. So the section leader sat behind him, wearing full space armor, and an ear-to-ear grin.

As Laurie skillfully maneuvered the troop carrier through the maze of satellites, orbiting ships, defense installations and cast-off junk which circled the planet, McCade popped a stim cap and hoped he was right. Still, it seemed like the only possibility that made sense. What if Bridger and Votava hadn't left Earth? What if they'd holed up somewhere waiting for the search to die down? But they'd still need transportation off-planet. How could they get it without alerting the authorities?

Votava's paper had suggested a possible answer. She'd written about a whole new generation of cargo carriers. They'd be huge. Each would carry what it presently took ten freighters to move, and as a result, shipping costs would be greatly reduced. The key to their design was that, except for central power-control modules, the giant vessels would make one-way trips. That meant many systems required by conventional ships could be simplified or eliminated. The result . . . even more savings.

But more important from McCade's point of view was that the ships would be unmanned. Computers already did most of the work involved in piloting ships anyway. Except for atmosphere landings or emergencies, human pilots were little more than expensive back-up systems. So the ship's computer would take it into hyperdrive and then out in the vicinity of the destination. All without aid of a human pilot.

Nonetheless Votava's paper indicated that cramped living quarters were included in the power-control modules for use by emergency repair crews. She'd been very specific about that. So much so that McCade had begun to wonder. What if Bridger and Votava were aboard one of the huge ships? Hidden away in the emergency living quarters which no one would think to examine. Waiting until the search died down. Sweating out the days and minutes until the giant vessel hurled itself into hyperspace. It made a great theory, McCade reflected as the tiny troop carrier skimmed along the flanks of a mighty battlewagon, bristling with turrets and launch tubes. And he was going to feel damn silly if it was wrong.

Bright sunlight poured into the cockpit as the troop carrier emerged from the battleship's shadow. Ahead, the huge cargo carrier gleamed in the sun. It wasn't pretty. Built to voyage only in deep space, it had none of the streamlined beauty common to ships designed to negotiate planetary atmospheres. It was long and cylindrical. The hull was not a proper hull at all, but comprised of thousands of cargo pods, each connected to those around it by standard fittings. As a result the ship had a bumpy, textured look. Their angle of approach hid it, but McCade knew from the diagrams he'd studied that the power-control module was suspended in the center of the hollow space running the length of the cylinder.

They were closer now. He could see four tugs, dwarfed by the freighter's tremendous bulk, cautiously starting to tow it out of orbit. It was the largest ship he'd ever seen. No wonder they'd christened it *Leviathan*.

There wasn't much time left. His foot tapped out an impatient rhythm until he became conscious of it, and forced himself to stop. Being a passenger was driving him crazy. As soon as the vessel was clear of other traffic it would enter hyper-space, where the little troop carrier could not follow. Days or weeks later it would emerge in the vicinity of Weller's World, a relatively primitive planet just inside the frontier.

"Sam . . . look." Laurie pointed to the main detector screen. It showed a luminescent outline of the cargo carrier and the four tugs. Now a sixth ship appeared. Its outline suggested an atmospheric shuttle, a guess confirmed moments later when the computer inserted "AS Type IV" in the lower right-hand corner of the screen. Until moments before, it had been hidden on the far side of the *Leviathan*. Now it had cleared the larger ship and seemed headed their way. At first McCade was unconcerned. Chances were it was on a perfectly innocent errand. In any case it was an unarmed model, and there wasn't much it could do short of ramming them.

However, as it got closer, it became increasingly apparent that the shuttle intended to intercept them. The com screen came to life with an excellent likeness of Cadet Votava. He noticed with amusement that she'd promoted herself to lieu-tenant commander. Nonetheless she was quite convincing. Her voice carried just the right mix of bored authority and arrogance.

"This is a restricted Naval Operation Area under code one-niner-zero-two alpha. Reverse course immediately or be fired upon." Her image faded to black before McCade could reply.

"We've got 'em," McCade said with grim satisfaction.

"Maybe," Laurie replied, turning up the magnification on the detector screen. The shuttle had slowed and opened its cargo bay. A dozen tiny figures dressed in space armor spilled out. One maneuvered a space sled. On it rested the unmistak-able form of a recoilless energy cannon.

McCade felt his pulse begin to race. The energy cannon was designed for surface action against enemy armor. Its use in space was extremely unconventional. But it would work. One of Bridger's ideas no doubt. Walt was right—the man was dangerous. That kind of creativity applied to an entire battle could be devastating. Meanwhile the cannon was a very real threat. It had its own integral tracking system, and more than enough power to vaporize the small troop carrier. A fact not lost on Laurie, who hurled the troop carrier into a series of gut-wrenching, heart-stopping, evasive maneuvers that made the hull creak. She seemed to enjoy it. McCade didn't, but was determined not to show it. If he'd been at the controls himself, it wouldn't have bothered him, but just sitting there watching, it made him feel queasy.

Laurie switched on the suit coms and her voice boomed into his helmet. "Attention all personnel ... button up and stand by for cabin depressurization. Section Leader ... by the numbers please."

McCade went over his gear, checking seals, power supply, oxygen and so forth, while behind him Van Doren and his men did the same. McCade glanced up to see the shuttle getting uncomfortably close. It appeared the energy cannon would be operational any moment.

"Section One, combat ready, Captain," Van Doren said formally. "On your command."

Out of the corner of his eye McCade saw Laurie was pleased by the honorary "Captain."

"Roger," she replied with equal gravity. "Ejection and enemy contact in approximately four minutes. Secure the energy cannon by whatever means possible. Take prisoners if you can ... but don't risk your men unnecessarily. I don't know who they are, but one thing's for sure, they don't look friendly."

"Aye aye, Captain," Van Doren answered calmly.

McCade flinched as a pulse of blue light raced by in front of them. A ranging shot. A vise closed on his chest as they went into a tight turn and raced straight toward the cannon. The troop carrier shuddered as an energy pulse slid down its side. A red warning light blinked on in front of McCade. The cabin was fully depressurized. Laurie's gloved hands danced over the controls. The troop carrier began to zigzag in a random pattern. The little ship shuddered and groaned under the strain. McCade felt the tug of the facial tic that always plagued him in moments of stress. He hoped Laurie wouldn't notice it and desperately wished for something to do.

Laurie touched a button and the top of the carrier split down the middle as the sides were retracted into the hull. McCade felt momentary vertigo as she put the small craft through another series of acrobatic maneuvers.

"Five, four, three, two, one," Laurie counted, and hit the ejection control. Together Van Doren and his marines were blasted out of the troop carrier in perfect formation. As the ship raced away, McCade watched the rear screen on full magnification. Laurie had placed them slightly above and behind the cannon. Once clear of the troop carrier, each marine released his seat and used his suit jets to blast down toward the enemy.

Van Doren was in the lead. His men were spread out in V formation behind him. Lines of blue light rippled and flared as both sides opened fire. A marine disappeared in a yellow-red explosion. Then the cannon and two figures near it flashed incandescent as they were hit by a shoulder-launched missile. "Got the sonovabitch," an exuberant voice shouted over McCade's suit com, followed by a scream as a marine was hit.

"I want radio silence, goddamnit!" Van Doren bellowed.

After that the battle was silent, men moving as though part of an eerie, slow-motion ballet which someone had forgotten to score. Shoulder weapons lashed out, slicing through armor as if it weren't there. Then, as the combatants got closer to each other, hand blasters came into play. Their less powerful beams often failed to penetrate the heavy armor, causing many to draw older and more effective weapons. McCade thought he could make out Van Doren swinging an enormous battle axe as he led his men into hand-to-hand combat. While difficult to use in normal gravity, the axe would be lethal in zero G, especially in the hands of an expert. And Van Doren was undoubtedly an expert. Then the screen went blank as the little ship passed out of high mag detection range.

The enormous bulk of the freighter loomed ahead. The tugs had cut their tractor beams and started to move off. Laurie frowned in concentration as they skimmed the side of the large ship.

"The lock's just ahead," she said. "Get ready."

The lock was located about halfway down the ship's length. A long tunnel running through the center of a support strut connected the lock with the power-control module suspended in the center of the hollow cylinder. McCade was thinking about the length of the tunnel.

"It's gonna be real fun trying to get down that tunnel if there's someone at the other end shooting at us."

"A cheerful thought," she said grimly as she brought the troop carrier down in a graceful arc, killing thrust, and gliding smoothly toward the other ship's lock. She flicked a switch activating a light tractor beam which locked onto the larger vessel and began to reel them in. Moments later they were snuggled up a few feet below *Leviathan's* lock.

McCade hit his seat release. His stomach lurched as he floated free of the ship. An eternity of emptiness stretched away in every direction. He felt the moment of panic that always accompanied free fall for him. They'd almost washed him out of the Academy for it. Forcing himself to concentrate, he fired his suit jets, and moments later was clinging to the other ship's lock, happy to have his hands on something solid again.

Meanwhile Laurie was using the troop carrier's com unit. "Merchant ship *Leviathan* . . . Merchant ship *Leviathan* . . . This is naval vessel MTC four-niner-two. Terminate departure immediately. Imperial Navy authorization code four-five-one delta zero . . . I repeat . . ."

McCade decided the lock had either been purposely jammed or shorted out.

There was a burst of static over his suit radio followed by a male voice which could only be Bridger. "Naval vessel MTC four-niner-two. Cut your tractor beam and depart at once. Make no further attempt to board this ship. I repeat . . . depart at once. This vessel will shift into hyperspace ten standard minutes from now. Repeat . . . ten standard minutes and counting. End of transmission."

McCade swore under his breath and struggled even harder with the lock mechanism. Laurie appeared at his elbow. She held a ship cracker cradled in her arms. It was intended for rescue work on damaged ships and could cut through almost anything. The ship cracker wasn't heavy in zero gravity, but it was bulky and awkward. Normally operated by a crew of three, it took both of them to hold and aim it. As Laurie pulled the trigger, a ruby red lance of energy leapt from the device's nozzle and bit into the ship's durasteel hull.

McCade began to sweat. He felt his recycling unit shift into a higher speed. He could just barely make out Laurie's face through her darkened visor. Sweat rolled off her face and her teeth were bared in a grimace. A dark comma of hair had fallen across the whiteness of her forehead. McCade thought she looked beautiful.

Moments later the beam cut through the lock's mechanism and the hatch swung open. There was no rush of atmosphere into space. The tunnel had been depressurized. McCade wondered why. He didn't like the possibilities. Motioning Laurie to stay back, he entered the tunnel. It stretched off into the distance, ending in another hatch which provided access to the power-control module. The tunnel was evenly lit and empty. The walls covered with a maze of pipes and electrical conduit. It looked too easy—too inviting. McCade took a few cautious steps forward, gesturing to Laurie for radio silence. Bridger could easily monitor their suit radios. McCade pulled his blaster and began to move swiftly down the tunnel. He noticed the weapon had none of his slug gun's comforting weight. He'd have to compensate for that.

He soon reached a junction where two smaller maintenance shafts joined the main tunnel from the left and right. Cautiously he peered into each. Both were dark beyond the first twenty feet. He signaled Laurie, and together they hurried forward. McCade figured they had five minutes at most before the ship hurled itself into hyperspace, taking them with it.

A figure dressed in space armor dropped from the ceiling. Apparently he'd been hiding in a vertical maintenance shaft. He fired his blaster before his feet hit the deck. That was a mistake. His bolt went wide. Smoke and electrical sparks poured out of a section of pipe and conduit to McCade's right. McCade fired his blaster in reply. A white-hot hole appeared where the man's chest had been. He was slammed back against the tunnel wall.

"Behind us, Sam!" Her voice was shrill.

Instinctively he dropped to the deck, and sensed more than saw the energy beam that passed over his head. Scrambling on all fours he turned to see Laurie go down. Beyond her lay a headless figure in space armor. Next to the body knelt another man who had a blaster centered on McCade's chest. McCade began to bring his own blaster up knowing he'd never make it. As he waited to die, some remote part of his brain reproached him for not checking the side tunnels more carefully. If he'd only had more time. . . . Then the man's left side disappeared as Laurie blasted him from the deck. McCade moved quickly to her side. She seemed so small, even in bulky space armor. Behind the visor her face was terribly white and drawn. A quick check revealed no sign of a wound, and her armor seemed intact.

"Laurie?" he said.

Her eyes blinked open, and she managed a weak smile.

Wordlessly he picked her up as gently as he could and started down the tunnel toward the lock. He'd taken only a few steps when a tremendous jolt threw them both to the deck. The lights went out, and a moment of total darkness passed before dim emergency lights flickered on. McCade knew he should get up but couldn't find the energy. The half-healed wound in his left arm began to throb. The pain cleared his head. He felt the deck move erratically under him. Then he understood. Bridger had detonated the explosive, emergency fittings connecting the power-control module to the cargo pods—and disappeared into hyperspace. Evidently he didn't want to take the boarding party with him—especially since they were winning.

The force of the power-control module's departure, plus the loss of its mass, put the remaining part of the ship into an erratic spin and tumble. As he struggled to his feet McCade wondered if the cargo pods would hold together. Awkwardly he gathered Laurie's inert form into his arms and started toward the lock. He'd taken only a few steps when the emergency lights flickered off and the artificial gravity disappeared. Somewhere an emergency generator had failed. Naturally the main field generators had vanished into hyperspace along with the power-control module. After a brief moment of dizziness, McCade managed to shift his grip on Laurie to use only one hand, so he could use the other to activate his helmet light. He pushed off the nearest bulkhead in the direction of a handhold. As he moved from handhold to handhold, he quickly decided weightlessness was an advantage rather than a problem. By towing Laurie behind him he could make fairly good time.

Occasionally, forward motion stalled as the hull tumbled and they were thrown into the nearest bulkhead. McCade worried that the violent motion of the ship might break the light tractor beam securing the troop carrier to the hull. If it did it would be one helluva walk home. Which reminded him of the marines. Their air would be running low. He tried to move even faster. Finally he made it to the lock. To his relief the troop carrier was still there. He paused, calculated, hoped for the best, and jumped. They damn near soared right by the smaller ship before he managed to grab an antenna with his free hand and haul them in.

He strapped Laurie into the copilot's seat, slid behind the controls, and plugged his suit into the ship. Fresh oxygen squirted into his helmet, and there was a burst of static as the radio came on, followed by an exchange of conversation between Van Doren and a navy shuttle. The marines were being picked up. He started the engines, cut the tractor beam, and plunged recklessly down into the atmosphere.

Four

McCade sat staring at the green wall, wondering why hospital walls were always green. "Of all the colors you could program a wall to be, why choose bile green? Ah! There's the connection," he mused wryly. "It's obvious, once you put your mind to it."

Wearily he swung his feet over onto the floor. He made an ancient gesture of derision toward the nearest scanner. Only Walt would put surveillance sensors in a hospital room. He stood slowly, and then shuffled over to the wash basin in one corner. He splashed cold water on his face and looked up into the bloodshot eyes which stared balefully back from the metal mirror. He watched in the mirror as the door behind him slid open. He wasn't surprised to see Swanson-Pierce. The other man's right arm was in a cast and sling. Somehow he made it appear dashing and elegant.

"Well, Sam old boy, you've been at it again, haven't you?" Swanson-Pierce said, settling himself into one of the room's two ugly chairs. "Bodies everywhere." He shook his head sadly. "Unauthorized use of a naval vessel, not to mention half a dozen Imperial marines, illegal boarding of a merchant ship, and a re-entry that broke every regulation in the book. It's quite a list. I've spent the entire morning trying to sort the whole thing out. God help us if the press gets hold of it."

"Blow it out your tubes, Walt," McCade said angrily, walking painfully over and sitting on the edge of the bed. He remembered the frantic plunge through the atmosphere, way too fast for the shields to shed enough heat, the emergency landing, confusion, and arrest. But nothing about Laurie. Trying to appear casual, McCade asked, "How's Laurie?"

Swanson-Pierce raised an eyebrow and replied, "The lieutenant is fine . . . no thanks to you. I left her moments ago in the base hospital. Evidently she suffered a mild concussion. She says someone bounced her helmet off a bulkhead." There was curiosity in the naval officer's look which McCade chose to ignore.

"I'm glad she's okay," McCade said. "She's a good kid. . . . She did all right up there." He remembered looking into the blaster and waiting to die. He fumbled through his pockets for a cigar. "And the marines?"

"One dead, four wounded, and one of those probably won't make it," the other man replied soberly, his eyes on the deck.

McCade winced. One dead and maybe another. For nothing. Bridger had escaped. His searching fingers found a cigar butt which he lit with a trembling hand. He sucked smoke deep into his lungs and blew it toward the deck. "And Van Doren?"

Swanson-Pierce's expression changed to amusement as he said, "Corporal Van Doren is fine." He paused for effect. "His Captain's Mast adjourned about half an hour ago. It seems he pleaded guilty to drunkenness on duty, issuance of illegal orders, theft of a navy vessel, illegal dueling, and interference with a merchant ship. All things considered, I think he got off easy, don't you?"

"You really think the press'll buy that?" McCade asked.

Swanson-Pierce shrugged. "They have so far. It's preferable to censorship, which always makes people even more interested."

McCade stared wordlessly into the naval officer's gaze, his

thoughts still on the marine who had died and the other who probably would.

After a moment Swanson-Pierce said, "Don't do it, Sam. It won't help. These things just happen sometimes, that's all. Besides, we've gained quite a bit actually. It's true they got away . . . but at least we know they haven't made contact with the Il Ronn. So we've got a chance." He paused. "You'll be interested to know your marine friends took a prisoner." He watched McCade expectantly.

The silence stretched out. Finally McCade gave in. "And what did you learn from that prisoner?" McCade asked through gritted teeth.

"I thought you'd never ask," the other man replied with evident satisfaction. "It seems he, along with his stalwart companion, were all port-trash of one kind or another. Ex-mercenaries, beached spacemen, laid-off miners and the like. I'm sure you know the type." His expression made it clear that he thought McCade probably knew the type intimately.

McCade ignored it. "Then they weren't assassins," he said thoughtfully.

"Exactly," Swanson-Pierce replied smugly. "Apparently Bridger hired an ex-mercenary named Iverson, who then recruited the rest. Unfortunately Iverson met an untimely end recently while operating an energy cannon. Clever idea that. Anyway it may interest you to know Iverson made the bomb which concluded our luncheon in such a dramatic fashion." He made a microscopic adjustment to his sling.

McCade frowned thoughtfully. "So let's see, these . . . what did you call them? Port-trash? They infiltrate Naval Intelligence Headquarters, plant a bomb on exactly the right auto-cart, and then make their escape. All without your fancy hardware and highly trained spooks noticing anything suspicious. I don't know, Walt. . . . It's not the kind of report I'd want to file." He shook his head in mock concern.

Swanson-Pierce recrossed elegantly clad legs nervously. "Well, ah, yes, naturally we're quite concerned. Unfortunately our prisoner doesn't know how the bomb was placed or detonated. He swore, however, that he helped Iverson put it together. We have our best investigators on the problem."

"Terrific," McCade said, crushing the cigar butt under his heel. "If Bridger knew, he'd be terrified. While they're at it maybe they can find out where everybody's getting little items like energy cannon, high explosives, and navy-issue space armor."

Swanson-Pierce coughed and looked slightly embarrassed as he studied the gleaming toe of his right boot. "Actually I think we know the answer to that one. Our prisoner says they all came out of the *Leviathan*'s cargo. Evidently part of a shipment for the marine detachment on Weller's World."

McCade shook his head in disgust. "Well tell me this. . . . If Iverson's men worked for Bridger . . . who sent the assassins? And why?" Both men stared at each other and silence filled the room.

Swanson-Pierce broke the silence. "You'll know when we do." He paused as he turned to leave. "They say you'll be discharged in the morning. I trust you've got everything you need?"

McCade nodded silently.

"Well, good hunting then." When the other man didn't answer, Swanson-Pierce slipped out of the room closing the door behind him.

McCade sat in the darkened control room staring at the viewscreen. Around him, *Pegasus* hummed and vibrated gently. The air was cool and dry, carrying the faint aroma of cooking. He watched, fascinated, as constellations wheeled slowly along their eternal paths and stars shimmered across the unimaginable distances of space. Of course they weren't real. As long as the ship remained in hyperspace, normal space wasn't visible. These were computer simulations. But they looked real, and he never tired of their beauty. The flickering light of the screen brought back memories of boyhood campfires when the dancing flames had captured his eyes and set his mind free to roam a sky full of mysterious stars. Now the stars no longer seemed mysterious. Just beautiful points of light, none of which were home.

"Hi, Sam!" Laurie dropped into the seat next to him. He turned, and the brightness of her smile washed away his somber thoughts. Her hair had fallen across her brow again and her eyes flashed as she shook it back into place. "Why so serious?" she asked.

He smiled. "Just remembering how things were when I was a boy."

"And how were they?" she asked, drawing her knees up under her chin, regarding him seriously.

McCade shrugged. "Pretty good actually. I spent my early years on Dorca III, and then my parents were transferred to Terra, and naturally I went with them. They were electrical engineers. They must have been good, because they both taught at the Imperial Academy of Arts and Sciences. Dad died a few years ago of a heart attack, and Mom went a year later. I wasn't surprised. She wanted to be with him." He stared at the viewscreen for a moment before speaking again. "I don't think they were very pleased about the way I turned out." He looked across at Laurie. "How 'bout you?"

A veil fell over her eyes as she replied. "Oh nothing special. . . . I never knew my parents. . . . They were killed in some kind of accident out near the frontier. So I spent a lot of time in various kinds of schools and academies. I did well, and managed to enter the Academy. . . . End of story."

McCade didn't believe it. Oh, what she'd said was probably true enough, but he felt sure she was leaving a lot out. Why? There was no way to tell.

Laurie sniffed the air dramatically, her eyes flashing once more. "Smells good! Wait till you see what Amos made for dinner! Who'd of thought a stuffy old marine could cook?"

"Lucky for us he's an expert with the ship's weapons too," McCade replied dryly.

"Phooey," she said. "I'm an expert with the weapons. . . . What we needed was a cook!" She made a face and disappeared toward the lounge.

McCade smiled after her. Swanson-Pierce had insisted she come. She'd volunteered, probably at Swanson-Pierce's request, and the medics had given their approval, also at the naval officer's request no doubt. In any case she'd been sent along to keep an eye on him. McCade had given in with a tremendous show of reluctance.

The main control monitor buzzed softly. He looked up to see that they would emerge from hyperspace in six standard hours. He punched the "acknowledge" button and began a routine scan of the major system readouts. Of course the ship's computer did the same thing thousands of times a second, but it made him feel better. And once in a while over the years he'd even found something wrong.

They'd been in hyperspace for three weeks. During that time they'd traversed a distance it would've taken pre-empire ships years to cross. That hadn't stopped the early colonists, though. They'd risen from Terra and disappeared into the blackness of space. Some won through to habitable planets. Many didn't. In time the colonized worlds broke free of Earth and formed their own governments. The Confederation followed. Some said it was the lack of hyperdrive, as much as constant bickering, which caused the Confederation to disintegrate. It takes speedy communication to hold a stellar government together. And since no one had managed to punch a com beam through interstellar distances, ships remained the fastest form of communication.

It was certainly true that the rise of the first emperor occurred about the time a workable hyperdrive was discovered. In fact most historians agreed that the first emperor couldn't have won without it. Even though they were vastly outnumbered at the start, hyperdrive enabled his ships to travel vast distances in a fraction of the time required by the Confederates, a tactical advantage he exploited brilliantly. Even so, he'd been forced to amass a great fleet, and fight battle after battle. The empire he'd built was founded on hyperdrive and the blood of those who didn't have it.

McCade's thoughts were interrupted as the intercom buzzed, followed by Van Doren's basso saying, "Chow's on, sir. . . . I mean boss."

"Thanks, Amos." McCade grinned. Van Doren was supposed to be his bodyguard, not an Imperial marine. But old habits die hard and Van Doren was still having trouble ridding himself of his military mannerisms. McCade had asked Swanson-Pierce to restore the marine's former rank, and the naval officer had agreed—but only if McCade would take the man along on detached duty. All the marines who'd been in the fight with Bridger's men were being reassigned far from Terra's inquisitive press—except for the two buried with full honors, McCade thought soberly.

For his part Van Doren was eager to go along. He wanted to be there when they caught up with Bridger. But by way of an added incentive he'd been told that otherwise his next duty station would be on a planet called Swamp. A small detachment of marines was stationed there to protect resident scientists from their specimens.

After an excellent meal of smoked Fola on a bed of steamed Zuma, with chocolate torte for dessert, courtesy of the ship's stasis locker, the three of them relaxed over coffee in the lounge. McCade rolled rich cigar smoke off his tongue filling the air with an evil-looking blue haze.

"Remind me to renew my anticancer treatments," Laurie said, wrinkling her nose in disgust and turning the lounge's air scrubber up a notch.

"If there *are* twelve torpedoes waiting at the nav beacon," McCade replied, "there isn't much chance we'll die of cancer."

She stuck out her tongue at him but knew he was right. They'd gone through *Leviathan*'s cargo manifest together before launch. Besides explosives, energy weapons and space armor, the huge ship carried five hundred Interceptor-class torpedoes bound for the Naval Arms Depot on Weller's World. After the giant hulk was caught and towed back to Earth orbit, a quick inventory revealed that twelve of the torpedoes were missing.

McCade considered the torpedoes as he sipped his coffee. Each needle-shaped black hull would be ten feet long. Aboard would be a very sophisticated minicomputer, an array of sensors, and a tidy little nuclear warhead. Usually they were carried and launched by Interceptors, small one-person fighters like the one tucked away in the bay where *Pegasus* normally carried her lifeboat. Trading the lifeboat for the Interceptor was a calculated risk. The lifeboat could save their lives in case of trouble, but so could the fighter; it all depended on which way things went.

To make matters worse, before they had left, naval armorers had confirmed that an expert could rig the torpedoes for an ambush. It had been done once or twice before. Was Bridger an expert? No one knew for sure—but they'd have to assume he was. He'd certainly had access to the necessary information.

If Bridger laid an ambush, the nav beacon would be the logical place to do it. Though technically a ship equipped with hyperdrive could enter and depart hyperspace anywhere, doing so entailed an element of risk. What if you happened to pick an exit point right in the middle of a large asteroid, for example? No one ever lived to report such incidents, of course, but there was little doubt they occasionally happened. As a result, a far-flung network of nav beacons had been established along the Empire's main trade routes. Each emitted its own distinctive code while entering and exiting hyperspace at one minute intervals. That way the beacon could be located by ships traveling in either normal space or hyperspace.

So while scouts and prospectors took pride in playing cosmic roulette and rarely had the luxury of using nav beacons, ships using established lanes always did. Therefore Bridger could expect his pursuit to emerge from hyperspace soon after he did and in proximity to the nav beacon. They'd considered sending an unmanned drone through first, but naval experts had agreed the torpedoes' sensors were too sophisticated to fall for such a ploy. And when McCade had suggested a destroyer, Swanson-Pierce had laughed, saying the Empire couldn't spare warships to chase after torpedoes which might or might not be there.

Van Doren spoke as if he'd read McCade's mind. "With all due respect, boss, you shouldn't worry so much." He patted the bulkhead next to him. "She's sound as an Imperial credit, not to mention that I've checked her personally, and when the time comes she'll show 'em a thing or two!" It was a long speech for the big marine. He leaned back, eyes bright under bushy brows, lips curved in a smile which held little humor. McCade smiled and nodded, wishing he shared the marine's confidence.

A few hours later McCade was reclining in the pilot's seat wearing full armor. Laurie occupied the copilot's position beside him, her face hidden by her visor. He wondered what she was thinking. Did she feel she should be sitting in the pilot's position? It had been a long time since he had taken a ship into combat. But damn it, *Pegasus* was his ship. He wouldn't always have Laurie to lean on. At least that's what he was telling himself.

Behind and slightly above them, Van Doren sat enclosed in a gun blister. Without sufficient crew to fully man the ship's secondary armament, most of it had been slaved to his position. Of course if there was an ambush, most of the battle would be fought by the ship's computer using the main armament. No human eye and brain could track tiny targets traveling at thousands of miles an hour. Not unless they got very close. Then the secondary armament would be their last chance.

"Do you think it'll work?" Laurie asked, her voice unnaturally casual.

"Sure I do," McCade lied.

After all, it could work, he thought. They had programmed the ship's computer to overshoot the nav beacon slightly. If there were torpedoes waiting, hopefully they'd be aimed at the next exit area immediately around the beacon. It would take the torpedoes a moment to detect *Pegasus* outside that area, recompute attack trajectories, and launch. That moment would be their edge.

McCade's eyes were locked on the main control monitor as the final seconds ticked away. At its center the nav beacon was represented by a white light. It appeared and disappeared as it jumped in and out of hyperspace. Then there was the second of disorientation and nausea he always felt during a hyperspace shift, followed by subtle changes in the viewscreens as the computer switched from simulated to actual images.

Now they were in normal space . . . and for a moment . . . so was the nav beacon. Close by, a yellow light blinked, probably *Leviathan*'s power-control module. Around it appeared a globe of red dots. Each represented a torpedo. Just inside the perimeter of the globe, almost touching a red dot, was a green light symbolizing *Pegasus*. Their plan hadn't worked. They were practically sitting on a torpedo. The torpedo vanished in a flash of intense white light before McCade could utter a sound. Van Doren's battle cry was still ringing in his ears when it was replaced by a calm but unfamiliar female voice.

"This ship is under attack. Please prepare for high-stress evasive action. The bar and all recreational facilities are closed."

McCade would have laughed, but a crushing weight was suddenly added to his chest. *Pegasus* accelerated and began to execute a series of intricate evasive maneuvers. Through blurred vision he saw the remaining red dots reorient themselves and begin inexorably to close on *Pegasus*. McCade felt a slight jolt as the ship launched torpedoes of its own. To his satisfaction he watched two red dots disappear in explosions so bright the ship's sensors were forced to dampen down or burn out. But a third red dot was closing fast.

"Enemy target now leaving primary defensive zone sector four-eight. Engage with secondaries," the calm computer voice said. "Due to immediate defensive energy requirements, there will be no hot water for showers until two standard hours after termination of engagement."

"I've got it," McCade said as he struggled to clear his vision and concentrate.

As his hand closed around the control grip for the bow energy cannon, he heard a double "Roger" from Laurie and Van Doren. The control worked much like the stick in an atmosphere flier. As he squeezed it, a target monitor came to life in front of him. When he rotated the handle to the right the target grid moved right on the screen. McCade lined up on the growing red dot. His thumb pressed the button at the top of the handle and pulses of blue light raced out to meet the torpedo. The powerful defensive screens of the *Pegasus* flared to the edge of burnout and then held. As McCade's eyes returned to the main control monitor, he counted five red dots still hurtling toward them. Apparently either *Pegasus* or Van Doren had nailed two more. But it wasn't enough. One or more torpedoes would almost certainly get through.

"Prepare for emergency damage control," the pleasant voice said. "Due to this vessel's current tactical situation, it seems advisable that both passengers and crew seek alternate transportation as soon as possible." McCade gritted his teeth and promised himself that if he survived, the computer wouldn't. Now he knew why the ship's previous owner had restricted the computer's use of voice simulation.

"Sam! There's a chance. Hit it now!" Laurie pointed at the bright red cover located in the very center of the control console.

McCade understood immediately. Without hesitation he flipped up the cover and hit the switch it protected. This time the disorientation and nausea of the hyperspace shift was a welcome relief. The moment the shift was complete, he hit the computer override switch again, felt his stomach lurch, and watched as the screen adjusted back to normal space. Their forward motion had carried them away from the nav beacon. The light created by the five torpedoes' mutual annihilation was just starting to fade behind them. McCade felt a muscle in his left cheek begin to twitch as he thought about the odds against surviving both the torpedoes and two random hyperspace shifts.

Laurie had removed her helmet. Sweat matted her dark hair. Her face was frozen in a silly grin. "We made it," she said.

"Thanks to you," he answered simply. Her eyes registered pleasure at the compliment. Suddenly he felt old. It'd been a long time since he'd been a hot young Interceptor pilot. He should've thought of a hyperspace shift himself.

"We're a good team, that's all," Laurie said. "Isn't that right, Amos?"

"Damned right," the big man answered, lowering his bulk from the gun blister. "I told ya she wouldn't let us down, didn't I, boss?"

"The bar is now open," the computer said.

McCade laughed. "You were right, Amos, she's a great ship."

A few minutes later they had swung around and were positioned near *Leviathan*'s power-control module. It looked like an oversized tin can. A few random cargo pods were still connected to it where the explosive fittings had failed to detonate. To all appearances it was deserted. Repeated attempts to make radio contact brought no reply.

"Well," McCade said grimly, "it looks like we're gonna have to do it the hard way."

Laurie looked concerned. "I don't think that's a good idea, Sam. They might have rigged her to blow the moment someone goes aboard."

"Right, boss," Van Doren added. "Why not get some swabbies up here and let them check her out. They've got the gear for this sorta thing. Or, better yet, let's just put a torp in 'er."

"Both your suggestions are tempting, Amos," McCade replied with a smile. "But the first would take too long, and the second would leave us with a lot of unanswered questions, not to mention some unhappy owners. No, I'm gonna have to board her."

"We're going to board her!" Laurie said.

"Right, boss," Van Doren added, eyes gleaming with anticipation. McCade sighed, and shook his head in mock exasperation.

Half an hour later McCade swung open the hatch to *Leviathan*'s lock. He paused for a moment, giving thanks that nothing had blown up, and then entered.

Back aboard *Pegasus*, Van Doren sat stoically in his gun blister, eyes searching, finger on the trigger. Below him Laurie fumed at the ship's controls. Neither was happy. But in McCade's judgment anything else would be stupid. If there was trouble it wouldn't help if they all got killed. This way they could come to his rescue if required. Besides, it was a one-person job. Or at least that's what he'd told Laurie. Deep down, a part of him wondered if he was grandstanding. Trying to make up for his failure to think of the hyperspace shift. Pushing those thoughts aside, he opened the inner hatch. What he saw was not pretty. Three bodies lay sprawled in a jumbled pile before him.

The first thing he noticed was that none of them were wearing armor. So the module had been pressurized when they'd come aboard. He checked for atmosphere and then opened his visor. A quick and unpleasant inspection revealed that none of the bodies were those of Bridger or Votava. There were two men and a woman. All three were dressed in coveralls bearing the logo of the Meteor Tug Company. They'd all been shot at close range with a small caliber slug gun. As far as he could tell they'd been unarmed. They hadn't been killed, they'd been executed. The coldness of it turned his stomach. Bridger was no longer a rational being. Any sympathy McCade had ever felt for the two fugitives was replaced by a hard knot of burning anger that settled in his stomach and wouldn't go away.

McCade allowed himself to fall back into a fold-down seat. He couldn't take his eyes off the bodies. Why? It didn't make sense. He tried to imagine how it had happened. The tug routinely coming alongside. The crew wondering aloud about the missing cargo pods. The slight hiss of escaping pressure as the locks made contact and then opened. A murmur of conversation as the crew entered, expecting to find an empty module. Instead, what? A confrontation? Probably. Followed by three cold-blooded killings. There was no doubt about who had done it. Then what? Bridger and Votava had used the tug to place the torpedoes and then headed for Weller's World. A planetary tug couldn't take them much farther anyway.

McCade fastened his armor, found a cigar butt and lit it. The smoke helped to disguise the fetid air. His thoughts drifted back to the cockpit of his Interceptor. The image of a pirate ship sharp and clear in the old-fashioned weapon sight, his thumb on the firing stud, and two voices fighting to command him. The first a woman's voice, a pirate, pleading with him to spare her ship, swearing she had only women and children aboard. The second voice was Bridger's, hoarse from hours of shouted commands, ordering him over and over again to fire.

The cigar butt burned his fingers. He dropped it and crushed it under his boot. He began to search the tiny cabin. Bridger and Votava had lived in the tiny space for almost two months. At some point the overloaded recycler had broken down and trash had started to pile up on the deck. Discarded clothing, rotting food and other less identifiable debris were all mixed together into an unpleasant history of their confinement.

As McCade sorted through it in random fashion, he began to notice scraps of writing. Sometimes it was on common note paper, but more often than not it was on other things, the margins of pages torn out of operational manuals, on the backs of napkins, disposable plates—literally anything. For the most part the writing was incoherent, and as far as McCade could tell, meaningless. The more passages he found the more they seemed to him to be the ravings of a lunatic. McCade was familiar with Bridger's handwriting, having seen it on his own commission as a lieutenant and his final court martial, as well as several more recent documents. It was Bridger's handwriting all right. But the mind controlling it was far from normal. Bridger was either physically ill or in the process of losing his mind.

McCade paused to read the scribbling in the margin of a sheet bearing the title, "CARGO MODULE SURVIVAL KIT INVENTORY N4689." Carefully written into the margin on the left-hand side was "Inventory. Inventory. Inventory. I'll show them inventory! Marvelous inventory! Glorious inventory! Inventory sufficient to wipe out once and for all the devil's servants. Inventory too long on the shelf. Inventory I shall use to cleanse the heavens!"

It didn't make any sense, and yet it did. McCade was reminded of the metal plate. Once again he felt sure Bridger had cracked the secret hidden there. And in doing so he'd obtained weapons of some kind. "Inventory sufficient to wipe out once and for all the devil's servants," he'd said. That sounded pretty lethal. Of course if the man was operating on about half power, then he could be hallucinating too. He searched for another fifteen minutes. He found lots of additional scribbles, but nothing that made sense. Finally he gave up.

When he called *Pegasus* on his suit radio Laurie's anxious voice made him feel guilty for not calling earlier. He explained the situation, sealed his suit and started for the lock. Then something caught his eye. Bending over he picked up a handful of photographs from the litter on the deck. They'd been partially obscured by an outflung arm. Holding the pictures under an overhead light, he quickly scanned them. All were human. Outside of that he couldn't find any special commonality. Men, women, young, old, civilian, military... there were all kinds of people. Why would Bridger and Votava have what seemed like a random assortment of photos aboard?

Getting down on his hands and knees he searched the deck for any he might have missed. Then he noticed a corner of something sticking out of a clenched fist. Gritting his teeth he pried open the cold, stiff fingers. He removed a crumpled photograph and smoothed it out. To his surprise Laurie's familiar brown eyes stared back at him. A chill ran down his spine. What in space was her photo doing here clutched in a dead man's hand? Was he trying to communicate something? If so, what? Laurie certainly hadn't been present when he died. It didn't make sense. But then these days, what did?

He stared at the picture for a long time. Finally he stood and tucked it away. He'd decided not to show it to her right away. For some reason he couldn't quite put his finger on, he felt guilty about that decision. He sealed his suit and entered the lock. Moments later he stepped out into the starry void.

Five

EVEN THOUGH IT was more than a klick away, he could
make out every detail of the sprawling complex through the
powerful lens. The scope was a military model mounted on a
tripod. Just one of the "extras" he'd conned Laurie out of back
on Earth. Not that it'd done them much good so far. McCade
leaned back for a moment to rest his eyes.

They'd been watching the Il Ronn legation for two days
now. So far there'd been no sign of Bridger or Votava. In fact
there'd been no signs of life at all. If it hadn't been for the
comings and goings of the occasional hover limo, he would
have concluded that the place was deserted. Considering the
on-again, off-again state of hostilities between the human and
Il Ronn empires, he was surprised the aliens were even allowed to have legations on human worlds. But it seemed both
sides allowed the other a limited diplomatic presence on certain worlds. If nothing else, it made mutual spying more con-
venient and comfortable.

That was part of what he'd learned at Naval Headquarters shortly after landing on Weller's World. To McCade's surprise, Naval Headquarters was located in a slightly dilapidated dome bordering the spaceport. Usually the Imperial Government went in for more imposing edifices. But even here the inside was brightly painted and efficient. After a short wait in a pleasant reception area, they had been shown into the commanding officer's spartan office. The officer who rose to greet them was a lieutenant. He introduced himself as John Paul Jones. Named after the ancient naval hero, McCade supposed. The fact that such a junior officer was in command showed McCade how thin the navy was stretched along the frontier.

But even if the lieutenant was short on rank, he still managed to be intimidating. His skin was a shiny black. Intelligence gleamed in his dark eyes. He carried himself gun barrel straight, with a belligerent thrust to his chin as though daring someone to hit it. He was in a position of considerable power out here and he knew it.

Laurie identified herself and briefly explained their mission. She also identified the fugitives, but didn't indicate why they were being sought. Jones didn't ask. Like every other officer along the frontier, he'd received instructions to watch for Bridger and Votava. If he had questions about why, he kept them to himself.

He dealt with their situation quickly and efficiently. A team was sent up to sort out the mess aboard the remains of the *Leviathan* and a search was simultaneously launched for the tug. It didn't take his people long to find it. Since Bridger and Votava hadn't dared land at the spaceport, or bring something as large as the tug itself down through the atmosphere for a landing in the wilds, they'd left it in orbit. The tug's lifeboat was missing.

"Chances are they brought it down somewhere in the back country," Lieutenant Jones said. "The farms out there are hundreds of klicks apart and the chances of being seen are just about nil. Then it'd just be a matter of walking and hitchhiking into a town. Logansport's the biggest."

They did their best to pump Jones about local conditions. But outside of giving them some very basic information about the planet and the Il Ronn legation, he was not very communicative. He had barely enough personnel and resources to cope with his regular duties and wanted no part of whatever these two were up to. So they thanked him and followed the directions on the map he'd provided. The Il Ronn legation was located just outside Logansport. They figured that to make contact with the Il Ronn, Bridger would have to go there sooner or later. It was thin, but they didn't have anything better to go on.

So they had put the legation under surveillance, but so far they hadn't seen much. The Il Ronn didn't enjoy the planet's climate and stayed cloistered within their bio-conditioned complex most of the time.

For the hundredth time that day McCade swept the powerful lens over the whitewashed building. All windows were still barred and shuttered. Plus there were other more effective but less visible security measures in effect. Van Doren had attempted a recon the night before. He'd never seen so many sensors. He'd been able to get within a hundred feet of the complex but no farther without risking almost certain discovery. The Il Ronn certainly liked their privacy. And for all he knew, Bridger and Votava might already be in there, having been whisked in right under his nose in a privacy-screened limo.

It was frustrating, and he hoped Laurie was having better luck. He hadn't seen her since the day before. She'd suggested that he and Van Doren man the surveillance post while she tried to contact the local intelligence network. McCade had agreed. They could use all the help they could get. In the meantime, McCade and Van Doren were each doing fourteen hours on and fourteen off. The days on Weller's World were a little longer than Terra's. It wasn't that bad, as stakeouts go. During his years as a bounty hunter McCade had been through much worse.

In fact, after weeks on the ship, it felt good to be dirtside again. A cool breeze relieved the afternoon heat and rustled the slightly bluish foliage that formed a protective canopy overhead. Weller's World was actually quite pleasant. Blessed with broad temperate zones above and below its equator, it was basically an agricultural planet. Rural enterprises of all sorts flourished. Genetically modified Terran crops and animals had been crossed with native flora and fauna to produce hybrids. Over time, some of the hybrids had proved to be quite valuable. Especially those that could be used in the manufacture of pharmaceuticals. The export of hybrid agricultural products provided farmers with cash crops. They spent the money on the machinery required on their labor poor world. Since the machinery was manufactured on planets nearer the Empire's center, Weller's World also made a good market. Gradually the planet had become something of a local trade center too. Being located at the far end of the Empire's trade routes has numerous disadvantages . . . but it has some good points too. For one thing the settlers on the frontier worlds in that sector had started bringing their exportable goods to market on Weller's World. Better prices were available deeper into the Empire, but first you had to get there. At the very least, getting there would cost more. Plus there was the ever-present danger of running into pirates. No, it was better to keep the trip as short as possible. Besides, the people on Weller's World were a rough and ready bunch among whom the frontiersmen felt more comfortable.

So every day one or two beaten up old ships, pre-Empire, some of them, would lower themselves wearily onto the scarred surface of the spaceport. From their dank holds a wild assortment of strange and exotic goods issued forth to be sold at daily auction. With a show of reluctance well-dressed local merchants bought goods for a pittance, which they'd later sell for a small fortune farther into the Empire. But the profit didn't end there. The frontiersmen were eager to spend their credits on electronics, tools, chemicals, vehicles, weapons and more. Such things meant the difference between life and death on their planets. And before they left there'd usually be one night on the town, a wild, uproarious night, to be remembered and exaggerated later. A night of profit for a legion of saloon keepers, drug dealers and prostitutes. Yes, the merchants of Weller's World were doing very well. Plus there were whispers of darker transactions. Of mysterious ships landing in the bush. Of cargos sold, only to reappear in the market a few days later. There was little doubt that some local merchants had strong ties to the pirates. Very profitable ties at that.

There was a rustling behind him and McCade turned, slug gun half out of its holster, to see Van Doren worming his way into the small clearing.

"It's just me, boss," Van Doren said in a stage whisper.

"Sounded like a whole brigade," McCade said, grinning.

"You're just jealous of my manly proportions," the marine replied, rising to his full height within the protective screen of vegetation. "Anything new?"

"Nothing," McCade answered, indicating the legation. "But I figure we should see some action soon."

"I sure hope so," Van Doren said. " 'Cause sittin' here all night ain't my idea of a good time."

McCade yawned. "Speaking of which I'm heading back to town for some shut-eye. Have a good one."

McCade returned the marine's wave and crawled out through the bluish foliage to the nearby farm road. Hidden in the bushes where Van Doren had left it was an old-fashioned electro-cycle. He wheeled it up onto the reddish dirt road, climbed aboard and whirred off toward Logansport.

He awoke panting. His heart was racing. The room felt hot and muggy. His sweat had soaked the sheet under him. The dream had seemed so real. He'd been running through the streets of Logansport. Somewhere ahead of him was Bridger. Behind him a torpedo followed. The closer he got to Bridger, the closer the torpedo got to him. From somewhere up ahead, Bridger's insane laughter floated back to him. It grew louder and louder until it filled the streets, and the people on the sidewalks began to laugh too.

There was a slight noise from the right. He froze—straining to see and hear. His right hand crept by inches toward the butt of the needle gun under his pillow. The cool metal felt reassuring in his hand. There was the scrape of a shoe on the rough wood flooring. A figure moved slowly into the path of the moonlight streaming in through his window. Both moons were full tonight. The face that moved into their combined light was Laurie's. He watched, mesmerized, as she slowly and deliberately brought a handweapon up and aimed it at his chest.

McCade's hand flashed forward. He emptied the needle gun's magazine into her chest. She made a strangled sound and collapsed to the floor. McCade rolled out of bed, hitting a chair, which went over with a crash. Scrambling to his feet he snatched the slug gun from the dresser and aimed it into the pool of darkness where she'd fallen. Then he reached over and hit the lights.

A seething pool of greenish protoplasm met his eyes. There was no sign of Laurie beyond pieces of her clothing, which were mixed in with the strange green substance. The door banged open and Laurie burst in, a small sleeve gun in her hand. She aimed it at the mess on the floor. "I heard a noise! What is it?" she asked, nose wrinkled in distaste.

McCade regarded her with a raised eyebrow. "Believe it or not . . . it looked exactly like you until a moment ago. No offense," he added dryly.

"What's it doing here?" Laurie asked.

McCade shrugged. "Beats me. . . . I woke up as you—I mean it—was about to equip me with a second navel." He nudged the fallen gun with his toe.

"You are both cretins of the first order," a hoarse rasping voice said. It came from the pool of matter on the floor. It had changed. Now McCade saw that a small, ovoid shape had resolved itself from the surrounding protoplasm. It spoke through a small round aperture in its glistening surface. "You've killed me," the voice said pitifully. "Even now I'm dying a slow, painful death. How sad. How degrading to die at the hands of bipedal tool users."

McCade and Laurie glanced at each other in amazement. "Better you than me, friend," McCade replied calmly. "What the hell are you anyway?"

The ovoid seemed to shudder and convulse slightly. Its outline blurred and for a fraction of a second McCade saw his own face. Then the ovoid reverted to its former appearance, though slightly smaller, as if the effort had somehow diminished it.

"A Treel," Laurie said.

"Finally, a glimmer of primitive intelligence," the hoarse voice said. "You see before you a sight few are privileged to witness. A Treel in the full magnificence of his natural state. Even though I am mortally wounded, notice the incredible beauty of my body."

"I'll admit I've never seen anything like it," McCade said. "Who sent you? Why did you try to kill me?"

For a moment he thought the Treel wasn't going to re-

spond. Then it shivered, blurred, and he found himself looking at Cadet Squadron Leader Votava.

As the alien jerked, evidently suffering another convulsion,
Votava faded into green protoplasm. Suddenly lots of things
made sense. He'd heard of Treels, but never seen one before.
Few had. Treels spent most of their time looking like something else. That's how they managed to survive.

Their native planet swarmed with deadly life forms. Treels
could imitate them all, from a rough likeness right down to the
last biological detail if they wished to. That could include
internal organs, voice print, fingerprints, the whole ball of
wax. But evidently McCade's darts had wounded this one so
badly it couldn't sustain an impersonation for more than a few
moments.

"We are the only perfect race . . . for in us the great Yareel
saw fit to demonstrate the unity of all life." With that the alien
began an eerie chant in his own tongue.

A host of thoughts crowded each other, fighting for domi-
nance in McCade's mind. A Treel. As he'd just seen, a Treel
could impersonate any living thing which didn't exceed its
own mass. But the Treel had to model its impersonations on
something. The photos he'd found aboard the *Leviathan*.
Photos the Treel had used to perfect his imitations. He remembered the photo of Laurie he'd found clutched in the dead
man's hand. So the man had tried to identify his killer. But it
hadn't been Laurie. She'd been aboard *Pegasus* with him. No,
for some reason the Treel had chosen to look like Laurie when
the tug's crew came aboard. Why? So they wouldn't recognize
Votava from the fax sheets Naval Intelligence had sent out. It
made sense. How long had the Treel posed as Votava,
McCade wondered. Days? Months? Years? Yes, years probably. He remembered the discrepancy between the psych pro-
files before she left Mars, and after she entered the Academy.
Somewhere between Mars and Terra the Treel had murdered
the real Votava and taken her place. Then in the role of Votava, the Treel could have gone to work on Bridger. Feeding
his anger and hate. And then when he'd learned the secret of
the metal plate, urged him to use his new knowledge. Anger
buried McCade's other emotions. A cold-blooded killer that
could take on the appearance of anyone it chose. The perfect

assassin. Suddenly another piece of the puzzle dropped into place.

Turning to Laurie, McCade said, "Now we know how the bomb was placed on that autocart." And why I found your picture aboard the *Leviathan,* he thought to himself. "It was no sweat for the Treel to place the bomb while impersonating someone who belonged in the building, someone like you." Laurie looked puzzled for a moment, and then nodded her head in understanding.

"That's right, Sam," the Treel said in a perfect imitation of Laurie's voice. "You aren't as stupid as you look."

"Why?" Laurie said. "Why have you done these things?"

The Treel made a hoarse coughing sound. A distorted likeness of Votava's face came and went. The Treel rasped, "My native planet lies just inside the Il Ronn Empire."

"They threatened you?" Laurie asked. The Treel's protoplasm convulsed into a shaky likeness of a stern-looking Il Ronn before again collapsing into a shapeless mass. A dry racking cough issued forth and for a fleeting moment McCade felt sorry for the strange being.

"Yes, primate, you speak truly," the Treel croaked. "While great of intelligence and beautiful to look upon, my race is few in number. Were it otherwise, we too would rule a great empire! But that is not the destiny Yareel granted us. We seldom mate, and then only on our native world. The Il Ronn have threatened to destroy our planet if we fail to serve them. The inevitable result would be the extinction of my race."

"I'm sorry," Laurie said. "We oppose the Il Ronn. Perhaps we could help."

"You're too late," came the hoarse reply. "Soon the man you call Bridger will lead the Il Ronn to the War World and then, invincible, they shall prevail throughout the galaxy."

"Bridger . . . where is he?" Laurie asked urgently, cutting McCade off.

She was answered by a hoarse sobbing which McCade supposed might be laughter. "It worked twice! We used the same trick twice!" The Treel chortled.

"You mean he's here? Right here in the hotel?" McCade asked.

The alien's laughter turned to hoarse coughing. "Yes . . .

here. Like me he lies ill unto death. But soon they will come and take him. They will extract the information they require. Then woe unto man." Once again the eerie chant began.

McCade opened his mouth to ask what the War World is, exactly, but never got the chance. Instead Laurie turned, aimed her needle gun and fired. He felt the sting as the dart went into his thigh. A wave of nausea rolled over him. Drugs . . . she'd used drugs. He felt betrayed. He searched for sorrow in her eyes as he sank into dark oblivion, but found none.

He surfaced briefly at times before again sinking back into unconsciousness. During those moments he gathered distant impressions. First of being carried by rough hands and then of being thrown into some kind of vehicle, followed by a long jolting ride. Later he thought he remembered a snatch of conversation.

"I say let's waste 'im, I don't fancy cartin' 'im all over town."

"No, damn it. She said ta put him in parkin' orbit for a while . . . gently like. Ya mark me, lad, she'll put ya ta the local an' I mean smart like. . . ."

Somehow listening was more effort than McCade could bear, and he slipped back into the restful darkness.

He awoke with a splitting headache. The simple action of turning his head sent a lance of pain through his neck. His left thigh hurt too, where the dart had penetrated muscle and then dissolved. He was lying on a cold stone floor. High on the wall across from him a dim street light cast its feeble glow through a barred window. Other prisoners surrounded him. Some lay on the floor, as he did. Others slept in makeshift beds. In a far corner a man quietly wept. The smell of vomit and urine was overpowering. Water dripped steadily from the ceiling and fell a drop at a time into the puddle beside his head.

With tremendous effort he tried to sit up. He was rewarded with an explosion of pain forcing him back against the cold damp floor. He lay there a long time, thinking. Obviously Laurie worked for someone besides Naval Intelligence, and had for a long time. The question was who? The Il Ronn? No, that didn't make sense. The Treel disguised as Votava had acted as their agent. So who was left? The pirates, that's who.

Suddenly the assassins made sense. They'd bothered him

from the start. Bridger and Votava—strike that—the Treel hadn't sent them. They'd used mercenaries. No, someone else sent the assassins. Someone who knew the naval base and could help them get in. Someone who could tell them where McCade would be and when. Someone like Laurie. But why? He might never learn Laurie's personal motives, but those of her employers were obvious. The pirates had found out somehow about Bridger's breakthrough.

He remembered his computer research into Bridger's activities and his conclusion that Bridger had broken the secret of his "Directory." In spite of the computer's assurances that no one else had asked for the same information, obviously they had. Laurie must have done the same research and had reached the same conclusions. At that point either she or her superiors decided that the last thing they wanted was for McCade to catch Bridger and turn him and his secret over to Naval Intelligence. They wanted Bridger and the knowledge locked away in his head just as the Il Ronn obviously did. So, Laurie hired assassins to kill McCade, while her fellow pirates no doubt launched an intensive effort to find Bridger themselves.

But the assassins failed. So Laurie decided to use him instead of killing him. Let him lead her to Bridger. And that's exactly what he'd done. Suddenly he wanted to get his hands on her, to hurt her, to punish her for his own stupid vulnerability. And yet he knew that given the chance he still wouldn't do any of those things.

So far things hadn't gone well. McCade smiled grimly to himself in the darkness. But the Treel had added one small scrap of information to his limited hoard. What had he said? Something about Bridger leading the Il Ronn to the "War World." The name was certainly ominous, and bore some rather obvious possibilities.

Had Bridger's "Directory" somehow given him the location of an entire world? One developed by the Builders and dedicated to war? If so, and if the weapons on such a world were still in tact, the implications could be enormous. There was little doubt that the Builders had possessed a science and technology superior to anything yet developed by either humans or Il Ronn. Logically therefore the weapons developed by such a race would be truly awesome. Whoever found them first might well have the means to control all of explored space. Whatever it was, the Treel had learned of it, probably as a result of Bridger's demented ravings, and had by now communicated that knowledge to the Il Ronn.

The whole thing scared the hell out of him. If such power existed, who should control it? The human empire? The Il Ronn empire? The pirates? The more he thought about it, the less he liked any of the possibilities. Gradually the light from the window grew brighter, and his fellow prisoners began to stir. He managed to sit up.

"Got a light?" came a voice from behind him.

Automatically his hand went to his lighter and to his surprise it was there.

As though reading his mind the voice said, "If it ain't lethal, they let ya keep it."

Turning, McCade confronted a bear of a man who dwarfed the rickety chair on which he sat. McCade lit the man's cigar, and then searched his pockets for one of his own.

"Here, sport, try one o' mine," the man said, offering McCade an expensive, imported cigar still sealed in its own metal tube.

"Thanks," McCade said, looking the man over as he unsealed the cigar and carefully rotated it over the flame from his lighter. The man had a head of unruly black hair, with a beard to match. His eyes were small and bright, tucked deeply into creased flesh. His teeth flashed white when he smiled, something he did a lot. He was dressed frontier style. A dark woolen shirt was covered by a leather vest. His pants were made of a black synthetic that looked very tough. He wore lace-up boots. McCade noticed an empty knife sheath sticking out of the right one.

McCade inhaled and blew out a rich stream of smoke. "You have good taste in cigars."

The big man's laughter boomed through the cell. "Friend, I have good taste in everything. Ships, women, wine, food and cigars, in that order. And believe me, I've had my share o' the last four lately. After all, it's gotta last me another year."

"You're from off-planet?" McCade asked.

"Sport, do I look like I belong on this dirt ball? Hell no I don't. I'm from Alice," the other man said proudly. That's halfway out ta the Il Ronn Empire. Hit dirt here three days ago with a load o' rare isotopes. Was I ever glad to get rid o' that stuff. Hotter than an asteroid miner's dreams, it was. How about you, sport? What brings ya ta the anal orifice o' the galaxy?"

"Nothing much," McCade replied vaguely. "Just trying to turn an honest credit."

The other man nodded sagely and winked one of his tiny eyes knowingly.

"Sam McCade." He stuck out his right hand and watched it disappear into the other man's massive grip.

"Glad ta meet ya, sport. My mother named me Fredrico Jose Romero. But friends just call me Rico."

"Well, Rico," McCade said, "maybe you could tell me where the hell I am?"

"Welcome ta the Longansport municipal drunk tank, Sam ol' friend. Ya don't remember being picked up?"

McCade shook his head. He remembered the needle gun in Laurie's hand and the sting as the dart entered his flesh. By now she had Bridger and was long gone.

"Well I'll bet those spaceheads remember picking me up." Rico rubbed a huge fist with a look of satisfaction in his beady eyes.

McCade nodded agreeably. "How do we get out of here, Rico? I've got things to do and people to see."

"No sweat, friend. . . . In a few minutes they'll open up this toilet and let us out."

"No trial or anything?" McCade asked.

"Nah," Rico replied, dropping his cigar butt into the puddle next to McCade. It sizzled and went out. "That'd be bad for business. Not only would it slow the manly art o' drinkin' . . . it'd mean more taxes ta run the court. An if there's anything the local merchants don't like, it's more taxes." Rico's words were punctuated by the clanging of metal as a large section of bars was slid back by two men in police uniforms.

"All right . . . hit the bricks," the shorter of the two said. "This ain't no friggin' hotel."

Singly and in small groups, the men stood, collected their weapons from the jailers, and shuffled out through the gate. McCade noticed that the blade Rico slipped into his boot sheath was double-edged and over a foot long. Together

McCade and Rico followed the others out through a maze of dank hallways and into a sun-filled street. McCade squinted as he glanced around to get his bearings.

"How about breakfast on me, Rico," McCade suggested, rummaging through his pockets and finding some crumpled local currency.

"That'd be fine, Sam ol' friend," Rico answered. "It seems I'm temporarily broke."

They flagged down a public ground car. McCade punched his hotel's name into the vehicle's computer and the ancient conveyance lurched into motion. Fifteen minutes later they entered the hotel's lobby and were greeted by an anxious Amos Van Doren.

"Boss! Nobody relieved me, so I got worried and came lookin'.... Couldn't find you or Laurie neither. Hotel says she checked out but you didn't, so I figured I'd wait. You okay?"

McCade assured Van Doren he was and suggested that Rico start breakfast without them. The big man nodded amiably and smiled as he ambled off in the direction of the hotel's restaurant. McCade headed for his room with Van Doren in tow; on the way, he related the events of the night before. The marine's reaction to Laurie's affiliation surprised him.

""Somethun' 'bout her always bothered me, boss. Couldn't put my finger on it. Always seemed like a cat waitin' on a mouse, know what I mean?"

McCade didn't. And that bothered him. Laurie seen through Van Doren's eyes sounded like a different person from the woman he'd known. One she'd never let him see. Or one he'd been blind to. It made very little difference. As McCade opened the door, he saw the room was neat and tidy. There was no sign of the Treel. Not even a stain to mark where the alien had been. Laurie must have disposed of him somehow. With pirate help no doubt.

So by now Laurie had located Bridger and lifted off-planet. Soon the pirates would interrogate Bridger and, regardless of resistance, they would succeed. Of course Bridger was ill. Very ill, according to the Treel. Sufficiently ill to delay interrogation? McCade hoped so. He needed time. He had to find out where the pirates had taken Bridger. And that wouldn't be easy. They had lots of worlds to pick from. Meanwhile the Il Ronn were no doubt looking for Bridger too. It should be an interesting race.

Thoughtfully he strapped on his gun belt. It, along with his other gear, had been left untouched.

Together he and Van Doren headed for the lobby. McCade paused by a bank of public com units. "How about *Pegasus?*" he asked. The marine looked embarrassed. McCade realized Van Doren hadn't thought to check on the ship. "That's okay, Amos. . . . Join Rico for breakfast. You'll like him. I'll call the spaceport."

A few minutes later McCade joined the other two in the restaurant. He wasn't happy, and it showed.

"Problems, old sport?" Rico asked around a mouthful of food.

McCade nodded. "It seems our ship lifted without us." Inside he was seething. Laurie had not only snatched Bridger out from under his nose, she'd also used his ship to lift him off-planet.

If Rico was curious, he didn't show it, but blood suffused Van Doren's face, and the eyes beneath his bushy brows grew hard and bright.

"I'm sorry, boss."

"Don't be," McCade said. "There wasn't any way you could've known."

"Maybe I could help," Rico said, chewing thoughtfully. "If ya have credits fer a charter, that is . . . and providin' it don't take too long."

They haggled back and forth while McCade waited for his food. A process Rico clearly enjoyed. Finally they shook on a fee which McCade thought surprisingly low. So low it made him suspicious. In fact, he began to wonder if Rico wasn't just too good to be true. If so, it could work to their advantage. As things stood, he'd lost Bridger and didn't have the faintest idea of where to start looking. Maybe Rico would provide a lead.

So they talked and joked, finally finishing breakfast about an hour later. Rico headed for his ship while McCade and Van Doren went to check out of their hotel. Adding insult to injury, Laurie had stiffed him with her bill as well. Fortunately he'd insisted on a thick wad of expense money before they'd lifted from Terra. It was still in his luggage where he'd left it.

As they headed for the spaceport, McCade briefed Van Doren on his suspicions regarding Rico, and they agreed on a plan. The big man met them as they approached his ship.

"There she is," Rico said proudly. "The *Lady Alice*. Ain't she somethun'?"

McCade had never seen a more decrepit-looking ship. She was a pre-Empire freighter. Her hull was pitted and scarred by a thousand re-entries. One of her landing jacks was leaking black hydraulic fluid, and she had a list to port.

"Yeah," McCade replied dryly. "They don't make 'em like that anymore."

But Rico was oblivious to such sarcasm. As they climbed aboard, McCade began to understand why. On closer inspection he saw that, contrary to outward appearances, the *Lady Alice* was in perfect shape. Outmoded systems had been replaced with new. The ship's interior was spotless, and glistened with fresh paint. As they passed a weapons blister, McCade noticed the brand new energy cannon mounted in it. For some reason, Rico wanted the *Lady Alice* to look like she was on her last leg. Interesting, McCade thought, I wonder why?

Six

RICO INVITED MCCADE and Van Doren to strap into the crew positions just aft of the pilot's seat. He offered no explanation for the ship's lack of a crew. Not that a crew was absolutely necessary, of course.

Thirty minutes later they had cleared the atmosphere and were in deep space. Rico unbuckled himself and swiveled his chair around to face them. He had a friendly grin on his face and a very unfriendly-looking stun gun in his huge right hand. His grin slipped into a frown, however, as he looked down the barrels of the slug guns held by both McCade and Van Doren.

"Uh-oh . . ." Rico said. "I've got a feelin' you're ahead o' me, sport. Would ya believe I was just kiddin'? No? I was afraid o' that." He dropped the stun gun.

McCade couldn't help laughing. The man's incredible effrontery was somehow disarming.

"No hard feelings, Rico. . . . But why?"

Rico shrugged. His smile disappeared. "Figure it out for yourself. I don't have nothin' ta say."

"Maybe I could change his mind, boss," Van Doren growled.

"Somehow I doubt it, but thanks anyway, Amos," McCade replied. Turning to Rico, he said, "I've got a hunch you didn't just happen to be in the drunk tank when I was. You arranged to be there." He paused and regarded the other man thoughtfully. "The frontier worlds have been organizing, haven't they? And somehow you got wind of this Bridger thing and dealt yourselves in."

Rico's face remained impassive, but McCade would have sworn he saw a flash of confirmation deep in the other man's eyes.

"Okay," McCade said. "I'll take a last try. You were taking us somewhere. Somebody wants to ask us some questions. Well, what if I told you that's fine with me? In fact, that I want to go?"

And why not, McCade thought. I don't know where they took Bridger . . . but I'll bet you've got a pretty good idea.

Rico looked thoughtful for a moment and then nodded. "That's right, ol' friend . . . but we ain't goin' there while you're pointin' them slug throwers my way."

McCade slid his gun into its holster and motioned for Van Doren to do likewise. The marine hesitated for a moment, glancing back and forth between McCade and Rico. Finally he holstered his weapon, but with obvious reluctance.

In spite of himself McCade's hand strayed toward his own gun as Rico bent over to retrieve his. A broad grin creased Rico's face as he tucked the stunner away into a shoulder holster.

"Don't worry. No more surprises. Shake?"

Rico offered McCade a hairy paw. McCade accepted. But when Rico and Van Doren shook hands, he noticed that eyes locked and shoulders tensed. Muscles bunched and writhed in massive forearms. After a moment both men sat down, apparently satisfied. When they looked his way, McCade was blowing smoke rings toward the overhead, evidently oblivious to the whole thing.

It was a three-day trip to Alice. Most of it was spent in normal space, with only a short hyperspace jump in the middle. At first McCade spent his time trying to pump Rico for information. He soon found that was a waste of time. The other man steadfastly refused to answer questions, saying, "That's not for me to say. Them that's waitin' is all great talkers. Me, I'm more a doer."

So McCade quit trying, but Rico's silence tended to confirm his theories. For one thing it suggested a strong centralized organization, rather than a loose collection of individuals acting on their own. And organization implied specialization and discipline. Both hallmarks of government. Something the frontier worlds were not supposed to have. Either petition the Emperor for admission to the Empire or forget it. That was the law. McCade wondered if Swanson-Pierce knew about Laurie's defection, or that the frontier worlds were organizing. Somehow he doubted it. There seemed to be a great deal that Naval Intelligence wasn't aware of.

If Rico was close-mouthed about his people and their aims, he was just the opposite on the subject of Alice. McCade had never met anyone so in love with a planet. And from Rico's description he couldn't figure out why. Evidently a good portion of the planet's surface was in the last stages of an ice age. Giant glaciers dominated both poles and stretched icy fingers north and south. A narrow temperate zone girdled the equator.

Naturally the first settlers built their homes in the temperate zone. But they quickly realized their mistake. The area just above and below the equator was volcanically active. Two enormous continental plates met there. As they collided, mountains were upthrust, lava flowed, and frequent seismic activity destroyed surface structures as quickly as they could be built. So the settlers retreated south and settled where the glaciers met the temperate zone. This area had its hazards too, primarily the incredible cold, but it was still preferable to the volcanic region. According to Rico, the land had a wild, frozen beauty. What's more, it was rich in minerals and there was plenty of it. A man could carve a future out of land like that —limited only by his own courage and imagination. Fusion power plants, land crawlers, energy weapons, and automedics might come in handy too, McCade thought to himself.

In spite of Rico's endless anecdotes about the planet's frigid surface, McCade wasn't ready for the cold that embraced them as they left the ship. It searched out the tiny gaps in their clothing and entered, driven by the relentless wind. It cut through the parka Rico lent him and chilled him to the bone. Rico himself seemed unaffected, smiling through a beard quickly frosted with ice. Well after all, McCade reflected sourly, the big man was wearing a powered heatsuit.

To his relief they scrambled quickly into a heated crawler, which jerked into motion, toward the distant hills. Looking out through scratched plastic, McCade watched with surprise as the *Lady Alice* sank slowly into the ground. Then he realized the ship had landed on an elevator, which was lowering it into an underground hangar.

Seeing his interest, Rico said, "Winter storms. Cold enough ta freeze the balls off a icecat. Sixty kilometer winds. Other possibilities too," he added vaguely. "Summer now so no sweat."

Terrific. Sweat's gonna be the least of my problems, McCade thought. He looked at Van Doren and they both shook their heads in amazement. As they drew away from the spaceport, McCade began to notice carefully camouflaged weapons emplacements. Without exception they were aimed at the sky. He didn't like the implications. Then he began to see blackened craters, burned out domes and wrecked crawlers. Smoke still poured out of what had obviously been some kind of tracking station.

He turned to question Rico, but the big man was in whispered conversation with the driver, a handsome woman in her late forties. When he leaned back, Rico's face was black with anger. McCade started to ask him what had happened, but then thought better of it. So they rode on in silence. McCade and Van Doren watched the passage of frozen scenery, while Rico sat slumped, deep within his own thoughts.

After what seemed like an hour, but was probably less, the crawler approached a snow-covered hill. It looked no different from twenty others they'd passed, but just when it seemed certain that they would crash into the hillside, an armored door as white as the snow around it slid aside, revealing a lighted tunnel. As the crawler entered, the door slid closed behind them. The noise of their passage bounced off the walls, then, without warning, the tunnel opened up into a large chamber.

McCade saw rows of parked crawlers, power sleds and snowmobiles. They looked like they'd seen hard use. In one corner mechanics swarmed over an armed crawler that evidently had been hit by an energy weapon. He couldn't tell if they were repairing it or stripping it for parts. In either case they were obviously in a hurry.

Moments later they pulled up to a loading dock. As they stepped out, McCade and Van Doren found themselves looking into the business ends of four weapons held by some very steady hands.

"Put 'em away, ya bozos!" Rico said, stepping between the four men and McCade. "Can't ya see they're comin' peaceable? Sides which they could probably eat ya for breakfast." As the men sheepishly holstered their weapons, Rico turned to McCade. "Sorry 'bout that. How's they ta know ya'd come quiet?"

"It's okay, Rico," McCade said, glancing at Van Doren. The big marine looked doubtful, but dropped his hand from the butt of his slug gun.

"These spaceheads'll take ya ta your quarters, if'n they don't get lost along the way," Rico said with a derisive snort. "After ya've had a chance ta clean up I s'pose the bigwigs'll talk your ear off. See ya later!" With a jaunty wave, the big man lumbered off.

With two ahead and two behind, McCade and Van Doren followed the guards through a maze of corridors. Some were nicely finished and others still showed signs of recent construction. Eventually they were shown into adjoining cubicles. They were clean, but spartan. McCade lay down on the hard mattress, planning to think.

It seemed only moments later when an insistent knocking woke him. Glancing at his wrist term he saw that over five hours had passed. As he swung his feet onto the floor, the door opened and a man stepped in. He was tall and slender, dressed in frontier fashion. His movements were smooth and quick. The bones in his face were prominent but well-formed, granting him predatory good looks. His eyes were like cold chips of black stone through which McCade could see nothing. McCade didn't like him . . . and somehow knew the feeling was mutual.

"The Council wishes to see you," the man said. His expression made it clear that attendance wasn't optional.

"Good," McCade replied. "And I'd like to see them. Just give me a moment to clean up." McCade started for the tiny bathroom.

Suddenly the man was in his way. He's damn fast, McCade noted to himself.

"The Council wants to see you *now*," the man said. Before McCade could reply, he heard the unmistakable metallic sound of a slug gun going to full cock. Looking toward the sound he saw Van Doren aiming his massive handgun at the man's head. "Maybe you'd like to meet your *maker*—now," the marine said calmly.

The man paled and tensed his body. For a moment McCade thought he might challenge Van Doren's reflexes. Then, with a visible effort, the man forced himself to back down. He's no coward, McCade thought. There was implacable hatred in the eyes staring back at him.

"It's okay, Amos," McCade said, forcing a smile. "I'm sorry. I'm afraid Amos takes his duties as my bodyguard too seriously."

The other man nodded his head in a short, jerky motion, turned on his heel and left the room, slamming the door behind him.

"You should've let me blow his head off, boss. That one'll be trouble later . . . you mark my words," Van Doren said.

"You're probably right, Amos," McCade said wearily. "But I'm afraid the Council might become annoyed if we blew their envoy's head off. I do appreciate your desire to be efficient however." Van Doren shrugged his shoulders and returned to his cubicle.

A few minutes later McCade entered the hall freshly showered and shaved. He felt better because of it, plus it wouldn't hurt to make a good impression on the Council. Whoever they were. Van Doren was right behind him.

The tall man was waiting impatiently. "You come with me," he said, pointing to McCade, "and you stay," indicating Van Doren. McCade noticed that the man had strapped on a gun of his own. His right hand hovered over its well-worn grip.

Van Doren's hand was inches from the butt of his own gun when McCade said, "Let it be, Amos. They've got all the cards right now, so let's play it their way." He tossed the marine a mock salute as he followed the tall man down the hall.

It was a short journey. A few minutes later they were ushered past a heavily guarded door and into a large circular room. It was dominated by a semicircular table of some highly polished native wood. Behind it sat four people. For some reason he wasn't surprised to see that Rico was one of them. The big man nodded in his direction and winked one of his tiny eyes.

Then McCade's attention was drawn to the woman on Rico's right. She was beautiful. Or had been. A terrible white scar slashed across her softly rounded face from high on the left side of her forehead down across her right cheek. None the less, it was her large hazel eyes that dominated her face. They regarded McCade with cold curiosity.

"Welcome, Citizen McCade," she said. "Rico has told us a great deal about you. Please allow me to introduce the rest of us. On my far right is Professor Wendel. He'd head of our scientific team."

The professor was an elderly man who wore his thick white hair in a neat ponytail behind his head. His bright blue eyes twinkled as he inclined his head toward McCade in greeting.

"On my immediate right is Col. Frank Larkin," the woman continued. "The colonel is in charge of our armed forces."

McCade judged Larkin to be in his middle fifties, but he could have been older. His head was shaved in the tradition of the elite Imperial Star Guard—the special marine brigade responsible for the personal safety of the Emperor. His hard eyes inspected McCade as though on parade and his nod granted nothing more than recognition.

"And of course you've met Rico, our Master at Arms," she said, "and Vern Premo, our comptroller." She indicated the tall man who now lounged against one wall. He was staring past McCade toward the woman with open avarice in his eyes.

"I'm Sara Bridger," she said coldly. "Chief Political Officer for the Council. I understand that you want to kill my father."

Confusion filled McCade's thoughts and emotions. It couldn't be. Sara Bridger had been captured by pirates and was probably dead by now. Yet he knew it was true. Without the scar she would be the same woman he'd admired aboard the old *Imperial*. Older but still beautiful. The tiny lines around her eyes and mouth added character, while taking nothing from her beauty. A beauty transcending even the scar.

"Well?" she said, unconsciously tracing the scar with a fingertip.

"I have no desire to kill your father," McCade replied evenly. "However, he is a fugitive from Imperial justice."

"You speak of 'Imperial justice.' Where is it?" she asked bitterly. "Why does the navy allow the pirates and the I1 Ronn to slaughter our people? Where was Imperial justice when the pirates came yesterday, raping and burning? Last night we buried fourteen of our friends. Some were only children. Their only crime was trying to defend their homes. Was that just?"

Her eyes burned with hatred and her cheeks were flushed, serving to emphasize the whiteness of the scar. McCade realized she was close to exhaustion.

"I'm sorry," he said simply.

With visible effort she brought herself under control. "What crimes has my father committed?" she asked, steel lying just under the soft surface of her words.

"Desertion . . . and possibly other crimes I'm not free to divulge," McCade answered.

"You'll tell her whatever she wants to know!" The angry voice was Premo's. No longer lounging against the wall, he was standing, his body rigid with anger as he clenched and unclenched his fists at his side.

"That'll be enough o' that," Rico said levelly, "or would ya care ta take ol' Rico on?" For the first time McCade saw caution in Premo's eyes.

Sara Bridger broke the uncomfortable silence that followed. "Rico's right, McCade." She aimed a critical glance at Premo.

"You'll not be forced to speak." Her expression hardened. "But you must understand that, until Rico's arrival a few hours ago, I thought my father was living happily on Terra. Now I learn he's being hunted like an animal throughout the Empire. Hunted by men like you. Men who kill for money!" Disgust and revulsion played across her features.

McCade felt his hands start to shake as he remembered the marines who'd died and the bodies he'd found aboard the *Leviathan*. The muscle in his left cheek twitched uncontrollably as he spoke. "Your father has already murdered innocent people. It's quite likely he intends to murder more. If I have to kill him to stop that, I will. And you're right, I'm doing it for money. But you know what? In your father's case, I'd do it for free."

The blood drained from Sara Bridger's face, leaving it as white as the scar that bisected it. Hatred burned in her beautiful eyes. Without a word she rose and left the room.

"For that you'll die!" Premo spit the words out one at a time. McCade spun toward him, his hand over his gun and the promise of eternity in his wintry gray eyes.

Somewhere a klaxon went off. Everyone froze as a calm male voice came over the PA system. "This is a class three attack, including light armor and infantry. All active and reserve personnel report to your units immediately. All noncombatants report to your class three duty stations."

Everyone bolted for the nearest door. Premo's look promised another meeting as he turned on his heel and marched out.

When McCade turned back, the other Council members had already left, with the exception of Rico. He was lighting a cigar while regarding McCade with a raised eyebrow.

"Seems like you don't make friends too easy, ol' sport," he said, rising from his chair. "Wanna come with me'n take your antisocial tendencies out on some pirates? Sounds like they're at it again. Two attacks in two days is a little much. It's gettin' outta hand." Without looking to see if McCade followed, he turned and went out the rear door the other Council members had used.

McCade had to stretch to match the other man's gigantic strides. "What's Premo's problem anyway?"

Rico shrugged. "Who knows? Premo's Premo. I know it's hard ta believe . . . but in some ways he ain't bad. Jus' keep in mind that when it comes ta Sara, he's crazier'n a Tobarian Zerk monkey."

"I've got a feeling he's going to remind me," McCade said dryly.

"Here we are," Rico said as they turned a corner. Rico led McCade into a lift tube. Moments later they emerged into a smaller version of the chamber he'd seen before. This one had only four crawlers in it and there wasn't room for any more.

As they got closer McCade noticed all four were armed. They hadn't been designed for combat, so they didn't have turrets. That meant the energy cannon mounted toward the front of each vehicle could only be aimed forward. A large caliber slug thrower had been installed in a blister at the rear of each crawler to deal with threats from behind. A smaller caliber automatic weapon was mounted in a blister on top of the massive machine.

"Had six o' these ta start with . . . but the pirates pared my section down ta four in the last six months," Rico said as they approached the lead crawler. He inspected its tracks and patted the machine's scarred flanks lovingly as they walked around it.

Up close the crawler towered over the two men. Intended to withstand the rigors of planetary exploration, the crawlers had been built to take lots of punishment. So with the addition of some extra armor plating and weapons blisters they made respectable heavy tanks. Just how respectable McCade was about to find out.

As they rounded the front end of the crawler, McCade saw a slim figure in overalls and a helmet straighten from inspecting a huge bogey wheel and turn to toss Rico an informal salute. "Unit Two ready for action, sir," she said. "Chuck and Sparks are aboard."

"Thanks, Paula," Rico answered as he scrambled up the rungs leading to the top hatch. "Meet Sam McCade. . . . Is Yamana still sick?"

Paula nodded toward McCade and replied dryly, "He only broke his leg last week, Rico."

"Well, ya can't 'spect me ta remember everything, damn it," Rico said, pausing at the top. "Sam here'll take Yama's place in the tail position. . . . That okay?"

McCade indicated it was. A few minutes later with help from Paula, he had strapped himself into the tailgunner's position and the crawler got under way. His weapon was an electrically driven, multibarreled slug thrower. A descendant of the ancient Gatling gun. Each of the six barrels fired hundreds of armor-piercing shells a second. It could be elevated for aircraft or depressed for surface action. McCade wondered which to expect.

Cold white light flooded his blister as the crawler emerged

from its camouflaged hiding place and rumbled out across ice and rock. He watched as the other three crawlers spread out to take up positions on either side of Rico's unit. A dispassionate voice broke the steady static on his earphones. "Command to section Charlie Four... we have six unidentified armored units approaching your sector... range one klick... bearing one-two-oh. Have fun."

"Roger," Rico replied. "Let's go get 'em, Charlie Four."

The crawler's speed increased with a commensurate increase in the amount of vibration. McCade felt like it would shake his teeth out. He noted that, as usual, the muscle in his left cheek had begun to twitch, and it felt as though someone had poured cold lead into his stomach. He wished he was manning the energy cannon so he could see where they were going... and what was coming. Not knowing was the worst part. But Rico had quite understandably put him in the least critical position. A voice he'd never heard before broke radio silence with, "Unit three has visual contact with four unknowns, range approximately 750 meters bearing one-two-oh. Request permission to fire primary."

"Negative," Rico answered. "Hold fire. Units four and six confirm sighting."

For what seemed like an eternity there was only static on McCade's headset. Then, "Unit six confirms." And a moment later, "Unit four confirms... enemy has opened fire."

"Commence evasive action... and fire!" Rico shouted.

McCade felt the entire crawler jerk in sympathy with the recoil of their primary armament. For at least the tenth time he wished he could see what was going on. Instead he had an unobstructed view of where they'd been. For what seemed like hours McCade listened to shouted commands punctuated by shouts of victory and groans of defeat. He was thrown from side to side during violent evasive maneuvers and jolted up and down as the crawler hurled itself across gullies in the ice and rock. Meanwhile he tried to build a picture of the battle in his mind.

The initial charge against the six pirate units netted Rico's smaller section two kills at the cost of unit four. Now the four remaining enemy units were locked in individual duels with what remained of Rico's section. Coordinated group action was impossible in the broken terrain. McCade's thoughts were interrupted as Rico shouted into the intercom, "Look out, Sam! That bastard's tryin' ta get behind us!"

McCade was thrown to the right as Rico put the crawler into a tight turn. If they could turn fast enough they'd be able to match the pirate unit and prevent it from getting behind them. But their adversary had the advantage and used it.

McCade watched the huge black shape fill his sight. He forced himself to hold back until it filled his sight from edge to edge. Then he pulled the triggers on the twin grips and heard an eerie whine as his gun opened up. He watched his tracer arc up and then down to meet the oncoming enemy crawler.

His stomach muscles tensed as the other unit returned his fire. The pirate unit's tracer probed and searched, trying to complete a deadly connection between the two crawlers. The blue pulses of their energy cannon wove in and out of the white tracer, forming an intricate pattern of color and movement. Then the crawler lurched under him and he knew they'd been hit hard. Their speed dropped and McCade realized the engine noise had too. Evidently they'd lost an engine.

His fears were confirmed when Rico said, "We just took a round in the starboard engine. Prepare ta bail out."

McCade gritted his teeth and continued to hold the triggers down. Now that his own crawler had slowed it was easier to hit the enemy. Now Rico's top blister gunner had joined him in his efforts to hit the pirate's tracks. Suddenly the enemy unit slowed. They knew Rico's primary armament could only aim forward. So they planned to sit and pour it on while Rico's remaining engine slowly turned the crawler to meet them. Then using their superior speed, they'd get around behind Rico again and it would start over. Things don't look good, McCade thought grimly. Then he noticed the tendril of smoke coming from the inside of the enemy unit's track. He concentrated his fire on that spot and was rewarded with even more smoke. Then flames replaced the smoke and the other crawler stopped moving. Rico completed his turn at that moment and McCade lost sight of the enemy. He felt the recoil of Rico's energy cannon and heard the muffled sound of an explosion. They'd won.

But instead of victory yells, there was silence on the intercom. Then McCade realized he hadn't heard any radio transmission from the other units in Rico's section for some time.

He was about to ask what was going on when he felt a hand on his shoulder. He looked up to see Paula holding a finger to her lips and motioning for him to follow. McCade released his harness. After some contortions he managed to turn in the cramped space of the blister and follow Paula through the narrow accessway into the crawler's main cabin.

Rico greeted him with a whispered hello and a friendly pat on the back that nearly drove him to the deck. Two other men nodded their greetings. One sat at the crawler's controls. He didn't look old enough to drink yet, much less drive a crawler into battle. He had a friendly grin, and the name Chuck was scrawled in gold thread across the left breast of his bright green jacket. A middle-aged com tech sat in front of a bank of com units and detectors. He wore a set of earphones on his balding head. After a cheerful wave he turned back to his screens.

"Nice job back there, ol' sport," Rico whispered as he motioned for McCade to join him behind Sparks.

"I had some help," McCade replied, pointing up toward the top turret.

"Yeah, Paula ain't bad. . . . Here, take a look at this," Rico whispered.

McCade joined Rico in looking over the com tech's shoulder. A battle map appeared on the screen in front of them. On it were four blinking green lights. It appeared all the units except Rico's had been knocked out. Then Rico pointed at a steady red light almost on the edge of the screen. It was rapidly moving away from the battlefield. One of the enemy units was escaping.

"Okay, Chuck," Rico whispered. "Let's go. Take 'er nice 'n' easy."

To McCade's surprise he felt both engines start up. Rico smiled knowingly. "It's just amazin' how them engines come 'n' go like that."

The crawler lurched into motion. Once they were moving, the ride smoothed out. McCade watched as obstacles appeared and disappeared on the forward viewscreen. Just when he thought the crawler could go no farther, Chuck would deftly steer them around the problem. Turning back to the battle map, McCade saw that a steady green light now pursued the red.

"I don't get it, Rico," McCade whispered. "He's still in

range. Why don't we open up on him? And why am I whispering?"

"First, 'cause we wanna follow him. . . . And second, 'cause we don't know how good the spacehead's audio sensors are."

"He isn't likely to hear us talking over the engines, Rico."

"That's where you're wrong, ol' friend. Least I hope ya are. Like I tol' ya before, we used ta have six units, but they've been wearin' us down. They always work it the same way. A ship lands, off-loads armor and infantry, they hit and run, then it's up and away. Ta stop 'em ya gotta nail their ship. So on Weller's World I bought me some shielding. Blocks noise and heat. After we landed, the crew worked like a gang o' Celite stevedores ta install it. Only had enough for the engines though. Twenty feet out we're as quiet as an icecat's shadow, and as cold as his rear end."

An enormous grin bisected Rico's hairy face and his tiny eyes twinkled with merriment. "Imagine the look on those bozos' mugs when we blow their ship out from under 'em."

Then McCade understood. Rico was planning to follow the pirate crawler back to its mother ship. Then with the pirate vessel sitting vulnerable on the ground, they would stand a chance of beating down its screens and destroying it. It was a good plan and obviously one the man had worked on for some time. However, McCade saw room for one added refinement and, if it worked, they'd end up with a usable ship instead of a wreck.

The two men held a whispered conference. Rico was quick to adopt McCade's suggestion and quickly passed appropriate orders to his crew. After that there was nothing to do but wait. Time seemed to crawl by.

Outside, an endless parade of broken rock, ice and stunted vegetation crossed the viewscreen in monotonous succession. After what seemed like an eternity, they topped a rise and paused, hidden among upthrust spires of rock. Ahead the pirate crawler picked its way down the slope through the accumulated scree toward the valley below.

"He's talking to the ship on a sealed beam," the com tech whispered. Rico nodded.

Below, the pirate ship dominated the valley. To McCade's eyes its long, lean shape seemed pleasantly symmetrical against the jumble of ice and rock strewn around it. A ring of hastily erected earthworks surrounded the ship. But now the weapons pits stood vacant. All personnel had been pulled back in preparation for lift-off. Now they waited for the single crawler steadily creeping across the valley floor.

McCade turned to see Paula sitting at the controls of the energy cannon. Rico and the other crew members had already evacuated the crawler, leaving Paula and McCade to complete the plan. In McCade's view that was only fair, since it was his plan and entailed additional risk. Paula refused to go, pointing out that the plan called for precision shooting, and adding that she was the best shot on the crew. No one had disputed her claim.

McCade watched as a cargo hatch was slowly retracted into the pirates' hull, leaving a large rectangular opening for their crawler to pass through. A ramp was extruded from the area just below the hatch, and as it touched the ground the crawler began to move up it. As it did so Paula squeezed the trigger. Light blue pulses of energy leapt across the intervening space to smash into the crawler and the open cargo bay. Just as McCade had hoped, both the crawler and the ship had been forced to shut down their defensive screens long enough for the vehicle to embark. The unprotected crawler was quickly reduced to a pool of molten metal. Even though the ship's hull was made of sterner stuff, it too had begun to glow. The plan had worked. The pirate couldn't close the cargo hatch with the crawler in the way, so they couldn't lift ship.

McCade tapped Paula on the shoulder. She nodded and slipped out of her seat. Two steps later she dropped through the emergency escape hatch and disappeared. McCade hit the transmit switch, sending a prerecorded high-speed burst of code racing for Council Headquarters. Then he too dived for the escape hatch.

Seven

McCADE AND PAULA were crouched under the crawler, huddled between massive treads, when the first missile hit. There was an ear-splitting roar and the ground shook convulsively as waves of intense heat rolled over them. But the crawler's tremendous bulk and defensive screens sheltered them from the worst of it. Paula bent over, clutching her head with both hands. McCade grabbed her arm and they crawled toward the rear where a rectangle of daylight was visible between the huge tracks.

McCade waited for a moment, and then used a pause in the missile barrage to crawl out and run for the nearest pile of jumbled rock. He half-guided, half-dragged Paula behind him, leading her around the clumps of burning vegetation. Just as they dived into the shelter of the rocks, more missiles arrived, hitting the crawler and completely obliterating it. McCade gave thanks they weren't using nukes. However nukes would have destroyed their ship as well.

"Nice of ya to drop in," Rico said, rounding a large

boulder. "But I'm gonna miss 'er," the big man said, gazing sadly at the burning remnants. "She was a good ol' girl. Plus ya wouldn't believe how many forms I'm gonna have ta fill out. The Council's real good at inventin' new forms." He grinned broadly.

Five shots rang out in quick succession. Rico nodded in the direction of the sound. "That'll be Chuck 'n' Sparks keepin' their heads down for us. Chuck's a real artist with a huntin' rifle. They won't be clearin' that wreckage for some time."

"You okay, Paula?" McCade asked. She looked a little better and smiled wanly as she struggled to her feet. McCade put out a hand to stop her, but Rico shook his head. Paula paused for a moment and then disappeared in the direction of the sporadic rifle fire.

"Paula's married to Chuck," Rico said in explanation as he settled himself on a flat piece of rock.

McCade nodded as he accepted one of the other man's expensive cigars. "How soon can we expect some help, Rico?"

The big man examined the chronometer strapped to a hairy wrist. "Well assumin' ya triggered that call for help on your way out . . ." He looked questioningly in McCade's direction and receiving a nod, continued. "Then we oughta have air cover any time now. . . . and maybe ground support a half hour later.

McCade savored the cigar smoke as he blew it out into the cold, crisp air. Even in the shelter provided by the rocks the cold wind found them and seeped through McCade's parka to chill his skin.

"No offense, Rico," McCade said, "but this world is no paradise. What are the pirates after anyway?"

Rico shrugged his large shoulders. "Beats me, Sam ol' friend. Course we've always had a coupla raids a year. After refined metals mostly. But lately they've been hittin' us a couple times a week. Now suddenly it's one a day." He shook his head in amazement. "Funny part is they don't seem to be after the usual stuff. Course they take it if they find it . . . but it's like they're lookin' for somethun else."

"How long has this been going on?" McCade asked.

"Last coupla months maybe," Rico answered around his cigar.

McCade considered the other man's answer. The more he thought about it, the more he doubted it was coincidence. The pirate attacks had increased about the same time Bridger had gone over the hill.

Suddenly there was excited shouting from Paula and Chuck, followed by a roar and a sonic boom. Both men leaped to their feet and ran toward the valley wall. A breathless Paula intercepted them.

"They launched a boat from the far side of the ship!"

McCade swore to himself as Rico cursed out loud in a dozen tongues. Of course. A ship that size carried at least two lifeboats in case of emergencies or for use as shuttles. One on the port side and one to starboard. They'd picked the one on the far side to avoid detection by Chuck, Paula and Sparks. Launching a boat from a grounded ship called for consummate skill, lots of guts, and a large measure of desperation, but they'd done it. Damn! He should have thought of it. Now he'd lost his chance to ask the pirates a few questions.

There was a rolling thunder of sound as a flight of three atmospheric fighters swept over to circle the valley. "That's the flyboys. . . . Day late 'n' a credit short like always," Rico said, shading his eyes against the glare as he looked up at the specks circling overhead. "Well there's still a chance. By now Larkin's got a couple ships on patrol just outside the atmosphere."

Not much later a large freight copter arrived and disgorged some troops. McCade noticed there wasn't a uniform among them, but they were obviously well trained and disciplined. Colonel Larkin's influence no doubt. From their smoke-stained clothes and bandages he could see they had already been in action.

Before long Rico's crew was aboard the giant aircraft and on their way back to Council Headquarters. McCade sat slumped in thought, gazing at the frozen terrain passing below without really seeing it. At some point during the flight he fell asleep. When he awoke the copter was touching down.

Rico had to shout to be heard over the sound of the engines. "Looks like the battle's over, sport. The pilot says the all-clear was sounded about ten minutes ago. There was one other ship besides the one we got. It lifted 'n' got clean away. Guess it's time ta pick up the pieces again."

· McCade was hungry. Rico directed him toward the cafeteria. It was packed with a swirling mob of people. Many had taken part in the fighting and wore bandages to prove it. Nevertheless they engaged in a lot of good-natured kidding. With a shouted greeting, Van Doren's grinning face suddenly separated itself from the crowd. After wading through the line, they shared a table together.

With considerable prodding McCade learned that the marine was now something of a local hero. It seemed that while most of the Council's forces were drawn off into a series of small skirmishes, the pirates launched a surprise attack against the admin complex. The Council had relied mainly on the complex's camouflage to protect it. As a result the pirates had cut their way through the mostly unarmed clerical staff with ease. Until they ran into Van Doren, that is. Aware that a battle was raging somewhere, but unable to find either it or McCade, the marine was searching for the action when it found him. After launching a one-man counterattack, he managed to rally enough clerks and security guards to hold the main corridor until help arrived. As a result the pirates failed to penetrate the core of the complex.

Van Doren made it sound like a stroll through the park. But the awed looks and frequent congratulations of the other diners testified to the marine's accomplishment. In fact, McCade mused a few hours later as he sat waiting in an empty conference room, if it hadn't been for Van Doren, they wouldn't have had anyone to interrogate. He'd managed to take the day's only prisoner.

Larkin's planetary defense forces had vaporized the lifeboat as it left the atmosphere, although the second ship had escaped. So Rico's disdain for the "flyboys" had not been entirely deserved. Meanwhile the other pirates who'd survived had escaped into the wilds. If you could call that "escape." In any case, McCade felt frustrated. He seemed to be getting nowhere fast. In order to find Bridger, he'd have to get off-planet. He had a plan for that. But once in space, what then?

McCade turned to his right as a door there slid open. One by one the Council filed in. Wendel and Larkin nodded politely in his direction. McCade noticed Larkin's uniform was ripped and soiled. His right arm was in a sling. Evidently the ex-marine believed in leading his troops instead of following them as so many Imperial officers liked to do. Rico tossed him a jaunty salute as he entered, in contrast to Premo's look of barely disguised hatred. When Sara Bridger entered the room, she appeared even more exhausted than before. To McCade's surprise, she favored him with a formal smile as the room lights dimmed.

A bank of screens came to life in front of them. Each provided a different view of a bare, cell-like room dominated by a tubular hospital bed. On its gleaming surface a naked man lay spread-eagled, his powerful arms and legs restrained by leather straps. They'd shaved his head and body hair. McCade noticed the bony ridge bisecting the man's skull from front to back. It hinted at Tillarian blood. The Tillarians were a proud, some said egotistical, race who banned all those of mixed blood from the home system. Which probably accounted for this man's presence among the pirates.

Wires and tubes ran in and out of his body like multicolored parasites feeding off a corpse. It certainly beat torture, but McCade still felt sorry for the man. An efficient-looking female technician stood nearby, monitoring a bank of complicated controls. When she spoke McCade noticed that her speech had a husky, rhythmic, almost hypnotic quality. She asked a series of simple, nonthreatening questions. Name, date of birth, and so on. But the pirate met each question with a nonsensical string of words and numbers. Apparently he'd been memblocked. The question was how deep? Superficial blocks could be broken by an expert. Deeper ones could be broken too—but the process was usually fatal.

With consummate skill the technician probed, searching gently for a way around the block. She chose her questions with care, occasionally pausing to make minute adjustments to the flow of chemicals and drugs into the pirate's body. It took more than two hours before she found a way around the block and began to receive coherent answers. By that time she'd convinced the pirate that his mission was over and he was being debriefed by his commanding officer.

McCade added another cigar butt to the growing collection at his feet as the man related a good deal of boring detail which preceded the attack on Alice. Finally the pirate's narrative reached the part McCade had been waiting for.

"The assault began according to the plan outlined by our

shop steward. Using diversionary skirmishes for cover, my foreman led us into the administrative complex. Initially we encountered light resistance. Then in corridor five, we ran into trouble. Suddenly we ran into an organized defense and accurate sniper fire. Evidently the dirties were able to rush elite security forces into the area."

McCade smiled at this description of Van Doren and his file clerks.

"So after suffering heavy casualties, we were forced to withdraw," the pirate concluded.

"And you did the right thing," the technician said soothingly. "Now, what were the objectives of your mission?"

For a moment McCade thought the pirate would balk. The question wouldn't normally be asked during a debriefing, and for a moment the man's face registered doubt. Then the technician lightly touched her controls and the pirate's features gradually relaxed.

"Our first objective," he said in a singsong voice, "was to capture Council member Bridger."

McCade looked at Sara, but her expression was lost in the dark. Premo leaned over to whisper something in her ear, to which she nodded.

"Objective two was to capture or kill any other Council members present. Objective three was to retrieve any intelligence that might be available. Objective four was to damage and destroy as much of the administration complex as possible."

The pirate's words confirmed McCade's suspicions. The recent increase in pirate attacks was somehow connected to Bridger's disappearance. Why else would they place such importance on capturing his daughter? His mind raced as the interrogation continued. By the time it was over the technician would have skillfully extracted information on everything from the quality of pirate rations to the strength of their fleet. It was interesting stuff, but more than McCade needed to know.

The Council obviously felt the same way. The room lights came up and the Council members began to talk excitedly among themselves. The bank of screens faded to black and disappeared into the wall. Then the Council swiveled their chairs around to face McCade. Sara Bridger spoke first.

"McCade, I'm sorry about the way I acted the last time we met. I'm afraid I was tired and more than a little upset." Her hand strayed to the thin white line across her cheek. "You see, the news about my father came as quite a shock. In any case your bravery and that of your friend is strong testimony on a planet where deeds still speak louder than words." With that she frowned and paused before going on. "Which isn't to say I approve of either your profession or your methods," she added sternly.

"Understood," McCade replied levelly, catching a glimpse of her capacities as a politician. He admired the way in which she had apologized and then neatly regained the upper hand.

"Now," she said evenly, "perhaps we could pick up where we left off. The Council hopes that whatever you can tell us, combined with what we just heard, may shed some light on our present situation."

McCade had already considered the alternatives and decided in favor of complete honesty. Quickly and concisely he outlined the events leading up to his arrival on Alice. He left nothing important out, briefly touching on the Battle of Hell, his subsequent court martial, and how this had led Swanson-Pierce to try and use him. McCade saw Sara Bridger's already pale face grow even whiter at his mention of the Battle of Hell. Premo was furious. He started to rise, but her hand reached out to restrain him. With obvious reluctance, he fell back into his seat.

"Go on, McCade," she said, forcing a smile.

So he did, explaining how Bridger had evidently managed to decode his Directory, which in turn had apparently provided him with the location of the War World. McCade thought he detected a flash of pride in Sara Bridger's eyes at the mention of her father's accomplishment. But it was quickly gone in the buzz of conversation that followed as the Council members speculated about the War World and its potential impact on the citizens of Alice.

After a few moments of this, Sara asked for their attention. "Quiet, please. I'm sure we all agree that this War World is cause for concern. But let's hear the rest of Mr. McCade's comments." She nodded in his direction.

She was calm and attentive during the balance of his narrative, even laughing when he described his meeting with Rico.

By the time he was finished, he'd glossed over her father's relationship with the Treel in its guise as Cadet Votava, but in all other respects he'd been entirely honest.

The room fell silent for a moment. Then Colonel Larkin said, "So the Empire allows the pirates to exist as the price for peace. A price to be paid by us. I'd suspected as much but never had the guts to face it." He shook his head sadly, remembering all the good men who had died fighting token battles with the pirates.

"Not for much longer, it would seem," Professor Wendel interjected. "If the pirates pry the location of the War World out of your father, Sara, we won't be around very long thereafter."

"Not that we're gonna be that much better off if the Il Ronn or the Empire gets to him first," Rico added with a characteristic grin.

"*If* McCade's telling the truth," Premo concluded sourly.

Almost imperceptibly everyone turned toward Sara Bridger. Her eyes burned brightly in the whiteness of her face. Her hands were clenched talons in her lap. "It must be stopped," she said, her voice almost a whisper. Her face was haunted and desperate as she turned to McCade. "We must find him and stop this before they can use him. Even if it means killing him."

"No!" Premo spoke with such violence that spittle flew from his lips as he leaped to his feet. "I won't have it! He's lying! Can't you see that, Sara? He's trying to get you off Alice for some plan of his own. . . ." Suddenly one clawlike hand dived for the gun at his side.

As if by magic McCade's slug gun seemed to materialize in his hand. But before he could squeeze the trigger there was a loud cracking sound and Premo crumpled to the floor, his weapon falling from nerveless fingers. For a moment longer, life lingered in his eyes as he looked reproachfully up at Sara Bridger. Tears streamed down her cheeks and a wisp of smoke curled from the barrel of the small wrist gun in her hand. Then Premo was gone. Her eyes were still on his body when she said, "Tell the Council what we'll need, McCade . . . and they'll give it to you. Now if you'll all excuse me . . ." With a strangled sob she ran from the room.

McCade felt confused as he watched her go, wishing he

could comfort her, but afraid to try. He took a step forward, but stopped when he realized that to follow her he'd have to step over Premo's body. He looked up to find all their eyes directed his way.

"Well, ol' sport," Rico said, "like the lady said, what'll ya need?"

Eight

FIVE ROTATIONS LATER he was free of Alice but still
trapped by a lack of information. Nonetheless they'd settled
on a plan of action that might lead them to Bridger. It might
also get them killed. His seat vibrated for a moment as the
drive cut out for a fraction of a second before cutting back in.
The pirate ship had seen hard use without much maintenance.
It had taken the better part of four rotations to repair damage
to the cargo hatch, remove the charred remains of the pirate
crawler, and bury the pirates who'd been left behind when the
crammed lifeboat had lifted off. They'd chosen to fight it out
with Larkin's troops rather than surrender. McCade suspected
they would have found little mercy in the hands of the hard-
eyed colonists anyway.

To make matters more complicated, there wasn't any way
to tell when the ship had last been surveyed. That information,
along with the ship's log, inventory, crew list, and anything
else stored in the memory of the vessel's computer had been
bulk-erased by the escaping crew. They'd left a tidy little

bomb behind as a token of their esteem as well. Fortunately
Larkin's forces had found and disarmed it. Anyway it all
added up to a lift-off in a ship held together by habit and
prayer. There just wasn't enough time to do anything more.

McCade rubbed his eyes. They felt tired and dry. His body
demanded sleep, but his mind wanted one more look. Once
more he ducked under the hood of the lounge's small holo
player and tried to focus on the planet that swam before his
tired eyes. Its dull surface reflected little light. It looked like a
lifeless hulk, a dark place, a purposeless rock on an endless
path through space.

But McCade knew from the sketchy information gleaned
from the central data banks on Alice that it hadn't always been
so. When discovered by a far-ranging survey ship, clear back
in Confederation times, there had been life on the planet. It
hadn't been particularly attractive life, but it was life nonetheless. Dense jungle had wrapped most of the planet in a steamy
embrace. Giant mountains had thrust their lofty peaks to the
edge of space itself, and everywhere streams and rivers had
fed lakes and seas filled with life-bearing primordial soup. A
planet not unlike Terra in its early stages. But all that was
gone now. Replaced by millions of square miles of featureless
black rock. Confederation engineers had scoured the planet's
surface clean with hell bombs. In spite of their efforts tiny
microscopic organisms would doubtless start the long climb
once again, but it would be thousands of years before their
efforts became visible.

McCade turned the magnification up to max. The planet's
surface leaped up to reveal more detail. Right on the border
between day and night, slightly north of the equator, a fortress
could be seen. It was huge, covering more than a hundred
square miles. Originally it had been constructed as a forward
base from which the Confederation could defend itself against
an Il Ronn invasion. It was as close to impregnable as man
could make it. Energy for their weapons flowed from the
planet's core. The surface was sterilized to deny invaders even
the questionable hospitality of the jungle. In fact anything
which might have conceivably served an enemy was gone.
Mountains, rivers, seas, vegetation—everything.

The years passed and the Il Ronn never came. Instead the
Confederacy destroyed itself and the Empire was born. And

then the fortress *was* put to use. Staffed with Imperial marines, it made a good prison for those who refused to accept the Empire.

Thousands of prisoners disappeared into the sprawling complex. They rechristened the planet "The Rock" after a famous prison on old Earth. There the prisoners waited to die. They had little other choice. Like its ancient predecessor, the Rock offered little chance of escape. No one could survive long on the planet's sterile surface, and nothing larger than a supply shuttle was ever allowed to touch down.

As for taking over the complex itself, why bother? Rings of orbiting weapons platforms circled the globe and covered the surface of its four moons. Originally part of the planet's defenses, it had been a simple matter to aim them at the Rock itself instead of space. However, doing so had turned out to be a mistake. One which few of the marines manning the weapons lived to regret.

At first the attack seemed like one last glorious but suicidal gesture on the part of a ragtag rebel fleet. Badly mauled by Admiral Keaton in the Battle of Hell, they'd split up hiding among the frontier worlds, eventually coming back together at prearranged times and places. They knew the war was lost, and that knowledge drove them to one last desperate act, an attempt to free their imprisoned comrades. But much to their own surprise the rebel fleet met with an easy victory. The Imperial marines fought valiantly, but they weren't prepared for an attack from space, and they were grossly outnumbered. Within hours a half-million cheering prisoners stood on the barren black plains surrounding the prison.

It didn't take their leaders long to realize there was no place to go. They had insufficient ships to lift all the prisoners off the Rock, and in any case they lacked a destination. Elements of Keaton's fleet waited should they head toward the Empire, and in the other direction lay the Il Ronn, whose raiders were already making themselves felt. So once again the Rock's weapons were turned around and aimed toward space. What had been their prison became their home.

But they couldn't sit back and relax. The supplies on hand wouldn't last forever. The planet's surface wouldn't grow crops for a thousand years, even with terraforming . . . and without plant life even the atmosphere required maintenance.

So food and supplies would have to come from somewhere else.

What remained of the rebel fleet began to raid commerce along the frontier to obtain food and supplies. Those they raided called them "pirates." Disliking the term "pirates," they called themselves "The Brotherhood," although in truth the Brotherhood was more like an executive council made up of representatives from occupational organizations.

Then one day the Il Ronn attacked with unimaginable savagery. For two rotations the battle raged. The Il Ronn unleashed missiles and bombs of incredible power. But the rock's former inmates defended their home with courage and determination until finally the Il Ronn learned what Admiral Keaton had known all along. Without a civilian population to worry about, without industry to defend, a well-fortified planet can be held against any fleet. What was left of the Il Ronn armada limped off to lick its wounds.

Meanwhile one of the many small scout ships which Keaton referred to as his "eyes and ears," raced for fleet headquarters with its report of the Il Ronn defeat. Not long thereafter Admiral Keaton was shown into the Emperor's garden. The aging but still vigorous emperor lounged in the comfort of his stim bath. The two men talked for many hours. Keaton argued persuasively in favor of using the pirates as a first line of defense against the Il Ronn. The older man resisted at first, asking questions and pointing out potential consequences. But in the end the Emperor nodded his leonine head and it was agreed. It was one of his last major decisions. A few months later he was dead, and his son had assumed the throne.

McCade pulled his head out from under the privacy hood and fumbled for a cigar. Finding one, he lit it and leaned back to watch smoke swirl up toward the nearest intake vent. Getting on to the Rock, finding Bridger if he was there, and getting off alive wasn't going to be easy. Nevertheless it had to be done. Where else would Laurie have taken Bridger?

It didn't show up on the dated holo he'd been looking at but, according to the pirate prisoner, the Rock was even stronger now than it had been before. Since taking over, the pirates had expanded and improved the original structure, adding not only more comfortable quarters and recreational facilities, but more defenses as well. Chief among those were unmanned computer-controlled weapons platforms located about one light out from the Rock in every direction. Every pirate ship had an individual code printed into the atomic structure of its frame. As ships approached the weapons platforms, the code was automatically checked. If correct, the ship was allowed to pass. If not it was immediately blasted out of existence.

That's why McCade had chosen to use the pirate ship in spite of its questionable condition. Hopefully the code printed somewhere in its frame was still operational. If so they would pass the weapons platforms unmolested. If not they would die a quick death.

Wearily, he stood and made his way out of the small lounge, through the narrow corridor, and up to the control room. To his surprise Sara Bridger sat slumped in front of the huge command screen. On it, nearby stars and systems followed their stately paths as they had for billions of years. It was the first time she had left the privacy of her cabin since they'd lifted off Alice.

"It's beautiful, isn't it?" she said without looking around.

"Yes, it is," McCade answered, dropping into the seat next to her.

She swiveled around to face him, a tentative smile touching her lips. "Hello, Sam."

McCade felt something tighten in his chest when she said his name. Coming from her it seemed special somehow. A peace offering and an intimacy rolled into one. "Hello yourself," McCade replied with a smile. "How're you feeling?"

"Much better, thanks. I think it was the sleep I needed most. It seems like weeks since I've slept eight hours in a row. When the pirates weren't actually attacking, we were repairing the damage they'd done on the last raid and getting ready for the next one."

McCade nodded sympathetically. "Strangely enough, it seems you're what they were after." As quickly as the words left his mouth he regretted them. The light in her eyes dimmed as she turned back to the screen.

"Yes," she said. "Now that I know about the War World, it's obvious the pirates hoped to capture me for use as a hostage against Father's cooperation." She sighed. "I wonder how they knew I was alive and living on Alice."

"I imagine you have at least one pirate spy on Alice, if not more," McCade answered. "Nothing else makes much sense."

"Yes," she replied. "I imagine you're right."

She stared at the screen in silence and McCade couldn't think of anything to say. So they sat together in what eventually became a companionable silence. When she finally spoke, her voice had a hollow quality, as if coming from far away.

"Sam, tell me about the Battle of Hell."

"There really isn't much to tell."

"You told the Council that my father court-martialed you. . . . Why? I . . . I'd like to know, for personal reasons."

McCade was silent for a moment as the memories came flooding back across ten long years. With them came the hate and resentment that he had fought to control, but never quite conquered. Then he said, "Your father had me court-martialed for disobeying a direct order."

She turned her chair back toward him, her eyes locking with his as she said, "I think I know what that order was . . . but I'd appreciate your telling me."

So he did. Again he saw the pirate ship in the cross hairs of his sight as his thumb rested lightly on the firing stud. Again he heard the woman's pleading voice as she said, "Please, in the name of whatever gods you worship, I implore you, don't fire! My ship is unarmed. I have only women, children and old men aboard. . . . Please listen to me!"

Then the second voice, hoarse and commanding: "Fire, Lieutenant! That's an order! She's lying. Fire, damn you!"

Again he felt his thumb lift off the firing stud and watched as the pirate ship slid out of sight along his starboard side. Then the flare of the explosion in his rear screen as the pirate vessel was hit by one of the Imperial's main batteries at extreme range. Then the enemy ship was gone as its desperate captain took it into an uncalculated hyperspace jump.

For a moment Sara was silent. Then she said, "It happened exactly as you described it." Seeing his look of surprise, she said, "That's right. . . . My mother and I were aboard that pirate ship. We'd been put aboard shortly after they took the *Mars*. In fact I got this"—Her hand fluttered up to touch the scar—"fighting them at the main entry port along with the crew. And in a way I suppose it saved me from a 'fate worse than death.'" She smiled wryly. "They decided that even with surgery I'd never be pretty enough for the slave market. So they put me aboard a ship loaded with wealthy hostages. I guess they hoped to eventually ransom us, or if things went badly, use us as bargaining chips.

"Anyway, when our ship was caught by the *Imperial*, our captain piped the radio transmissions over the intercom. I think she knew what was coming and didn't want us to blame her. I'll never forget the look on my mother's face as she heard my father's voice commanding you to fire."

Tears ran down her cheeks.

"He wasn't a bad man," McCade said quietly. "He just couldn't deal with losing both of you. It drove him a little crazy."

"Thank you for that," she replied with a grateful smile. "Coming from you it means a lot. And you're right, he wasn't a bad man when I knew him. But whatever the reasons, he's become one. What he did during the Battle of Hell was wrong. And so was what he did to you afterward. And then to aid the Il Ronn against humans—worse than that, to give them the War World—there's no excuse for that." She paused. Though tears ran freely down her cheeks, her voice was calm and cold. "So if we find him, and I can't do it myself, promise me you'll kill him. It would be the greatest favor you could do for the man he once was."

McCade started to speak, but she shook her head. "Promise me," she insisted.

Reluctantly McCade nodded his agreement. There was no point in telling her that he would have done so in any case, assuming of course that Bridger wouldn't come with them.

She was silent for a moment, her eyes searching his as though looking for something important. "As you said, we escaped by taking a jump into hyperspace and then back out."

McCade put up a hand to stop her, but she shook her head and continued to speak.

"The ship was badly damaged. One of the two life rafts was destroyed. Those who could crowded into the remaining raft. Some of the wounded volunteered to stay behind. The captain insisted on staying with them." She shook her head in amazement. "It was funny really. That pirate captain would have cheerfully transported us all into slavery. But she wouldn't leave any of us on a crippled ship. Shortly after we got away, the ship blew up. We ran out of food rather quickly. There were so many of us packed into the little raft. At first we thought ourselves lucky to have plenty of air and water. Most people can last for quite a while without food. Then we learned the truth. For most of us, air and water would only prolong the suffering. We were way outside normal shipping lanes and the chances of being found were almost nil."

"The babies died first. And then the elderly. I think mother died inside as she listened to Father scream his insane orders. With her spirit gone, her body followed soon after. One by one I struggled to get their bodies into the raft's tiny lock . . . and into space . . . until eventually there were only three of us, a girl of about twelve and an old man. We tried to cheer each other up, we sang songs, and the old man told us about his life as a prospector. But eventually we ran out of things to say and retreated within ourselves. Privately I cursed the strength that kept me alive. Finally I felt myself sinking into welcomed darkness with a feeling of joyous release, certain my turn had finally come. But it wasn't to be. Instead I awoke, looking into Premo's face. He was a passenger aboard the ship that heard the raft's emergency beacon and picked us up.

"She was a tramp freighter. It seemed as though we stopped at every other asteroid to drop off supplies for some miner or lonely scientist. So Premo and I had lots of time to talk. He actually did most of the talking, while I listened. It was good actually. . . . I needed time to think.

"Like many of those who end up on frontier planets, Premo was a misfit . . . and on the run from something. I never asked what, and he never said. But he was brilliant in his own way . . . very knowledgeable about business and finance. As you saw, he was also a jealous and sometimes stupid man . . . in love with me in spite of this"—she indicated her face—" even though he knew I didn't feel the same way.

"But underneath all that, Premo was a dreamer, a man who saw the frontier worlds as an opportunity to start over, and avoid the mistakes of the past. He told me about Alice. About how it had just been opened and how beautiful it would be. What could be accomplished there and why it was important.

Well, I must have listened, because when we arrived I got off and never looked back."

"You never thought about going home?" McCade asked.

"Oh at first I did. But every time I thought about it, I imagined coming face to face with my father. What would I say? Tell him he'd murdered my mother along with hundreds of other people? No. It seemed pointless. Eventually I came to think of him as dead. And it worked—until you came along." She sighed. "You saved my life that day, Sam, and I'll always admire you for what you did, but maybe it would have been better if you'd followed my father's orders. If you had, I wouldn't have Premo's blood on my hands." She held her hands up and turned them over as if actually seeing blood on them. She stood and then shuddered before half walking and half running from the room.

McCade also stood, intending to follow, to tell her how glad he was that he'd saved her life, but stopped as the intercom buzzed.

"Weapons platform comin' up, boss. . . . We oughta know if we're gonna pass inspection any minute now." Van Doren's voice was cheerful. McCade wondered if the big marine was really unaffected by the possibility of death, or just couldn't imagine that it could happen to him.

"I'll be right there," McCade said over his shoulder as he stepped out of the control room and slid down the ladder to the level below.

Van Doren sat before the computer's master keyboard. As McCade approached, the marine touched a sequence of keys with surprisingly nimble fingers and then sat back to watch the screen.

"Any moment now we'll get the incoming pulse. It should register clear as a bell on our sensors. If the code's still working the pulse will read it. If not it's taps. . . ."

"Thanks, Amos. It's always nice to know I can count on you for a cheerful word in times of crisis."

Van Doren grinned in response, his eyes peering at the screen from beneath bushy brows. The seconds ticked away with maddening slowness. There was a noise behind him and McCade turned to see Sara enter. "I thought I should be here for the big moment," she said with a wan smile. Somehow it seemed natural to put his arm around her.

When the pulse came a moment later it seemed anticlimactic.

"Brotherhood Vessel 4690 *Zebra* cleared for planetfall" flashed on the screen and then faded away.

McCade let his breath out slowly, only then realizing he'd been holding it in. The arm he'd put around Sara suddenly felt awkward and out of place. He allowed it to fall and moved to Van Doren's side as he said, "Let's see if Rico's still with us."

Van Doren punched a couple of keys and a screen came to life above him. It was adjusted to maximum magnification. At its farthest edge a green light blinked on and off. Rico was still there, shadowing them in the *Lady Alice*. Before long he'd have to stop and lie doggo. Otherwise the weapons platforms would blast him. If challenged he would claim a mechanical failure which would soon be repaired. The neglected appearance of his ship would support his story. Rico would wait for six rotations. If they hadn't made it off the Rock by then, he'd rejoin the Council and together they'd figure out what to do next. The unspoken understanding was that McCade, Sara and Van Doren would be presumed dead.

"All right," McCade said, "it's time for phase two. Activate all the screens, Amos, and crank the sensors up to max. We'll see who else is in the neighborhood."

The marine pressed a series of keys. One by one the entire bank of screens in front of him came to life. Now they could see all the ships in their vicinity out to the range of their detectors.

There was a lot of activity. Which would be good for Rico, McCade mused. Hopefully he'd be able to lose himself in all the comings and goings. Screen by screen McCade eyed the possibilities. Pirate ships of all shapes and sizes swarmed around the planet like bees around a hive. Their radio traffic poured from the speaker over McCade's head. For the most part it was open and unscrambled, with only occasional bursts of code—an indication of how secure they feel, McCade thought. From the snatches of conversation, he began to build an interesting montage of activity.

Some of the ships were damaged from distant encounters with the Il Ronn. Others had been victorious and were making planetfall loaded with loot. Then there were the outward bound ships, hungry and on the prowl. Those they wanted to

avoid at all costs. There were other ships too. Possessors of
special one-time passes which enabled them to pass the
weapons platforms untouched, but which had to be reactivated
in order for them to leave. They were the smugglers, for the
most part. Traders in stolen and illicit goods. Disliked by
everyone, even the pirates, but used by all. They made their
dark living buying loot the pirates didn't need or want, and
then selling it on frontier worlds at below market prices,
sometimes to those from whom it had been stolen to begin
with.

And McCade knew that among the merchandise they
bought and sold were sentient beings. Thinking and feeling
creatures like Sara and her mother, snatched from merchant
vessels or native planets to live out short lives on some jungle
plantation or deep in a mine. But those were the lucky ones.
There were special customers for beautiful young women.
Customers with desires so dark and twisted no sane woman
would willingly comply with them. McCade shivered involun-
tarily, forcing his mind back to the ships which filled the
screens.

It took money to buy the kind of ships the smugglers
needed. McCade knew that all too often it was supplied by the
so-called legitimate merchants on planets like Weller's World.
All without interference from the Imperial Navy. Just another
payment on the price of peace. In any case, McCade thought
grimly, very soon one of the smugglers would be out of business. They'd known from the start it would be suicide to try
and land the pirate ship. By now it was overdue and probably
listed as missing in action. If it suddenly showed up, there'd
be pirates swarming all over it in seconds. No, it would be
much better to arrive in the guise of smugglers.

"Let's pick a small one," Sara said, scanning the screen.

"That's for sure!" McCade replied fervently. Even with the
element of surprise operating in their favor, they'd be hard-
pressed to take on a crew of five or six.

"How 'bout this one, boss?" Van Doren indicated his
choice with an electronic arrow.

"Looks like a small freighter," Sara said approvingly.

"Okay. Let's take a look," McCade said as he headed for
the control room. As he dropped into the pilot's position he
saw the two ready lights for the port and starboard weapons

blisters pop on one after the other. Van Doren and Sara were in their places.

Gingerly he took control of the ship away from the computer. He'd had very little time with her controls and didn't know all her quirks yet. He locked onto the blinking light still marked with an arrow and sent the ship toward it in a long graceful curve. Carefully he examined nearby traffic, looking for anything suspicious. But as far as he could tell, nobody was interested in their activities. As they closed with their target, it became apparent that the two ships would meet in a relatively empty area. That suited McCade just fine.

"This one looks like a keeper," McCade said into the intercom. "I'm about to say hello, so stand by. . . ."

With that he opened the standard ship to ship channel, audio only, and hailed the other vessel. "This is Brotherhood Patrol Ship 4690 *Zebra*. Heave to and prepare to be boarded."

The reply lit up the com screen to his right. The freighter's captain sent both sound and pix. His face was narrow and his skin bore an unhealthy pallor. A forced smile revealed rows of uneven yellow teeth through which his voice issued forth as a servile whine. A tiny gold disc hung at his throat. "Of course, of course. Always happy to oblige the Brotherhood. Is Your Excellency looking for anything in particular? I have an excellent bottle of Terran whiskey aboard," he added slyly.

"Just a routine inspection," McCade replied with what he hoped was the right mixture of boredom and authority. "Can't be too careful you know. Come to think of it, I am a bit parched. . . . I'll be over shortly."

The weasellike face nodded knowingly. "It'll be a pleasure to serve Your Excellency." With that the com screen faded to black.

McCade wiped the light sheen of perspiration from his forehead and heaved a sigh of relief. It had worked. The two ships were now in visual contact. The freighter was half the size of the pirate vessel. To McCade's surprise it was relatively new and appeared to be well maintained. A measure of the profits to be made, McCade thought sourly. "Contact in about two minutes," McCade said into the intercom. "Stand by."

When the ships were a few hundred feet apart, McCade

triggered the tractor beams, which locked the two vessels together. Through a series of gentle adjustments, he brought the two ships together with an almost imperceptible bump. They were touching lock to lock.

McCade ran through a mental check list as he stood and glanced around the control room. Everything seemed in order. He touched the key placing all major systems on stand-by, and headed for the lock where Sara and Van Doren were waiting. They had already pressurized the space between the two locks. McCade checked his slug gun, and the stunner hidden up his right sleeve in a spring-loaded holster. The other two smiled their readiness. McCade nodded and activated the inner hatch. With a sigh the lock cycled open, and as they stepped through he felt the familiar tug from the muscle in his left cheek.

As they entered the other ship, they were greeted by a Finthian Bird Man. He seemed to be molting. Large patches of his golden feathers were missing, revealing sections of greenish skin. His saucerlike eyes regarded them gravely.

"Welcome aboard the *Far Trader,* gentlepersons." His beaklike nose rose and fell as he spoke, his voice emanating from the translator at his throat. "Captain Fagan will receive you in the lounge if you'll step this way?"

Together they followed him through a maze of corridors and up a ladder to the next deck. Along the way they kept a sharp lookout for other crew members. They saw only one. A fragile-looking woman with gray wispy hair busily tending a hydroponics tank. As they passed Sara shot her in the back with a stun gun. The woman hardly made a sound as she crumpled to the deck. Sara never even broke stride. McCade shook his head in amazement as he followed the oblivious Finthian down another short passageway.

Moments later they entered the ship's lounge where they were greeted by the sallow Captain Fagan. Seated next to him was a three hundred pound sauroid whose smile, if that is what it was, revealed an enormous array of wicked-looking teeth.

"Welcome aboard our humble ship, Excellencies. This is my first officer, Mr. Slith. How may we serve you?"

"By keeping the amount of time we have to spend on this tub to a minimum," McCade replied arrogantly. "So let's get on with it. I'll need a print-out of your cargo manifest and a crew list. Oh yeah, and a fax of your log for the last seventy-two standard hours too."

"Immediately, Your Excellency," Captain Fagan sniveled as he punched McCade's requests into the keyboard at his side. Seconds later a printer began to whir as a sheet of plastic emerged from a slot.

Sara walked over and ripped off the sheet. She handed it to McCade with such a show of deference that he struggled not to laugh. With what he hoped was an arrogant sneer, McCade accepted the print-out and skimmed over it. Counting the captain, he saw that the *Far Trader* carried a crew of five. Sara had accounted for one on the way in, there were three present in the lounge, so there was another loose somewhere on the ship, a Cellite with the unlikely name of Sunshine.

McCade motioned to Amos and the big marine stepped to his side. "Check this out," he said, pointing to the Cellite's name on the crew list.

"Right away, boss," Amos said, and disappeared into the corridor.

Captain Fagan's features seemed to tighten. So you have something to hide, McCade thought. Not too surprising really.

"Is there a problem, Excellency? I assure you if there is, it was purely accidental. In all my years of trading with the Brotherhood I've never..."

"Stow it," McCade said. "It's just routine. Say, didn't you mention some Terran whiskey?"

"I did, Your Excellency," Fagan gurgled happily, reaching for the bottle at his elbow.

McCade flexed the muscles in his forearm and felt the spring-loaded holster deliver the small stunner into his hand. He brought it up and shot Fagan between the eyes. The little captain crashed to the deck, taking the bottle of whiskey and some glasses with him. McCade heard the thump of another body hitting the deck behind him and knew without looking that Sara had taken care of the Finthian Bird Man.

McCade swung left until the giant sauroid filled the sight. He pulled the trigger and waited for the alien to slump to the deck. Instead the giant creature stood with surprising ease and smiled, although on second thought McCade felt sure it wasn't a smile. He pulled the trigger again, as did Sara, who was also aiming her stunner at the scaled first officer.

"Uh-oh," McCade said. "I think he's got some kind of natural shielding against stunners."

"Brilliant," Sara said through gritted teeth, the knuckles of her right hand white where her fingers gripped the stun gun.

A strange electronic squawking sound came from the sauroid and for the first time McCade noticed the small box strapped to the alien's throat about where the human larynx is.

"Prepare to die, interloper!"

With that the huge creature produced a power knife and launched itself straight at McCade.

Nine

MCCADE JUMPED BACK. As he did, Sara threw herself between him and the charging alien. The sauroid batted her aside without apparent effort. She crashed into a bulkhead and then fell to the deck. The huge creature kept on coming, but Sara had slowed it just enough to give McCade a chance. He drew the slug gun and fired twice. The heavy slugs hit Slith square in the chest and the impact rocked him backward. However, to McCade's astonishment, the alien recovered and charged again, roaring his rage through the translator—although it really didn't require translation.

The slugs hadn't penetrated the sauroid's armored skin, but they'd made him a bit more cautious. As he neared McCade, the *Far Trader*'s first officer slowed and began to circle. McCade was very conscious of the power knife which hummed in Slith's scaled hand. He knew it wasn't a knife in the conventional sense. Oh, it could cut all right! In fact its sealed energy beam could cut through durasteel as though it was warm butter. With amazing speed McCade's massive opponent lashed out. He heard the knife sizzle past his left ear as he desperately back-pedaled to get out of the way. McCade swore under his breath. He'd watched the alien's eyes, expecting them to telegraph the next move, and they hadn't. So he switched his attention to the knife, which wove back and forth in an almost hypnotic pattern.

McCade moved left, and then right, catching Slith off balance and placing Fagan's unconscious body between them. He felt the edge of the table pressing him from behind. He had nowhere to go. He had to get the knife. He knew that. He'd hunted fugitives of all races. They almost always armed themselves with weapons effective against their own kind. It was a natural tendency. McCade had done it himself in choosing the slug gun. So he had to get the knife.

Slith lunged toward him again. McCade was ready and leaped aside. The power knife made a buzzing sound as it sliced through the table top a fraction of a second later.

Then came the break McCade was waiting for. The sauroid put a huge foot on the whiskey bottle and it rolled out from under him. That plus his forward momentum brought him down. As his right hand hit the floor McCade jumped on it with both feet. The knife popped free. Grabbing for it, McCade turned too late. He felt his feet go out from under him as his opponent hit them with the sweep of one powerful arm. As he hit the deck McCade saw that Slith had regained his feet and was already diving toward him. Instinctively he threw up his hands in a puny attempt to fend off the three hundred pounds of armored flesh falling toward him.

The knife was still clutched in his right hand. It sizzled as it slid smoothly into the Sauroid's chest. Then the alien's incredible weight hit him, forcing the air from his chest in one explosive breath. Blackness tried to drag him under. Desperately he tried to suck in air and push the dead weight off at the same time. Finally the scaled body rolled off. For a moment he just lay there, chest heaving as he gratefully sucked in air and waited for the darkness to clear from his sight. He staggered to his feet just as Van Doren burst through the hatch, slug gun in hand.

"Jeez, boss . . . you're always having fun while I'm gone."

"Yeah, well, the next lizard we run into is all yours, Amos."

Across the lounge, Sara stood and dusted herself off.

"You okay?" McCade asked.

"A little shaky," she answered slowly. "I'll bet I feel better than he does though." She indicated the dead alien.

"Thanks," McCade said. "What you did took a lot of guts."

She accepted the compliment without comment, but she looked pleased. "Now what?" she asked.

"Now we off-load the captain and his stalwart crew to the other ship," McCade said. "Amos, how'd it go with Sunshine?"

"Sleeping like a baby, boss."

"Okay, let's get to work."

It took the better part of an hour to get *Far Trader*'s crew through the lock and safely tucked into bunks aboard the other ship. It took all three of them, plus a power pallet from the cargo hold to move Slith. Without ceremony he went out an ejection port into eternal orbit around the Rock.

Then they were ready. McCade sent a coded radio command and the pirate ship took off for Alice. Its manual controls were locked off and would remain so until the proper code was entered by Colonel Larkin on Alice. If the ship hung together long enough to get there.

As McCade nosed the *Far Trader* down toward the Rock, he blew cigar smoke at the com screen and waited for the inevitable challenge. He didn't have long to wait. The com screen swirled to life with the likeness of an attractive but bored-looking young woman.

"Vessel, registration number and code please."

McCade's blood ran cold. The first two questions were easy—but the third was a real lulu. Evidently Fagan had been provided with a verbal code as well as the one-time-only electronic pass recorded into the ship's hull. As he gave the ship's name and registration number, his mind raced. Would Fagan have provided the code or the pirates? If the pirates had he might as well forget it. There were billions of possibilities. But Fagan might have been asked to provide the code. And he seemed like a simple sort who'd go for something uncomplicated, something he couldn't forget. His eyes desperately ransacked the control room, searching for anything that might provide a clue. *Far Trader*'s control room was almost military in its spartan orderliness. There was no sign of the personal bric-a-brac common to most control rooms he'd seen. Then his eyes came to rest on the stylized likeness of Sol mounted high above the controls almost on the overhead. Suddenly he remembered the tiny golden disc Fagan had worn around his neck. He was a member of the Solarian Church. Evidently a devout one.

The face on the screen no longer appeared bored. Now it was tense, with formerly soft lips pulled into a tight smile. *"Far Trader,* this is your final warning. State your code or be fired on."

"From Ra flows life," McCade said, intoning the traditional Solarian greeting. To his enormous relief, the tension drained from the woman's face, leaving only annoyance.

"Next time don't screw around so long," she said sternly. "Put it down on the light side outer ring of port twelve. Await an escort and ground transportation on grounding. Welcome to the Rock." With that the com screen snapped abruptly to black.

McCade forced his muscles to relax and reached up to wipe away the sweat that coated his forehead.

"I'll never know how you pulled that off," Sara said in amazement over the intercom.

"It was either dumb luck or Ra really is with us," McCade said, looking up at the golden disc.

Four standard hours later they sat on the ground awaiting the promised escort and transportation. Everything he'd seen in braking orbit and descent had reinforced the Rock's reputation for impregnability. They'd managed to get on the Rock, but as it was for so many others before them, the problem would be getting off again.

McCade used the time while they waited to look around. On one side black rock stretched away to the horizon. On the other, ships stood in orderly rows like a crop waiting to be harvested. As he swept the powerful lens over the forest of ships, McCade was amazed by the sheer scale of what he saw. There were all kinds: freighters, converted military ships, alien craft of all shapes and sizes, plus some small and very expensive-looking speedsters.

They were surrounded by bustling activity. Crawlers came and went, snaking between the ships with trains of loaded power pallets bobbing along behind. Cranes lifted mysterious crates in and out of dark holds. Vendors moved to and fro, hawking everything from food to spare parts. Aliens from a hundred worlds made a swirl of color against the drab rock as they hurried about on their various errands.

At regular intervals black towers stood, their broad bases forcing traffic to ebb and flow around them. At the top of each hundred-foot structure a bulbous turret bristled with antennas and weapons. Behind one-way armored glass, McCade imagined pirate sentries carefully monitoring the activity below.

He turned away from the scope and buzzed Van Doren on the intercom. "Amos, in our role as smugglers, it occurs to me we should know what we're smuggling. Take a look in the hold and let me know what you find. I'll be surprised if it's the ten thousand eternafiber blankets mentioned on the cargo manifest."

"Right, boss. . . . Back in a jiffy."

Turning back to the scope, McCade swept it over the spaceport again. This time he scanned the ships a mile or two away. Suddenly he swore out loud and jerked the scope back a bit. He wasn't mistaken. There she sat just as pretty as the day he'd first seen her. *Pegasus*. For a moment he just sat there, tracing her lines and running his eyes over her for signs of damage. There weren't any.

Thoughtfully, he turned away from the scope, rummaged through his pockets for a cigar butt, and then lit it with short angry puffs. So Laurie made it home. Therefore Bridger was here too. At least they were in the right place. Bridger had apparently been sick when they took him off Weller's World. Too sick to talk? Sick enough to die? There was no easy way to find out. So they'd do it the hard way.

Sara's head appeared in the control room hatch. "I think we've got company, Sam."

He nodded as a soft tone announced someone at the main entry port. A glance at the main security monitor revealed a man accompanied by an autoguard. The man was smiling and had the look of a prosperous, middle-aged business executive. His one-piece suit was expensive and beautifully cut.

By contrast, his companion was a masterpiece of forbidding intimidation. For psychological reasons its creators had granted it vaguely human appearance. If something six and a half feet tall with a ball turret for a head and energy weapons for arms could be called human. By making it slightly larger than most men, and ugly to boot, the machine's designers had ensured that those who could be scared off, would be. But for those who were not so easily impressed, the autoguard possessed a more than adequate ability to defend itself. Capable of taking on and defeating a section of Imperial marines, such machines were incredibly expensive. However they were also impossible to bribe or blackmail, which accounted for their popularity among the Empire's rich and powerful.

Violence is definitely out, McCade thought as the entry port cycled open. As he stepped out, the visitor introduced himself.

"Joseph Sipila, Longshoreman's Union, at your service, gentlebeing," the pirate said, grinning broadly, "and welcome to the Rock." His handshake was warm and firm. McCade found himself liking the man against his own better judgment.

Glancing at his wrist term Sipila said, "Captain Fagan perhaps?"

Inwardly McCade heaved a sigh of relief. There had been the chance that Sipila and Fagan were old friends or something. McCade had a story ready just in case, but was glad he wouldn't have to use it.

McCade nodded eagerly, adopting something of Fagan's servile manner. "Yes, Excellency, my crew and I are at your disposal."

"Disposal? Fido here handles my disposals, don't you, Fido?" the other man said cheerfully. With that he laughed uproariously and slapped the autoguard on the back.

"Quite so, I'm sure," McCade said, forcing a chuckle of appreciation.

"Well, enough of that," Sipila said. "We can't stand here jawing all day long. . . . No profit in that, is there, Fagan? Goodness no. Now let's see what you've got for us. . . ."

"Here's the sample you asked for, boss," Van Doren said smoothly, appearing as if by magic at McCade's elbow and placing an electronic component of some sort in his hands. Wordlessly McCade handed it over to Sipila, who accepted it with obvious pleasure.

"A guidance module for the Dragon air to ground missile! Good work, Fagan. These are on the Brotherhood's priority list. Should bring a nice price in the market. Anything else? No? All right then, have your crew off-load onto those power pallets over there, and a crawler will be along to tow 'em for you. You can ride to market in the crawler or call for a limo and an escort."

"I'm sure the crawler will be fine, Excellency," McCade whined. "There's no need to bother anyone else on our account."

"Fine then. I'll be off. Don't do anything I wouldn't do!" Grinning and slapping McCade's back, Sipila took his hulking companion and disappeared in the direction of another ship.

McCade felt the tension drain out of his muscles as he turned to the other two and in his best Faganlike manner said, "Well you heard him! Turn to! We haven't got all day." It was best to assume everything they said and did outside the ship was being monitored by the men high above in the black towers.

In spite of *Far Trader*'s automatic cargo-handling equipment, it took time and sweat to pull the six tons of electronic components out of her hold and load them aboard the waiting pallets. When they'd finished, all three went back aboard the freshen up and talk privately. McCade took a long, satisfying pull at the whiskey and soda in his hand, mentally toasting Slith as he did so. The whiskey was from the very same bottle the unfortunate first officer had tripped on.

"So what'll we do when we get the stuff to market?" Sara asked, taking a sip of the drink in her hand.

McCade shrugged. "Beats me. Play it by ear, I guess. But I can tell you this much, we came to the right place."

Briefly he told them about spotting *Pegasus*. Then all three were silent for a moment. Van Doren's expression was sour as he thought about Laurie's theft of *Pegasus* and his failure to prevent it. Sara took nervous little sips of her drink as she imagined coming face to face with her father. And McCade felt his cheek begin to twitch as he thought about the odds against ever getting off the planet.

So when the crawler arrived, all three were relieved to be doing something. As it moved smoothly into motion, McCade glanced out the rear window to see the power pallets bob and sway in their wake. Each floated easily on its cushion of air in spite of the load heaped on it. The driver was a taciturn man of vaguely oriental descent. His most eloquent phrases were grunts of various tonalities. The identaplaque above his head identified him as one Marvin Wong, a teamster in good standing.

The view that flowed by was fascinating. The Rock wasn't all weapons and grim fortifications. Pleasant-looking housing complexes came and went in a series of domes, along with elaborate recreational facilities. Here and there scrubby-looking trees struggled to survive in the imported soil. Children played around them as adults looked on approvingly, smiling and talking among themselves. On the surface it made a cheerful and innocent scene, but somehow McCade found it disturbing. None of it had been earned. It had been taken. Taken from planets like Alice and people like Sara. While these children laughed and played, others on Alice cried over shallow graves carved out of the permafrost with hand blasters. He looked over at Sara, but her eyes remained locked on the back of the driver's head.

Before long the crawler entered a huge dome. It was by far the largest structure McCade had ever seen. Larger than even the Imperial Coliseum, which covered what had once been the city of Detroit. There was an open space at its center dominated by a graceful column soaring hundreds of feet into the air. McCade sensed what whoever occupied the top of that column dominated the activity within the entire structure. Around the perimeter of the dome, broad terraces gently climbed toward the roof. The uppermost levels were sufficiently high that people could be seen flitting between them in air scooters.

Moments later, with a grunt of farewell, the driver discharged them in front of a lift tube. He handed McCade a rectangle of highly polished metal, and then without further ado, engaged the crawler's drive and headed toward a tunnel leading underground.

As they stepped into the lift tube, McCade examined the metal card. He'd never seen anything like it. He supposed it was similar to a universal credit card. But unlike a credit card, its surface was absolutely smooth. Therefore it seemed likely that whatever information it contained was recorded in its molecular structure, similar to the system the pirates used to identify their ships. McCade's thoughts were interrupted as the platform stopped on its own. Somewhere a computer monitored all arrivals and delivered them to whatever level happened to be the least crowded at the moment.

As they stepped out, McCade was again struck by the sheer size of everything. Ahead the broad terrace swept off into the distance. Beings of all races moved across its surface. He noticed they tended to stand, sit, or squat in small clumps around gray, boxlike structures. Among them moved the swaggering members of the Brotherhood's planetary police organization. Something about the way everyone hurried to get out of their way made it clear they were not public servants.

Occasionally someone failed to see them coming, or was too slow in moving out of the way, and received a careless shove or touch of the nerve stick to hurry them along. McCade made a mental note to stay as far away from them as possible.

Toward the outer edge of the terráce, an endless row of shops sold food, clothing and recreation to the milling multitude. The variety required to satisfy the needs of so many races boggled the mind. They give you money for your goods and a place to spend it, McCade thought with grim amusement.

As they approached one of the gray, boxlike structures, McCade saw it was a combination computer terminal and com unit, not unlike those used in large maximarkets on Terra. A woman could be seen on the com screen, but there wasn't any audio. Then McCade noticed the earphones, which could be adjusted to fit a wide range of auditory organs. He picked up a set and put them on. As he did so the woman vanished and was replaced by a menu of possible races. He touched the word "Human" and watched as the woman faded back in, speaking perfect Standard. McCade knew that if he'd touched "Finthian," he'd be listening to the warbling voice of a Finthian hen.

He listened as the current transaction came to a close. One of the thousands of anonymous merchants surrounding him had just purchased five hundred all-terrain vehicles taken in a raid on a frontier world called Lucky Strike. Now he'd sell them to some other frontier planet desperate for manufactured goods. McCade glanced up at Sara. She had donned a headset and her furious expression made her feelings clear.

He slid the metal rectangle into the slot provided for that purpose. A list of those ahead of him in line flashed on the screen, along with an estimated waiting time. He decided there was plenty of time to get something to eat.

The restaurant Sara chose turned out to be excellent. Instead of the typical autochef, it employed actual cooks who clearly knew their business. After a series of exquisite courses, McCade sipped a final cup of real Terran coffee while Van Doren polished his plate with a piece of roll. During the meal Sara had entertained them with a number of fictional but hilarious accounts of her love life for the benefit of electronic eavesdroppers. At least McCade hoped they were fictional.

Glancing at his wrist term he saw it was almost time for their transaction. They paid the exorbitant bill by sliding the shiny metal card into the restaurant's cashcomp. Somewhere, much to McCade's enjoyment, a computer debited Fagan's account accordingly. Then they returned to the market.

"Next, gentlebeings, is lot 76940-A. Ten thousand guidance control modules for the Dragon air to ground missile. Since this lot is on the Brotherhood's priority list, open bidding is suspended. The Brotherhood offers the owner five thousand credits per module."

A tidy five million credits! McCade was amazed. No wonder merchants of every race flocked here.

"Accept or deny," the man droned.

McCade pushed the "accept" button. He wondered what would've happened if he'd pushed "deny." He had a feeling it wouldn't be altogether pleasant.

"Transaction complete," the man announced.

The metallic card popped out of the console. McCade removed his earphones and picked it up. He held a fortune in his hand. They could buy another cargo, load it on the *Far Trader* and lift. It's what Fagan would do. But I'm not Fagan, he thought, meeting Sara's gaze, and besides, maybe there're things worth more.

Her eyes widened and her face paled until her scar almost disappeared. McCade whirled to find himself staring down the tubes of a dozen blasters held by men in full armor. They stood in a semicircle with Laurie at its center. For the second time he searched her eyes for sorrow and found none.

Ten

AFTER BEING DISARMED, they were herded through a maze of hallways, corridors, tunnels and lift tubes that always headed down. The farther they went, the fewer people they encountered. Those they did pass ignored them. McCade decided prisoners must be a fairly common sight on the Rock. He remembered stories he'd heard about pirate prisoners winding up as slaves and shuddered.

Meanwhile the hallways and corridors through which they passed had grown darker and shabbier. Eventually lift tubes gave way to endless stairs leading down. McCade noticed it was getting warmer and more humid. Even the walls were sweating. Soon water dripped, gurgled, and slid off every surface, turning his clothes to wet rags which clung to his skin and rubbed it raw. What he had first noticed as a vibration in the soles of his boots had become recognizable as the throbbing beat of heavy machinery located somewhere nearby.

He glanced over his shoulder to see how the others were doing and got a hard shove for his trouble. A soaked Van

Doren and Sara were right behind him, but there was no sign of Laurie.

The stairs finally ended in a dark area of indeterminate size. McCade decided it was probably large, since their footsteps echoed as if off distant walls. Widely spaced pools of light marked a path through the dark. Somebody rammed something hard between his shoulder blades to hurry him along. On the edge of his vision, light and dark met in gloomy twilight and he could just barely make out endless rows of old-fashioned bars. Then he realized this section dated back to the time when the entire complex had been a prison. Since then they had quite naturally renovated the upper levels first, leaving the deepest areas for detention cells and heavy equipment.

The floor suddenly shelved upward, causing him to stumble and almost fall. Strong hands pulled him back up and roughly shoved him on. Then they rounded a corner and were ordered to halt. Dark forms moved to his right, accompanied by the squeal of unoiled hinges. He was unceremoniously propelled forward. Metal clanged behind him. He turned to see the bulky shadows move off into the dark.

Not far away machinery beat out a massive rhythm that made his head hurt. He thought he heard the sound of two more cell doors closing, but they were too far off for him to be sure. He tried yelling, but there was no reply. If Sara and Amos were anywhere nearby, they evidently couldn't hear him over the machinery.

Strangely enough, other than weapons, they hadn't taken his personal possessions. If his lighter had been a miniature blaster, they would have been sorry. Unfortunately, it was only a lighter. He used it to examine his cell. Except for a plastic bench set against one wall, and some pathetic grafitti left by previous tenants, the cell was bare. McCade lit a cigar and sat down on the bench. He flinched as his back came into contact with the damp wall, and then decided to ignore it. He tried to think meaningful thoughts, but they refused to come. Eventually he lay down on the bench and drifted into an uneasy sleep.

He awoke to the clang of metal as his cell door was opened.

"If you'd be kind enough to step this way?"

He was surprised by his jailer's civil tone. As he stood to go, he realized that his back hurt from sleeping on the hard bench. He stepped out of the cell and a grav light suddenly came to life. It sat bobbing in the slight air current above and behind the jailer's head.

"I'll give you a moment to get used to the light," the jailer continued in a congenial manner.

As the light gradually increased, McCade suddenly recognized the smooth countenance of Marvin Wong, the formerly taciturn driver who'd brought them in from the spaceport. So they knew the moment we landed, McCade thought to himself. He made a note to himself to find out how.

Aloud he said, "Your vocabulary has certainly improved since we last met."

Wong smiled his agreement. "Yes, Captain Fagan, or should I say Citizen McCade? All is not always what it seems. Now if you would please follow me." Wong turned and set off without even checking to see if McCade was following along behind.

For his part McCade saw little advantage in doing anything else. He had little doubt that others waited in the darkness should he try to run. Besides, things had taken an interesting turn. Wong set a brisk pace. The grav light bobbed along between them, its ghostly glow casting enormous shadows as they moved. Empty cells were visible on both sides, but McCade saw no sign of Sara or Amos. Maybe they had already been taken wherever he was headed.

They were moving upward. At first the floor sloped. Then they climbed what seemed like endless flights of metal stairs, finally emerging into a corridor replete with normal lighting and carpet. The air flowing from a nearby vent was dry and warm, but McCade's skin was still chilled under his damp clothes.

As they marched down the corridor McCade noticed doors which interrupted its length at regular intervals. After passing quite a few, they stopped in front of one. It looked like all the rest to McCade.

Wong rapped on it three times before turning to McCade. "Go on in . . . they're waiting for you." With that he turned and headed up the hall with the now darkened grav light following faithfully along behind.

McCade watched him go with detached amusement. Why were they so relaxed now, when earlier they'd felt it necessary to throw him into a cell right out of the Dark Ages? Maybe they were trying to soften him up. Well, he decided, there's only one way to find out.

He plastered a confident grin on his face and palmed the door. It slid aside to admit him. The room was brightly lit and dominated by a long conference table. An inscrutable black man dressed in dazzling white was seated at the head of it. His eyes were hooded like a hawk's and utterly devoid of emotion. On his left sat a wizened humanoid who looked like a gnome, and on his right was Laurie, a quizzical smile touching her lips.

"Please be seated, Citizen McCade." The black man had a deep, melodious voice, which added to his presence.

"Don't mind if I do," McCade said, plopping into the nearest chair and immediately swinging his filthy boots up onto the polished surface of the conference table. "Much more comfortable than some of your other furniture," McCade ventured, patting his pockets for a cigar.

The black man watched him with patient amusement as McCade located a half-smoked butt and lit it. As soon as it was going, the black man spoke again. "My name is Brother Mungo. On my left is Brother Urbus, and I believe you know Sister Lowe."

"I once thought I did," McCade said, inclining his head in Laurie's direction.

"Your feelings concerning Sister Lowe's execution of her duties do not concern me, Citizen McCade," Mungo said dispassionately. "Although it may interest you to know this conversation wouldn't be taking place if it were not for her intercession. Brother Urbus and I favored feeding your mass to the main reactor—a couple of microseconds of power is, after all, better than nothing . . . which is what I think you're worth. However Sister Lowe pointed out how the Emperor's minions forced you to do their bidding, and that you've been useful, albeit unknowingly so. With that in mind, we've decided to be lenient." Mungo smiled tolerantly.

"What? No hot irons, no deep probes?" McCade asked with a raised eyebrow.

"Whatever for?" Mungo said gently. "It's painfully obvious that we know more about Bridger's discovery than you do. Oh, I suppose we could wring a few pitiful details about Alice out of you, or Miss Bridger for that matter, but what's the point? Soon we will command the War World and the pathetic defenses of Alice will no longer be of interest. In fact, as it turns out we really don't need Miss Bridger either. Too bad we wasted all that effort trying to capture her." He shrugged. "That's the way it goes."

McCade fought the mixture of anger and despair that threatened to overwhelm him. Mungo's manner was insulting. Even worse was the fact that everything he said was true. McCade didn't know anything they didn't. They held all the cards. McCade blew a stream of smoke toward his boots and produced what he hoped was a nonchalant smile.

"You're quite right, of course. Can't win 'em all, I always say. By the way, just as a point of professional interest, how did you locate us so quickly?"

"Thanks to Sister Lowe, that was easy," Mungo answered with obvious relish. "She hid a tracer in the handle of your sidearm before you left Terra."

McCade's mind flashed back to her arrival on *Pegasus* to see his duffel bag flying from Laurie's hand to land in his lap. He remembered pulling the slug gun out and noticing it had been cleaned and oiled—and bugged, he thought bitterly. The moment they had landed, the tiny tracer had triggered an audible alarm and lit up a visual display somewhere. From then on Laurie had known exactly where they were every moment. How they must have laughed while he carried out his transparent impersonation of Captain Fagan!

"Enough of this silliness," Urbus said in a high, piping voice. "As Brother Mungo indicated, McCade, we see little point in your continued existence. However in deference to Sister Lowe, we're inclined to release you if you'll promise to get off the Rock and disappear. As Captain Fagan, I believe you'll have adequate funds at your disposal and a good ship. That is the bargain you made with Keaton, is it not? We'll even throw in your brutish companion for good measure." Unseen hands opened a side door and shoved Van Doren into the room. His hands were bound. In spite of that, he moved toward Mungo, but stopped when he saw McCade.

"Well?" The frown of impatience almost disappeared into the gnome's already wrinkled face.

To his own surprise McCade found himself seriously considering the little humanoid's proposal. He had everything to gain and nothing to lose. Five million credits plus a good ship would make a very good start indeed. Actually better than what Keaton had offered. Just as quickly he rejected the notion, wryly noting that Swanson-Pierce and Keaton had chosen their tool well. Whether it was the importance of stopping Bridger and the War World, the years of conditioning at the Academy, concern for Sara, or just his own stubborn personality, he didn't know. But somehow it seemed important to finish what he'd started.

Stalling for time, McCade said, "And Sara Bridger?"

Before either man could reply, the door burst open to admit Marvin Wong. His normally unlined features were creased with worry as he hurried over to Mungo and Urbus. Leaning over, he whispered urgently in their ears. Then at the sound of distant shots and confused shouting, he whirled and ran for the door. McCade turned to watch him go. He turned back to find himself staring straight into Mungo's glittering eyes. "Sorry, McCade. All bets are off. It seems we're taking a sudden trip, and you're excess baggage."

With that he produced a small blaster and aimed it at McCade. There were two loud reports as both Mungo and Urbus slumped sideways out of their chairs.

"Well, now the fecal matter's hit the fan for sure," Laurie said matter of factly as she withdrew the still smoking slug gun from under the table. She stood and leaned over to pluck the blaster from Mungo's nerveless fingers. Tossing it to McCade, she said, "We'd better haul our fannies outa here before somebody comes along and blows them off." Then she was out the door and running down the corridor.

McCade looked at Van Doren and shrugged. He didn't trust her, but there weren't a whole lot of options. Van Doren held out his bound hands. A second later the blaster had burned through the plastic restraints and some of the skin on the marine's wrists. He didn't seem to notice. Together they bolted after Laurie.

The fighting was getting closer. The loud ripping sound of

automatic slug throwers and the sizzle of energy weapons were punctuated by shouted commands and screams of agony. McCade and Van Doren caught up with Laurie where another corridor intersected theirs. She peered cautiously around the corner for a moment before snapping off a couple of shots at an unseen adversary.

"Where are we going?" McCade shouted over the noise of the conflict.

"You came to find Bridger, didn't you?" she yelled in reply without looking back. Just then a man wearing a red arm band backed around the corner firing short bursts from an automatic slug thrower. Laurie pulled him down beside her and said something in his ear, to which he nodded in agreement.

Turning to McCade and Van Doren, Laurie said, "Get ready. When I go, stay right behind me. And for God's sake, don't blast anyone wearing a red band."

McCade and Van Doren nodded in agreement. A moment later the man with the auto slug thrower stepped out from the protection of the corner and opened up. Laurie jumped up and ran across the intersection with McCade and Van Doren right on her heels. As they ran McCade heard a cry from behind as the slug thrower fell suddenly silent. He was already turning when Laurie's hand reached back to jerk him forward. Without hesitation she led them down corridors, up stairs and through a maintenance tunnel before coming to a halt and motioning them to silence.

As she carefully peeked around a corner, Van Doren retrieved an energy weapon from a tangle of bodies almost blocking the hall. Three wore uniforms with the words "Planetary Police" woven into the dark fabric. Lying dead a few feet away was a young woman, a girl really, a red band around her head and a snarl of defiance twisting once pretty lips. An empty slug thrower lay inches from her fingertips.

McCade turned in response to Laurie's touch. "There's two of them, Sam. They're guarding Bridger's room. Chances are his daughter's in there too. I don't see any way to take them except head on."

McCade risked a quick peek. What he saw confirmed Laurie's report. "I'll take the one on the left, you get the one on the right, okay?"

"Okay . . . but be careful."

McCade nodded and checked Mungo's blaster, making sure the safety was off and the charge indicator showed full. Looking up to meet Laurie's eyes, he winked. She winked back. Wordlessly they tensed, and then jumped into the open, instinctively spreading out. Both landed in the combat stance the Academy had drilled into them, feet apart, weapons raised with both hands. Laurie's guard was looking the wrong way and died without seeing who shot him. McCade's man was not only looking the right way, he was damn fast. His first shot blew air into McCade's left ear. His second went into the ceiling, as half his chest disappeared and he toppled over backward to skid a few feet on the slick floor. Seconds later they were across the hall and through the door of a small anteroom which had evidently been used by the guards. Plates of half-eaten food, ash trays full of cigarette butts, and cheap skin mags littered every surface.

"There could be more in there," Laurie said, indicating the door to Bridger's room.

"Right," McCade replied. "Amos . . . cover the hall. . . . Okay, let's open it very slowly." Raising the blaster, he aimed it at the center of the door.

Laurie picked up a plastic chair and used it to slowly push the door open. Without warning a hand suddenly grabbed the chair and jerked on it, pulling Laurie through the door and into the room. Denied a target McCade rushed through the door to find that Laurie's assailant had her down with a hypodermic needle touching her jugular vein.

"Freeze or I'll drain her dry!"

McCade laughed and lowered the blaster. "That won't be necessary, Sara. She's one of us—at least for the moment."

Sara stood and tossed the needle into a corner. She extended a hand to Laurie and helped pull her up. "You might knock next time," she said with a crooked smile.

"Laurie, meet Sara," McCade said, looking around. Against the far wall he saw a hospital bed, almost hidden by a jungle of tubes and wires.

"Charmed, I'm sure," Laurie said, rubbing her neck reflectively where the needle had pricked her skin.

"You two will have to get acquainted later," McCade said, striding over to the bed. "Right now we've got a few problems . . . like how to get Bridger out of here." Looking down, he hardly recognized the gaunt old man who lay there with eyes closed. His chest barely moved with each shallow breath. McCade waited for the rush of hatred and felt cheated somehow when it didn't come.

"He's dying of Millette's disease," Sara said, moving to McCade's side. "They brought me here hoping I could make him talk."

Millette's disease. A rare form of blood infection first contracted by Lt. Jim Millette a hundred years earlier during an unauthorized landing on a survey planet. Unaware that he was infected, the young scout spread it to a number of planets before the first symptoms showed up. Scientists throughout the human empire had been working on a cure ever since . . . without much luck. So each standard year a few people died. Soon, it seemed, Bridger would be one of them. It certainly explained why Bridger had grown increasingly irrational, McCade thought. One of the effects of Millette's disease was a gradual deterioration of brain tissue.

"He wasn't rational enough to tell them what they wanted to know," Sara said softly. "So they brain pumped him."

It took McCade a moment to absorb the implications of what she had said. Brain pumping was illegal even in the secret interrogation chambers deep beneath Naval Intelligence Headquarters on Terra. But where knowledge exists, there are always those who will exploit it for a price. And for the completely unscrupulous, the temptation was irresistible . . . the complete transference of another's memory and knowledge, a form of theft often more profitable than any other type of crime. However the process was not without risk. From what McCade had heard, the donor usually died from neural trauma and the recipient was quite often rendered insane. It takes an unusually strong individual to deal with the complete memories, loves, hates, likes and dislikes of another person superimposed on their own. It was said the second set of memories eventually faded, but few recipients remained rational long enough to describe how it felt.

"They made me watch while they did it," Sara said hollowly. "He recognized me, Sam. . . . I know he did. He saw me and smiled. Then this man made them begin."

"Mungo?" Laurie interjected tersely from across the bed.

Sara nodded and McCade felt her shudder. He put an arm around her. "Mungo was the recipient?"

Again she nodded and tears ran down her cheeks.

No wonder they were willing to turn me loose, McCade thought. They weren't bluffing. They really did have all the information they needed. All safely tucked away in Mungo's head. His estimation of Mungo went up a bit. Having all of Bridger's thoughts and memories in your head wouldn't be any picnic.

His thoughts were interrupted by shouted commands and the answering sound of Van Doren's energy weapon. Outside, two security men were stupid enough to turn a corner without looking first. The rest of their squad didn't make the same mistake. Firing from every scrap of cover they could find, they turned the anteroom into an inferno.

Slamming the door behind him, Amos said, "Time to go, boss. . . . Seems they won't take no for an answer." He aimed his weapon at the opposite wall.

McCade felt the blaster being jerked from his hand and turned to see Sara burn a hole through her father's head. Laurie screamed, "No!"—but jumped forward too late.

"Even he deserved that much," Sara said, handing the blaster back to McCade.

"Damn, you little fool!" Laurie said. "Now we'll have to do it the hard way."

"Let's go!" The voice was Van Doren's. Laurie was gone in a flash. McCade turned and pulled Sara after him. Van Doren had already followed Laurie through the glowing hole he'd created in the hollow plastic wall. McCade and Sara were right behind. Laurie led them through a maze of corridors and rooms, sometimes using existing doors and sometimes calling on Van Doren to make new ones. Before long, McCade was completely lost. So when Van Doren burned his way through another wall and they emerged into a conference room, he didn't recognize it at first. Then he saw Mungo and Urbus still sprawled where they'd fallen.

"This should be the last place they'll look for a few minutes," Laurie said. "Here, let me borrow that for a moment." She indicated McCade's blaster.

McCade made eye contact with Van Doren, who nodded. Curious, McCade handed Laurie the blaster. She took it, adjusted the beam to fine, turned and neatly sliced Mungo's head off. McCade stood stunned as Laurie bent over to pick up the head by one ear with all the nonchalance of a grocer handling a choice melon. The beam had cauterized the severed neck.

"What the hell?" McCade asked in amazement.

"If we freeze this quickly enough," Laurie replied matter of factly, "it may still be possible to retrieve what we need to know."

"Why you bitch!" Sara shouted, shaking with rage. "If I hadn't shot my father through the head, you would have done the same thing to him!"

"And why not?" Laurie replied calmly.

"That's enough," McCade said. "We don't have time for this. But before we go any farther, I'd like to know who's who. Let's start with the guys in the uniforms. The ones that keep shooting at us. Who are they?"

Laurie shrugged. "They're planetary police. Supposedly they work for the Brotherhood, reporting to Mungo, who was Chief of Security. Over time Mungo corrupted many of them. The one who calls himself Wong is a good example. Anyway they were acting on Mungo's orders."

"Not the Brotherhood's?"

Laurie shook her head. "As far as I know, the full Council doesn't know about the War World. As you no doubt realize by now, I was placed in Naval Intelligence as a sleeper years ago. But when Bridger disappeared, and I figured out why, Mungo was the first to know. He took Urbus in as a partner and they planned to use the War World for their own purposes."

"And the others?" McCade asked. "The ones with the red arm bands?"

"They're members of the Committee for Democratic Reform," she replied. "They want to overthrow the Brotherhood in favor of a democracy."

"And you're a member?"

Laurie nodded. "The founder actually. I thought it would be a good idea to have some troops of my own. . . . As you've seen, I was right."

The unvarnished cynicism of it appalled and surprised McCade. This woman seemed so different from the one he'd met in Swanson-Pierce's office.

"Then why are you helping us now?" Sara asked.

"Good question," McCade added, "but you'd better hurry

the answer. It sounds like they're getting closer."

Laurie shrugged. "I didn't think Mungo planned to take me with him. So I killed him before he could kill me. Plus I figure if we give them what they want, the Empire will go easy on me. Who knows? Maybe Swanson-Pierce'll give me my old job back."

"You make me sick," Sara said.

McCade watched as the blaster in Laurie's hand began to come up in Sara's direction. But before it had traveled more than an inch Van Doren hit her with a massive, openhanded blow that sent her reeling sideways as the blaster flew one way and Mungo's head another. As he helped her up, Van Doren relieved her of the small slug gun. Having retrieved the blaster McCade aimed it casually in Laurie's direction.

"There are some more questions I'd like to ask you," McCade said, "but this hardly seems like the time or the place. Pick up that head you're so fond of, and show us a safe way out of here. And by the way, if anything goes wrong, I'm gonna make sure you're the first to go."

Van Doren grinned his agreement as he stripped off his jacket and handed it to her. Laurie quickly wrapped Mungo's head in it and moved toward the opposite wall.

"I won't give you any trouble," she said. "I've got as much reason to want off this crud ball as you do." She palmed the wall.

With a slight hiss of equalizing air pressures, a panel slid aside to reveal a narrow flight of stairs leading down. As she stepped through, McCade was close behind. As they started down the steps, McCade noticed the same dampness they'd experienced coming down from the surface. From the look of it, the passageway hadn't been used for a long time. The ancient lum lights embedded in the walls cast barely enough light to show the way. Behind him Van Doren and Sara followed, their boots clattering on the metal stairs. As they continued to descend, McCade noticed intermittent vibrations strong enough to set up a sympathetic hum in the handrail.

Ahead of him, Laurie turned a corner. As he followed he saw that the tunnel opened up into a small bay which reeked of mold and decay. The pools of stagnant water and piles of unidentifiable debris made a marked contrast to the sleek bullet shape of the empty transcar sitting beside the platform.

Beyond it a short stretch of gleaming monorail reached out to join the main line which passed by outside.

Again McCade felt the vibration he'd noticed earlier. It was stronger this time. A second later a transcar flashed by with a whoosh of displaced air. It was doing more than a hundred miles an hour. Not bad for a back way out, McCade reflected. Mungo had left nothing to chance.

The transcar had been designed only for two, so the four of them were a tight fit. But after some struggle, and some profanity from Van Doren, they were all in. Laurie touched a destination on the map display and the transcar slid smoothly into motion.

Moments later they had joined the main line and now began to accelerate. Outside, the tunnel walls moved by with increasing speed until finally they became a blur. What seemed like only moments later the transcar began to slow, finally coming to a stop in a large terminal filled to overflowing with milling travelers.

One by one they struggled out of the car. As soon as they were all clear, the transcar moved away from the platform, picked up speed, and then disappeared into a tunnel.

As far as McCade could tell, they weren't under surveillance of any kind. People swirled around them, all seemingly intent on their own errands. After considerable twisting and turning through the crowd, they arrived at a turnstile. McCade slid the metal card into the appropriate slot until all had passed. Moments later they were aboard another sleek transcar and accelerating away from the station.

Laurie sat across from McCade, her features calm and composed, providing no hint that the untidy bundle on her lap contained a man's head. She seemed different somehow, but perhaps that other Laurie had never really existed outside his hopes and desires.

Both Sara and Van Doren stared out the windows at the tunnel walls and the occasional stations that they raced by. Together the four of them formed an island of silence in the sea of chattering passengers.

When the transcar slowed to a stop they followed Laurie off. Moments later they were packed into a crowded lift tube, heading for the surface. When the platform came to a stop, doors slid aside.

McCade instantly recognized the shiny black surface of the spaceport, the guard towers and the hundreds of ships which pointed up toward the night sky. As their fellow passengers streamed off in every direction, they started off toward the guard tower nearest to the *Far Trader*. They had gone only a couple of feet when suddenly a circle of glaring white light snapped into existence, pinning them against the black rock. Then came a voice that rolled like thunder and reverberated off the ranks of ships. It belonged to Marvin Wong. McCade should have been surprised, but somehow wasn't. Hadn't Wong said that all is not always what it seems? Anyway, the fact that the Brotherhood had been on to Mungo through a double agent wasn't too surprising either. McCade suddenly realized that the Brotherhood had simply allowed Mungo to do all the work for them. And if it hadn't been for Laurie's intervention, it would have worked.

"McCade . . . McCade . . . McCade . . ." Wong's voice echoed off the surrounding ships. "Stand where you are or die . . . die . . . die . . . You are under arrest by order of . . ."

McCade didn't wait around to hear the rest. Instead he aimed a quick blaster bolt toward the top of the nearest guard tower, hoping to momentarily ruin the sentry's night vision. But as he dived out of the circle of light, he realized they could probably use infrared sighting devices. Of course, with so many heat sources around in the form of people and ships, infrared would cut both ways.

Rolling up out of the somersault, McCade found time to wonder how they had been tracked. Mungo's men had taken the bugged slug gun from him, so it wasn't that. Then he knew. He reached into his pocket and pulled out the metal credit card. It twinkled with reflected light as he threw it as far as he could. As it landed, an energy beam leaped down from the tower to obliterate it. The others had formed up beside him.

Yelling to be heard over the confused shouting and an alarm klaxon, he said. "Let's add to the confusion!"

By way of demonstration, he snapped random shots at nearby ships and rolled away. The shots were quickly returned, with interest, by crew members of those vessels. They had no idea who was firing on them or why, but they weren't about to just sit there and take it.

The others quickly followed his example and within seconds a number of lively firefights developed between neighboring ships. Confused and frightened for the safety of their vessels, some captains opened fire on nearby guard towers with heavy ship's weapons, quickly reducing them to red-hot scrap metal. Other towers immediately retaliated, their energy weapons cutting down entire rows of ships like scythes harvesting wheat. Under the cover of the resulting total confusion, the four raced toward the *Far Trader*, only to see it vanish in a blinding explosion as a neighboring vessel began to fire randomly in every direction.

"Pegasus," Laurie shouted. "She's over there!"

They all veered to follow Laurie, dodging between ships and ground vehicles, using what cover they could, and occasionally shooting back when fired on. As he ran McCade felt the ground begin to tremble under his feet. Ship after ship was lifting on emergency power to escape the destruction now raging from one end of the spaceport to the other. They gave the remaining ships between them and *Pegasus* a wide berth to avoid being accidentally killed by someone's launch. Paranoid even at the best of times, both smugglers and pirates were giving free rein to their imaginations, and it was every being for itself.

Panting heavily Laurie reached *Pegasus* and palmed the main entry port. One after another they tumbled into the lock and waited impatiently for the inner hatch to cycle open. As they scrambled through, McCade yelled, "Prepare for emergency lift at full boost. Activate all weapons systems and strap in!"

He ran for the control room, palming the control lock as he slid into the command chair. He noted with satisfaction that Laurie hadn't bothered to de-authorize him. As bank after bank of indicators came to life, he routinely scanned each. Everything looked good. As his fingers danced nimbly among the controls, the outside viewscreens came to life. He felt Laurie slide into the position beside him. Her presence reminded him of how things had been before planetfall on Weller's World. The memory both pleased and annoyed him.

"All systems operational," Laurie said with calm professionalism.

"Prepare for emergency lift," McCade replied. "Lift."

With that he turned the large red knob over his head one rotation to the right and pushed it in.

The ship shuddered violently as her engines built thrust. McCade had one last second to survey the madness that had consumed the spaceport. Everywhere energy weapons and slug throwers spewed death and destruction. It couldn't happen to a nicer group of folks, McCade thought wryly. Then the ship's defensive screens flared as they took a direct hit. A fraction of a second later, *Pegasus* blasted off under full emergency power. McCade blacked out momentarily.

As they cleared atmosphere, his vision cleared and he felt the terrible weight come off his chest. Flicking the rear screens on, he saw pinpoints of light as more ships followed him into space. Whether they were following or just trying to escape, he couldn't tell. Switching the forward screens to high mag he was momentarily blinded by the explosion as a nuclear torpedo hit one of the fleeing vessels. At first he couldn't understand why, but as his vision returned he saw all too clearly. Most of the escaping ships had lifted without the one-way pass necessary to get by the weapons platforms which still guarded the approaches to the Rock. The platforms were doing a very efficient job.

As they got closer, McCade watched in fascination as ship after ship was snuffed out of existence, like so many moths attracted to an open flame. Then it suddenly stopped.

A group of ships formed a temporary alliance and together they attacked one of the platforms. Some of the ships were destroyed in the process, but by virtue of sheer massed firepower, they won. As the weapons platform flashed incandescent, the alliance broke and the survivors fled through the gap they'd created and headed for safer regions. Every other ship within one light realized what had happened and headed in that direction to take advantage of the newly created escape route. *Pegasus* was no exception.

"Uh-oh. Looks like we got company, boss. And I don't remember sending out any invitations." Van Doren had again chosen the top blister as his battle station.

Sara had ensconced herself in the rear weapons turret. Her voice came over the intercom loud and clear. "He's right, Sam. There's two of them closing fast. I don't think they're friendlies. Pirate destroyers by the looks of them."

McCade confirmed her guess by switching on the rear screens and boosting them to high mag. It didn't look good. Options and strategies flashed through his mind in quick succession. He tapped a request into the ship's computer asking for advice. The reply was immediate and to the point, delivered by the now-familiar voice.

"Surrender immediately. The pursuing vessels have overwhelmingly superior firepower and speed. They will destroy *Pegasus* approximately 10.5 seconds after initial engagement."

"Good. I was afraid we might be in trouble," McCade said. He met Laurie's concerned gaze with what he hoped was a nonchalant smile.

"Stand by for sudden deceleration followed by enemy action," McCade said. "Five from now. Five, four, three, two, one." With a quick flick of the wrist, he cut the power by half and felt himself thrown forward against his harness.

The two pirate ships seemed to surge forward as if by magic, splitting to position themselves on each side, placing *Pegasus* in a cross fire. McCade forced himself to wait, hoping they would interpret the sudden cut in speed as a sign of cooperation. Evidently they did, because as they drew abreast of *Pegasus* they didn't open fire. Of course it could be just an effort to capture someone alive. Or some *thing* dead, he corrected himself, thinking of Mungo's head now resting on the top shelf of the galley refrigeration unit.

Finally both ships were level with *Pegasus*. "Fire!" McCade yelled into the intercom as all the weapons that could be brought to bear fired in unison. Both destroyers were suddenly bathed in fire. Neither was in any danger. Their defensive screens were much more powerful than anything *Pegasus* could hope to equal. So when they fired in reply, they did so with the care and precision of someone who is invulnerable.

And stupid. For as they opened fire, McCade punched full emergency power again, bringing the already hot tubes to the very edge of burnout, and setting off a host of alarm buzzers and flashing lights. But McCade was deaf to the ship's protests as he watched the rear screens with the fascination born of extreme fear.

Without *Pegasus* between them to shoot at, the destroyers were suddenly shooting at each other. And before human hands and tongues could intervene, the battle computer on each vessel used part of a second to re-evaluate the source of the incoming fire, the strength of the opposing defensive screens, and initiate appropriate countermeasures. A second later one destroyer vanished in a brilliant explosion and the other suddenly slowed and then stopped, apparently the victim of a damaged propulsion system.

With a groan of relief, McCade slumped back in his chair, cutting the emergency power as he did so. As the cacophony of warning buzzers and klaxons slowly died away, the computer's dulcet tones flooded the intercom. McCade would have sworn there was an edge of criticism under the apparently neutral words.

"Recent damage to this ship and its operating systems, due to actions taken under manual override, necessitate docking at a class C or better maintenance facility within the next one hundred hours of operation. The bar is open."

Sara and Van Doren's laughter echoed his own as he punched in a course for Alice, handed over control to the ship's computer, and headed for the lounge, where he intended to order a double, no a triple, Scotch. He didn't see Laurie cancel the course for Alice and enter a new set of coordinates into the computer, or hear as she selected a certain ship-to-ship radio frequency and made contact with the massive battleship some distance away.

Instead he was seated in the lounge, watching as Sara carefully applied a salve and bandages to Van Doren's burned wrists, while the marine pretended it didn't hurt. Moments later Laurie joined them. Then, when everyone had settled down to their favorite refreshments, McCade proposed a toast.

"To a successful mission and safe arrival on Alice!"

Each smiled, raised a glass, and took a sip.

Eleven

HOURS HAD PASSED since their escape from the Rock, and McCade was feeling rather pleased with himself. Bridger had been stopped, *Pegasus* was his, and there was every reason to expect a bonus. He glanced at Sara, who was engaged in friendly conversation with Van Doren, and took another sip of his third drink. Yes, things were definitely looking up.

His thoughts were interrupted by the computer's soft chime. Laurie beat him to it and reached out to tap a few keys. The screen across from McCade came to life. Displayed on it was the likeness of a ship, along with the technical specifications pertaining to it. McCade didn't need the specs to know what it was. There's no mistaking an Il Ronnian ship of the line. A fraction of a second later, its incredibly powerful tractor beams leapt across thousands of miles of space to look on to *Pegasus*. The computer confirmed tractor beam lock-up as the Il Ronnian vessel began to reel them in like a fish on a line. McCade turned and was heading for the control room when Sara's voice stopped him.

"Sam, look!"

He spun around to see Sara pointing at Laurie. It seemed as though her face was slipping. Her beautiful features had become elastic somehow and seemed to flow and ripple in an impossible way. Suddenly she appeared to collapse and then dissolve into a pool of shivering protoplasm. The Treel! But it had died on Weller's World! Except it obviously hadn't . . . because here it was in the repulsive flesh!

"Give me the word and I'll blow her . . . I mean it . . . to mush, boss!" Van Doren growled, aiming his blaster at the Treel. Sara sat perfectly still, looking back and forth between the Treel and McCade in amazement.

"I don't think that'll be necessary, Amos," McCade replied calmly. "It appears our friend here already *is* mush."

"Jape as you will, rigid ones," the Treel replied, switching now to its own hoarse voice. "For seldom is true beauty understood by those unblessed by the great Yareel.

"However," the Treel added pragmatically, "notice who is in possession of this small but effective blaster." With that a pseudopod emerged from the alien's liquid presence, grasping a shiny new weapon only recently taken from the ship's small arms locker.

McCade gestured for Van Doren to lower his weapon. "Don't bother, Amos. I don't think your blaster's up to the job anyway. On Weller's World, I put enough needles in it to kill six humans."

"You speak the truth, primate," the Treel replied smugly. "Since my race is perfect, we are impossible to kill, however on Weller's World it suited my purpose to let it seem otherwise."

McCade didn't believe Treels were impossible to kill. He just hadn't figured out how to do it yet.

He lit a cigar and said, "So what's up?" He followed the question with a stream of blue smoke.

"I would have thought that obvious . . . even to you," the Treel replied. "We must deliver Mungo's head to the Il Ronn. In a few minutes they'll take us aboard, where they will extract what they wish to know from Mungo's brain. At that point my job will be over. Excuse me while I inform them of the situation here."

With that the Treel extruded another pseudopod which

promptly transfigured itself into a perfect likeness of Laurie's hand—right down to her fingerprints, McCade imagined. Nimble fingers entered a series of numbers and letters, which were no doubt part of a prearranged code.

Watching the alien's confident movements, McCade silently cursed himself for the worst kind of fool. It had finally dawned on him that Laurie, the real Laurie, the one who had both saved and betrayed him, was dead—and had been since Weller's World.

Carefully he searched his emotions, trying to find either sorrow or satisfaction. Both seemed justified. But neither emerged to dominate the other. Yet the Treel was running up quite a butcher's bill. A bill that would have to be paid one day. First there had been Cadet Votava, then the crew of the tug, Laurie, and God knows how many others who had died supporting the Committee for Democratic Reform.

"So you killed her," McCade said flatly. His voice calm, even conversational. But his eyes were cold and bleak. Looking at them, Sara suddenly understood the part of his life she'd never seen. The professional killer stalking his prey.

"Yes, I'm afraid so," the Treel replied calmly. Now that the message had been sent, the alien seemed relaxed and almost gregarious. "No sooner had she rendered you unconscious with her traitorous dart than she turned on me. Injured though I was, my marvelous body was still able to momentarily assume the form of a Linthian Rath snake, with predictably fatal results. It seems, like most of you rigid ones, she was duplicitous in the extreme, appearing to work for the Imperial Government, but actually in the employ of the pirates." The alien's gelatinous body undulated for a moment as though to aid its thought process. "I will admit, however, that while assuming her form I learned that she was quite loyal to the Brotherhood's full Council. I doubt that Brother Mungo could have corrupted her as he did me."

"And then?" McCade asked.

The Treel sloshed back and forth a little in what might have been a shrug. "Events conspired to frustrate my noble plans. Laurie's henchmen soon arrived, evidently to help neutralize you, a task she had already carried out with admirable efficiency, and I was barely able to hide her body before assuming her identity. The situation forced me to reveal Bridger's location in the hotel. He was comatose and badly in need of medical attention. The rest should be obvious even to one of your limited mental acuity.

"In my role as Laurie, I had to accompany Bridger to the Rock and wait there for an opportunity to, ah, serve my employer. Fortunately Bridger's illness delayed their attempt to gain access to his mind. For a while it looked as though I would fail. Bridger grew increasingly less coherent and finally they brain pumped him. Fortunately you blundered in, presenting me with an opportunity to obtain the desired information and to escape as well."

McCade did his best to shrug nonchalantly. "So just for the record . . . what is the War World like?"

"Who knows, rigid one," the Treel replied conversationally. "Bridger never did tell me . . . that is, Votava . . . anything you couldn't surmise from the name alone. It is evidently a world having to do with war. More than that I couldn't say. And for that matter I don't think Bridger could either, for all of his raving. All he knew for sure was that it exists. And where. Soon the Il Ronn will retrieve that knowledge from Mungo's frozen brain tissue and I shall be free of the entire matter. A freedom I shall relish, by the way."

With that the strange being seemed to withdraw into itself. Only the unwavering blaster suggested its continuing attention.

As they neared the Il Ronnian vessel, it grew in their screens to blot out nearby constellations with its complex tracery of hull, weapons platforms, power modules, and other less identifiable parts. A lighted rectangle appeared in the black metal hull as a hatch slid aside to admit them. Inside the enormous hanger bay, *Pegasus* came to rest next to a row of one-man interceptors. The human ship was only slightly larger than the alien fighters.

They were searched and then escorted, without ceremony, through a maze of passageways and corridors. Their guard consisted of a heavily armed squad of tall, thin Il Ronnian troopers. Their uniforms identified them as members of the Sand Sept, an elite fighting force roughly analogous to the Imperial Marines, and just as famous for their valor.

As they walked, McCade began to sweat. The temperature

within the ship was uncomfortably high. It served to remind McCade that the Il Ronn had evolved on a desert planet. Which of course explained their preference for hot, dry worlds.

Finally they arrived on what was clearly the ship's command level. The ten or fifteen Il Ronn present didn't even glance up from their glowing control panels and monitors as the humans were led through and ushered into a side compartment.

As the prisoners entered, McCade experienced a brief moment of disorientation. As quickly as it came, it was gone, and he found himself standing on extremely fine white sand which shifted under his feet. The sand was tinged here and there with streaks of red and it reached out to meet a violet sky. The sun beating down on his shoulders was incredibly hot. McCade looked at his two companions and shrugged. There was no one else in sight.

The Treel had been escorted off under separate guard shortly after they'd left the ship. Instinctively it had assumed the guise of an Il Ronn. McCade was amused at the obvious discomfort of the Il Ronnian troopers who had marched it off, with Mungo's cold-packed head tucked securely under one arm.

To their right, the air seemed to buzz and shimmer. A huge Il Ronn seemed to appear from nowhere, although McCade realized the alien was actually entering via the same hatch they had used. The sensurround was that realistic. Suddenly he realized he'd have a hard time finding his way out of the compartment without help. The alien paused for a moment as if inspecting them. Its eyes were lost in the black shadow cast by the prominent superorbital ridge above them. McCade was struck by the resemblance between the giant alien and ancient pictures he'd seen of a mythical being known as the "Devil."

He stood on long, spindly legs which ended in broad, cloven hoofs. McCade noticed these hoofs seemed to float on top of the fine white sand rather than sinking into it as his boots tended to do. The Il Ronn's leathery skin was hairless, and even had a reddish hue. It seemed to blend with the red streak in the sand behind it. Long, pointed ears lay flat against his head, and to complete the devillike image, the Il Ronn had a long tail ending in a triangular appendage. At the moment, this appendage hovered over the alien's head, providing shade from the blistering sun.

McCade knew he wasn't the first to notice the resemblance between I1 Ronn physiognomy and the traditional Judeo-Christian image of evil personified. In fact some scholars thought that the aliens' devillike appearance might account in part for the almost instant enmity which sprang into existence shortly after the first recorded contact between human and I1 Ronn. They suggested that after thousands of years of exposure to an evil image closely resembling the I1 Ronn, humans could not view them objectively. This was a favorite argument among those opposing war with the I1 Ronn.

Other scholars disagreed, suggesting that early depictions of the devil were not imaginary, but real, and were based on early visits to Earth by I1 Ronnian explorers. This theory couldn't be simply laughed off, since there was ample evidence that the I1 Ronn had developed a star drive thousands of years before Man. However, being a more deliberate and cautious race than Man, their empire expanded slowly, allowing humans to eventually catch up. Proponents of this last theory went on to point out the brutal tactics still employed by I1 Ronn scouts when contacting less advanced indigenous races. They maintained that if the I1 Ronn did establish and maintain a temporary colony on Earth, their dealings with humans might have earned them a well-deserved reputation for evil, which they eventually came to symbolize.

So in their view, the hostility between the two races was natural, and based as much on history as on current events. This particular argument was favored by those who felt all-out war with the I1 Ronn was inevitable. As far as McCade knew, the I1 Ronn themselves had never commented on either theory.

He noticed that unlike many traditional images of Satan, the I1 Ronn in front of him had no horns. But he more than made up for this biological oversight when he opened a lipless mouth to reveal a wealth of deadly-looking teeth. His voice was surprisingly melodious.

"Greetings. I am called Reez. Commander Reez of Star Sept Four. I apologize for receiving you here in the comfort of my own environment. But that is the privilege of the victor, is it not?

"I'll assume your silence implies acquiescence," he continued after a moment. "I would like to thank you for delivering such important information into our hands . . . even if it *was* only through your incompetence. I assure you we will use it to speed the inevitable end of your pathetic empire."

McCade was really sweating now—small rivers of perspiration running off his body. Reez evidently understood the significance of that.

"I see you find the heat of our native environment uncomfortable. However I fear even greater discomfort may await you in the slave markets of Lakor. I'm told that conditions there are quite rigorous. Pleasant though, when compared to your subsequent existence on some mine world." He paused to study Sara in a calculating way.

"You, my dear, are another matter. I suspect they'll find other uses for you. Ugly by conventional human standards, it's true . . . but on Lakor there is a market for everything, even ugliness. I'm sure someone would find your disfigurement exciting. How wonderfully twisted, don't you agree?"

The scar across Sara's face was white against her flushed skin. Both McCade and Van Doren were already in motion when a hand flamer materialized in the Il Ronn's three-fingered hand. They jerked to a halt. Reez shook his head in pretended amazement.

"My what an emotional race! You have already served me well, although unintentionally, and as a reward I offer you the opportunity to continue in that service. Who knows? After the fall of your empire, we will need cooperative human administrators. Such a role could be yours. So the choice is between comfortable service to me . . . and the slave markets of Lakor. Which will it be?"

To his surprise McCade found himself giving the alien's proposal serious consideration. After all, it wasn't his fault Laurie had turned out to be a double agent and everything had gone to hell. But two things kept getting in the way. First, he felt sure that if he agreed to serve the Il Ronn, he'd be forced to act against the Empire. True, he had no reason to love the Empire, but he did care about his own kind. Second, he couldn't help remembering the Treel. Life as a servant to the Il Ronn didn't seem all that attractive. In fact it just amounted to a choice between one kind of slavery and another.

Reez stood waiting, contempt and arrogance surrounding him like a cloak. McCade tried to look into the alien's eyes, but found only darkness. Mixed feelings of revulsion and fear made his pulse pound and he found it took all his strength to speak.

"I can't speak for my companions," McCade said, "but personally I'd prefer the slave market of Lakor to your company any day."

With that he spat into the sand between the alien's hoofs and thereby sealed his fate. His action was a wanton waste of water and to a people for whom water had religious significance, it was a deadly insult. It implied that the commander's father should have showered his sperm on the desert, rather than use it to fertilize his egg-mother.

For a long moment, Commander Reez stood perfectly still . . . and McCade was afraid he'd gone too far. He'd known that the same action by another Il Ronn would have provoked a death duel. But he'd allowed both his fear and courage to control him long enough to hit back the only way he could.

When Reez spoke, his voice was as cold as death. "So be it." He turned to Sara and Van Doren. As one they spat into the sand before him.

The Il Ronnian officer regained his composure with effort, but his voice was like the icy distance of space itself. "I will not grant you the swift death you obviously seek. Instead, you will die slowly, as befits your kind, working, as animals should, for the profit of their betters. A fate for which your entire race is woefully overdue."

The air buzzed and shimmered as the alien departed. Seconds later their guards appeared, and this time they were far from gentle. Commander Reez had evidently made his displeasure known.

They were shoved, kicked and pushed back through the labyrinth of tubes and passageways before being literally thrown into some kind of detention cell. A superficial examination of the cell revealed that no effort had been spared to make it both primitive and uncomfortable. For an Il Ronn that is. The cell had been cooled to a temperature which felt just about right to McCade. Gone too was the intensely bright lighting favored by the aliens. The dimmer, warmer light was quite a relief to human eyes. Nonetheless the cell was still far from comfortable. There was no furniture, no sign of sanitary facilities, and no source of the Il Ronnian's precious water.

Glancing around the bare, seamless walls, McCade searched for some signs of the sensors, which he knew to be there. He couldn't see them, but that wasn't surprising. Knowing that all conversation would be monitored, by unspoken agreement all three remained silent. If Van Doren was worried, there was no sign of it in his cheerful thumbs up. Sara managed a smile and a conspiratorial wink. McCade smiled back and closed his eyes. Suddenly he was very tired. He resisted the impulse only briefly before, realizing there was nothing he could do, he let himself drift off to sleep.

He awoke to find the other two already up. A quick inventory revealed that he was sore, hungry and scared. Then the acceleration began. They were smashed down against the metal floor with tremendous force. That lasted for a few seconds, which seemed like hours. Then without warning the acceleration and gravity disappeared. Shortly after that the cell began to tumble. Since there were no hand holds or ways to strap themselves down, they tumbled with it. They were all experienced at weightlessness and quickly adjusted to it. But not before collecting some bumps and bruises from the unpadded cell.

As he glided from one surface to another in response to the cell's tumbling movement, McCade tried to figure out what was happening. He couldn't believe the gigantic Il Ronnian warship was out of control and tumbling end-over-end through space. But if it wasn't, then they were no longer aboard. Suddenly the acceleration made sense. The cell wasn't part of the ship and never had been. It was probably a cargo module that had been modified to include breathable atmosphere. It was probably equipped with a microcomputer and some retro-tubes as well. Reez had simply swung by Lakor and unceremoniously blasted their module down toward the planet, having warned someone on the surface of some incoming merchandise.

It was quick, simple and efficient. But it was also uncomfortable and dangerous, McCade thought as the module tumbled again, throwing him toward the opposite bulkhead. A fact which Commander Reez had no doubt considered. McCade executed a somersault and hit the bulkhead feet first, legs properly flexed, and then pushed off toward what had once been the deck.

Meanwhile Van Doren and Sara were likewise occupied. The marine demonstrated surprising grace and agility for a man his size. However his moves were nothing compared to Sara's. She had managed to transform the situation into an aerial ballet. In fact, she was apparently enjoying herself. Watching her, McCade remembered her as she'd been years before. Young, beautiful and completely untouchable. Separated from him by an entire obstacle course of social and financial barriers. Junior officers weren't welcome in the quarters of mighty captains. Particularly those who couldn't even afford the null-G ballet lessons Sara had taken for granted. And now here they were. Trapped in a cargo module hurtling down toward some unseen world. A world on which they would all be just so much meat for sale.

Her movements were lithe and precise. Each flowed seamlessly into the next as though planned and rehearsed for months. Her face was lit with a beautiful smile which somehow made the terrible scar disappear. Watching her made him feel good. And that surprised and confused him. It scared him too . . . because it made him realize how much he would miss her if they were separated. Somehow, without his realizing it, she'd become both friend and ally without the years of association it usually took to produce either relationship.

His thoughts were interrupted by the realization that gravity had begun to return. As it did McCade felt himself gradually grow heavier and heavier. They had evidently entered Lakor's atmosphere. Unfortunately the module was still tumbling end-over-end. What had been almost a game was now deadly serious. With added weight it became much harder to avoid hitting the metal bulkheads. On top of that, McCade knew he was getting tired. He had begun to sweat. With each movement, the next grew harder to perform. He saw the other two were also having difficulty—Van Doren more than Sara.

The sensation of weight continued to increase. McCade's reactions slowed accordingly. He started to make mistakes. Each time he made a mistake he paid a price in pain. Finally both he and Van Doren lost control. They crashed into the surfaces and into each other, making it increasingly difficult for Sara to maneuver around them. Reez could not have administered a more efficient beating if he'd been there in person.

Sara fared slightly better. She watched with concern as the two men were inexorably beaten, knowing there was nothing she could do to help them. Only her training and perfect conditioning had saved her so far. But she too was beginning to tire.

McCade watched with a strange sort of dispassionate interest as the gray metal surface came up to meet him. Somehow he couldn't summon even the slightest response from his leaden arms and legs. He could do no more than note the impact as his body slammed into the bulkhead and his head bounced off hard metal. A tremendous wave of pain rolled through his body and threatened to pull him under. One more, he thought. One more should do it. Then I won't feel anything anymore. The prospect seemed wonderful.

Then the module stopped tumbling. It seemed as if Reez had known the precise moment at which they'd be unable to take anymore, and had programmed the module's tiny computer to fire the retros at just that moment. McCade knew that was impossible. Nevertheless, he cursed Reez in a dozen languages as the module slammed down through layer after layer of atmosphere, bucking and shaking as though it would come apart at any moment. Each time it shook, another wave of pain rolled through him until one finally carried him with it, down into a dark abyss.

Twelve

MCCADE WASN'T SURE which was better—being conscious or unconscious. Both had advantages. Being conscious was good because you knew what was going on. For example, he was vaguely aware of the impact as the cargo module splashed down, presumably in a large body of water. Then he felt rough hands jerk him out of the module and throw him down into the stinking bilge of an ancient hovercraft. With a stuttering roar, they had then bounced off across the water toward an unknown destination.

At that point the delicious darkness of unconsciousness beckoned. And who was he to refuse? True, you didn't know what was going on, but that had its good points too. For one thing, you didn't feel it when a short squat Lakorian kicked you in the ribs a couple of times just for the fun of it.

Unfortunately, toward the end of the ride McCade came to, and found he had to stay that way. Waves of filthy bilge water kept slapping him in the face. Cautiously he looked around, moving only his eyes. No point in letting them know he was awake. Directly in front of him he saw two Lakorian ankles. Each was as big around as his thigh. They seemed to end in broad, webbed feet, but he wasn't sure, since the swirling bilge water allowed only glimpses of them.

Beyond the Lakorian who was serving as helmsman, McCade could see Sara. She was tied hand and foot. Suddenly he realized he couldn't feel his own arms and legs. Sure enough they were tied too—very tightly. His circulation had evidently been cut off for some time. Just then the Lakorian helmsman stepped forward slightly, allowing McCade to see Sara more clearly. She seemed to be watching some activity behind him. He couldn't tell what it was. More Lakorians probably.

After a moment she glanced his way. A look of concern clouded her features. He caught her eye and did his best to smile. It hurt. After a look of relieved surprise, she nodded in reply. Allowing his head to move naturally with the movement of the hovercraft, he managed to look farther to the right. He could just barely make out Van Doren's boots. As McCade watched, they moved as the marine tried to find a more comfortable position. His legs were tightly tied at the ankles. At least we're alive, McCade thought grimly. But for how long?

Hours passed before they made landfall. If you can call a swamp "land," McCade thought sourly. The hovercraft stopped at the top of a mud ramp. Two stumpy Lakorians hoisted McCade and Sara over their shoulders, climbed out of the hovercraft, and then sloshed across an open space ankle deep in mud. It took two of them to lift and carry Van Doren. Head down over a Lakorian shoulder, McCade couldn't see much of their surroundings. It seemed like mostly mud and lush green tropical foliage. It started to rain.

Unfortunately the rain seemed to have no effect whatsoever on the rancid body odor of the Lakorian carrying him. In fact, if anything, it seemed to make it worse. McCade noticed from his vantage point only inches away from the alien's skin that it was exuding an oily substance. Whatever the substance was, it was making the water run off the creature's greenish skin, and it smelled terrible.

With casual violence the Lakorian threw McCade into the back of a huge trailer. He hit the floor and slid on the layer of filth which covered it, before hitting a number of other occupants. They snarled and screeched and grunted their objections in a variety of tongues. One large, bearlike being cuffed him back in the direction of the door, where he collided with Van Doren on the way down. The heavy metal door slammed shut as the vehicle jerked into spasmodic motion.

McCade rolled up against Sara. After considerable fumbling, they managed to untie each other. Then while Sara was working on Van Doren's bonds, McCade stumbled to his feet. His arms and legs ached with returning circulation and bruises. Trying for balance, McCade swayed over to the open bars, which provided warm, fetid air, dim, dappled light, and barely managed to hold up a shabby roof. It was raining harder now, and the water made a drumming sound as it pounded down on the metal over their heads.

Peering out between the bars, McCade saw they were being towed by a large tractor type vehicle with an enclosed cab. It was equipped with huge balloon tires that seemed designed to float the vehicle when necessary. Looking at the passing terrain, McCade got the feeling it would be necessary quite often in fact.

The landscape was an unending procession of lakes, pools, rivers and puddles, separated by islands of lush plant life. About half the vegetation was green, the rest was black and rotting. Immense tree trunks reached up through the tangled growth toward the sun. Vines and parasitic plants draped themselves around the huge trees, adding to the verdant maze.

Here and there animal life was visible too. Large, bovine creatures on six legs browsed on hugh piles of weeds they pulled from the bottom of shallow lakes. Above them small, spindly figures skittered and screeched at the passage of tractor and trailer. Once some unseen marine presence threw a casual tentacle into the trailer as if reaching for an hors d'oeuvre. However, after the bearlike alien grabbed it and bit off a four-foot length of rubbery flesh, the remaining stump was withdrawn with considerable haste. The bear spit out a mouthful of tentacle with an expression of distaste and returned to its taciturn silence.

For the first time McCade really looked at his fellow prisoners. Evidently the slave markets of Lakor didn't play favorites, because they were definitely a mixed lot. Besides the bearlike creature, there were a couple of bedraggled Finthians, their plummage covered with muck, a single Cellite, eyestalks drooping dejectedly, and a complete Seph grouping. McCade remembered having read somewhere that the Seph were tri-sexual. It took a grouping of three to reproduce. They were huddled together in a furry mass that occupied one corner.

"An unlikely group, aren't we," Sara said, her smile almost obscured by the dirt on her face. In spite of the dirt, he found her smile appealing and bent over to kiss her. Her lips were soft and met his with a pleasant pressure which he returned, with interest.

"Excuse me, boss . . . but I think you better see this," Van Doren said.

"It better be good," McCade said, smiling at Sara before turning to the bars.

"Good it probably ain't," Van Doren replied sourly, spitting through the bars. "Not on this pus ball. You gotta wonder why anyone comes here. And what's more, why are those folks out there runnin' around in the rain?" He pointed out through the bars.

At first McCade couldn't see a thing. Then after allowing his eyes to adjust, he began to detect shadowy figures moving swiftly through the foliage. They seemed to be carrying long, thin objects. They could have been sticks. They could also be weapons. The three of them continued to watch the shadowy forms for some time. Even on foot and moving through dense undergrowth, the unknown figures seemed to have no difficulty keeping up with the slow-moving vehicle. Sometimes they would disappear. But a few minutes later they would be back, moving through the rain like ghosts.

If the Lakorians in the tractor's cab were aware of the watchers, they gave no sign. Both tractor and trailer continued their ungainly progress through the rain forest, lurching from one pond to the next. Gradually night began to fall. As dusk deepened into the blackness of night, the tractor driver flicked on powerful floodlights to push back the dark. Meanwhile a variety of nocturnal animal and plant life had switched on luminescent lights of their own. The net effect hurt McCade's eyes. The watchers could no longer be seen, but somehow he knew they were still there. Watching and waiting.

After a while McCade, lying beside Sara on the filthy floor, fell into a fitful sleep. It seemed perfectly natural to put one arm around her, and she snuggled up to his chest. She too fell asleep, stirring only occasionally and waking him from his confused dreams. Then all hell broke loose.

An aerial flare went off, lighting up the entire area. Somewhere an automatic projectile weapon began to stutter, and tracers arced in toward the cab. Instinctively all the prisoners hit the deck. But none of the fire seemed directed toward the trailer. Energy beams flicked out from the tractor to rake the underbrush. In spite of the rain, the vegetation immediately caught fire as though doused with liquid fuel. Evidently some of the plants exuded an extremely volatile sap. At times McCade thought he saw figures darting back and forth behind the flames. As far as he could tell, the incoming fire wasn't making much of an impression on the tractor. It had evidently been armored against just such attacks. He also noticed that the watchers continued to direct all their fire against the tractor and not the trailer. Whether this was calculated to spare the prisoners, or simply in recognition of their impotence, he couldn't tell. But he couldn't help feeling that any enemies of the Lakorians were friends of his.

A hidden speaker somewhere in the trailer squawked to life. This was followed by some kind of speech in a language McCade didn't know. No sooner had it ended than it started over in Standard. "We are under attack by criminal elements. Do not be frightened. You will not be harmed. Remain calm. The perpetrators of this unlawful attack will soon be destroyed."

As soon as it was over it began again. This time it sounded like the warbling speech of the Finthians.

It was obviously prerecorded, and McCade found that interesting. For one thing it meant that such attacks were probably very common. Why else would they prepare an announcement? It also implied some kind of organized resistance to the present planetary government. By whom? he wondered. For what reason? There weren't any obvious answers. Meanwhile the battle raged on. Neither side seemed to be making much of a dent in the other. The tractor continued to lumber forward, pulling the trailer along behind. However the watchers seemed able to keep pace without apparent difficulty, and both sides continued a desultory exchange of fire.

Finally, as if bored with the whole affair, the Lakorians

opened up with an automatic flechette gun. Heretofore they hadn't used it, probably due to the extremely expensive ammunition it consumed. It sprayed thousands of explosive flechettes per second into the undergrowth. The countless tiny explosions combined to create a continuous roaring that sounded like a giant beast gone mad. Incoming fire dwindled to almost nothing right away. Whether the attackers had been decimated by the flechette gun, or had simply withdrawn when it opened up, McCade couldn't tell.

For a while they waited, expecting the attack to begin anew. But it didn't. One by one they dropped off again into exhausted sleep. Even the occasional roar of night feeders, disturbed by the passage of tractor and trailer, failed to wake them.

It was daylight when McCade opened his eyes. The rain had stopped, allowing occasional shafts of sunlight to penetrate the forest canopy and splash through the bars onto the huddled prisoners. Outside, a light mist ebbed and flowed along the contours of the ground.

Before long they began to pass occasional dwellings. Without exception, they were built on pilings, and were therefore immune to the comings and goings of the water below them. Most were circular and had domed roofs. The roofs were hinged in some fashion, allowing certain sections to be folded open. Quite a few were exercising that option, apparently to take advantage of the sun.

Gradually the tractor and trailer bounced and jolted onto increasingly busy thoroughfares, and it wasn't long before they entered a good-sized town. McCade noticed that even clearly commercial buildings never exceeded three or four stories. The water-soaked ground probably wouldn't support more weight than that, he thought. Of course, it could be a shortage of appropriate technology too. He remembered reading that buildings higher than three stories weren't common on Terra either, until after the invention of the elevator. Everywhere he looked he saw a strange juxtaposition of current technology and primitive culture. As far as McCade could tell there were no public utilities as such. If a homeowner wanted power, they could buy their own small fusion plant, otherwise forget it. That seemed to suggest a weak or nonexistent central government. Maybe the slave traders were in control. That would explain a lot.

All-terrain vehicles were popular, though. It was a rare dwelling that didn't boast a late-model vehicle sitting out front, often right next to the rotting wooden boat it had replaced. By the same token, the streets seemed more accidental than planned. It seemed as if they had been superimposed over and around an extensive canal system. The canals had evidently fallen into disuse. They were choked with water weed, and were apparently regarded as nuisances by Lakorian drivers. Equipped as they were with all-terrain vehicles, *they* tended to regard any ground not actually occupied by a house or tree as part of the road.

McCade wondered what would happen to the Lakorian economy if the slave trade suddenly disappeared. Most of the off-world income would disappear along with it. All-terrain vehicles would run out of imported fuel and be left to rust by owners who couldn't afford to import it privately. And, McCade thought to himself, a lot of folks would suddenly start repairing their boats.

The tractor-trailer twisted and turned endlessly through narrow and often obstructed streets before finally jerking to a halt in front of a raw-looking stockade. "Uh-oh, boss," Van Doren said. "This looks like home sweet home."

"Home maybe," Sara replied, holding her nose, "but sweet it isn't."

McCade silently agreed. An unbelievable stench surrounded the stockade. The reason was obvious. An open ditch followed the perimeter of the wall, creating an informal moat. The moat was filled to overflowing with rain water and the sewage generated by thousands of slaves, past and present. The stockade itself had been constructed using the time-honored system of digging a trench, standing logs upright shoulder to shoulder, and then filling in around the bottom with dirt. As the tractor drew near, a gate made of rude-looking planks swung open to admit it and then squealed closed as the vehicles lumbered clear.

The tractor ground to a halt in the large open space dominating the center of the stockade. The passage of vehicles and thousands of feet had turned the dirt there to mud. In the exact

center of the open space stood a wooden platform. Its surface
had been worn smooth by constant use and bore ominous-
looking stains. A striped awning had been rigged over it to
keep off the rain, granting it a sort of false gaiety. McCade
didn't need a tour guide to explain the platform's purpose. It
was empty now, but would be in use as soon as the slave
auctions began. Beyond the platform was a swirling mass of
flesh, feather and scale—citizens of a hundred worlds—talking, laughing, bickering and fighting. Passing the time as they
waited for the next round of buying and selling to begin.

For the first time since landing, McCade began to feel
afraid. Up to now he'd assured himself that some sort of
chance to escape would present itself and he'd be ready. But it
hadn't and now it looked as though it never would. There was
a screech of rusty metal as a Lakorian guard opened the gate
on their trailer. With a series of grunts, kicks and unintelligi-
ble commands, he forced them out. They stood in a bedraggled huddle ankle deep in the muck of the compound.
McCade tried to get his bearings and spot weak points in the
stockade. He hadn't found any when the sorting began.

Three stumpy Lakorian guards waded into their midst and
started pushing and shoving. With expertise born of much
practice, they roughly grouped their prisoners according to
race. No sooner had that been accomplished than they stepped
in and began sorting by sex. As a squat guard grabbed Sara
and jerked her away, McCade jumped on its back and tried for
a choke hold. He might just as well have tried to choke an oak
tree. A second guard peeled him off without much effort and
smashed him down into the muck with a single blow from
some sort of cudgel. McCade picked himself up just in time to
see Sara disappear into one of the low slave pens which lined
the inside of the stockade wall. His head buzzed from the
blow and his stomach knotted up in fear and anger. He had
tensed for a hopeless run toward the slave pens when he felt a
firm grip on his arm.

It was Van Doren. "Whoa, boss. Not now. We'll get our
chance later."

At first McCade was ready to throw Van Doren's hand off
and go anyway. But after a second he calmed down enough to
realize the marine was right. There wasn't any point to it.
Even if he outran the closest guards, he couldn't outrun the

energy weapons he'd seen mounted at regular intervals along the top of the stockade.

He nodded and felt Van Doren's hand fall away. The Lakorian guards were leading one of the Finthians, evidently a hen, away toward the pens. They had also taken one of the three Sephs. Evidently one qualified as a female and the other two as males. The two males were obviously distraught and uttered pitiful squealing noises. The single Cellite meanwhile stood in dejected misery. Next to him the bearlike alien remained impassive. McCade could detect no sign of fear or dejection in the shaggy brute's stance. He noted with interest that large brown eyes, black nose, and large rounded ears were taking everything in. It stood at least seven feet tall and probably weighed three hundred pounds. A powerful friend indeed if some kind of alliance could be forged.

Then it was their turn. The remaining Finthian, along with the two Sephs and the dispirited Cellite, were herded off in one direction, while McCade, Van Doren and the bear were taken in another. After sloshing across the compound, they were shoved into a pen, and an iron door slammed closed behind them.

It was dim inside the pen, lit only by one old chem strip and what little sunlight managed to find its way in through cracks and holes. The dirt floor was relatively dry and slanted toward a ditch at the back of the cell, thereby encouraging runoff. The ditch contained a sluggish flow of water, and judging from the smell, served as part of the open sewer system.

A few informal kicks quickly testified to the soundness of Lakorian construction techniques. So much for knocking the wall down. McCade found a spigot, from which he managed to coax a trickle of water. After slaking their thirst and scraping off what dirt they could, McCade and Van Doren plopped down and leaned against a wall.

"I don't suppose either one of you fellow homosaps has a dope stick secreted about your persons?" The voice was a rumbling basso and originated from their shaggy cell mate. The most surprising thing was that he spoke perfect, unaccented Terran.

"Sorry," McCade replied, patting his pockets. "Don't use 'em much. I might have a partly smoked cigar though."

"Any port in a storm, my granddaddy always said," the big creature replied as McCade handed him a half-smoked cigar.

Having found a shorter butt for himself, McCade lit up and leaned over to light the other's as well. Van Doren watched the ritual suspiciously as though sure their furry companion was up to no good. When both had their cigars drawing satisfactorily, the bear said conversationally, "You know, we're in a lot of trouble."

"Really?" McCade asked with a raised eyebrow. "You mean this isn't the Lunar Hilton?"

"Go ahead . . . kid around," the other said, gesturing with his cigar. "But don't blame me when you're sweating your ass off in some mine."

"I won't," McCade said with a smile. "But while we're on the subject of you, who are you anyway? Did I understand you to say 'fellow homosaps' earlier? No offense, but most humans come with a lot less hair."

"No offense taken," the bear said calmly. "I'm aware of my hirsuteness. But that's what you've got to expect if you're an Iceworld Variant. By the way, the name's Phil. Sorry about the little love tap I gave you in the trailer. It was just a reflex action."

McCade had heard of Variants but never met one. That wasn't too surprising since he knew they were damned expensive. Variants started out as normal humans. But after extensive biosculpting, something doctors on Terra specialized in, they ended up suited to one particular and usually exotic environment. In Phil's case, he'd been sculpted for work on the Iceworlds. Considering that Alice fell three classifications short of Iceworld status, McCade shuddered to imagine what such worlds were like.

"How come you didn't tell us this in the trailer?" Van Doren growled.

"I was waiting to see what kind of folks you were," Phil replied amiably. "Frankly I don't always choose to associate with fellow homosaps. But when you jumped that guard in the compound, I knew you were my kind of folks."

"This must be a little tropical for you, isn't it?" McCade asked.

Phil nodded in agreement as he blew a long column of

smoke into the humid air. "Frankly it's hotter than an Il Ronnian steam bath."

"Somehow they knew you were human, because they put you in here with us," McCade mused.

"Hey, boss," Van Doren said. "If he's a human Variant, then he's probably augmented too." The marine continued to regard Phil with suspicion.

"Good point. Phil?" McCade said evenly. "How about it?"

"Sure," Phil replied with the wave of a hairy paw. "I'm augmented. All the usual stuff. Back-up infrared vision, amplified muscle response, razor-sharp, durasteel claws, the whole ball of wax. Doesn't do me much good against energy weapons though."

"Nonetheless," McCade said, "it can't hurt. How did you wind up here anyway, Phil?"

Phil shrugged eloquently. "I'm a research biologist indentured to United Biomed. Me and Mac. He was my partner. Anyway, we were outbound to our station on Frio IV with a load of supplies. That's when the pirate jumped us." Phil took a long, final drag from the cigar before stubbing it out.

"We didn't stand a chance," he said soberly. "When they came aboard they gunned Mac just for the hell of it. Called him a freak." Phil shook his huge head, and his lips peeled back to bare the durasteel teeth that ran the length of his short snout. "God help 'em if I ever catch 'em," he said through a growl.

McCade nodded his understanding. "Tough break, Phil. . . . Pretty much the same as what happened to us." He waved his cigar butt vaguely.

"Yeah, sure," Phil said as one round ear twitched. He obviously didn't believe a word of it.

All three were silent for a while. McCade found he couldn't stop thinking about Sara. He tried to force thoughts of her out of his mind so that he could think, plan, find some means of escape. But it didn't work.

Time passed and when the door to their cell finally screeched open, McCade found himself face to face with Brother Mungo.

Thirteen

THE DOOR CLANGED shut. McCade stared at Mungo with disbelief. It couldn't be. He'd seen Laurie slice Mungo's head off. He'd seen her carry it around. And later he'd seen the Treel deliver it to the Il Ronn. Nonetheless Mungo sat across from him, head firmly seated on his shoulders, eyes on the dirt floor.

"Boss . . ." Van Doren broke the silence.

"Yeah, I know, Amos," McCade answered wearily. "It's our old friend the Treel again. Well, what brings Your Supreme Softness to our humble abode? Slumming?"

Mungo's hooded eyes came up to meet his. McCade forced himself to remember that it wasn't really Mungo. It wasn't even the Treel impersonating Mungo. The sadness in those eyes was the Treel's. Speaking with Mungo's deep, melodious voice, the Treel made no attempt to hide his identity.

"As usual, you jest, rigid one. Nonetheless I shall answer your question. The great Yareel has seen fit to frown upon me. A great sadness is upon me. My suffering is beyond all knowing. I am not here of my own free will."

172

"Wait a minute. This guy's a Treel?" Phil interrupted.

McCade nodded.

"No kidding!" Phil exclaimed. "I remember coming across them in exobiology . . . but a real one. Damn! They're really rare."

"This one isn't," McCade replied. "Every time we turn around we trip over him."

"Why's he wearing the chemlock?" Phil asked.

"Chemlock?" McCade looked, but didn't see anything unusual about Mungo's appearance.

"Yeah," Phil insisted. "Right there behind his left ear. See it. The little black box."

McCade moved closer to take advantage of what little light there was. The Treel ignored him. It was almost invisible against Mungo's black skin, but sure enough, there was a small container tucked behind the man's left ear.

"That's a chemlock," Phil explained. "It's feeding tiny amounts of chemicals into his bloodstream. If you try to take it out . . . boom! A charge goes off and so does his head. Somebody thought it up as a way to medicate psychopaths while allowing them back into society. Never seemed to catch on though. . . . People didn't like having them around. Afraid they'd blow up without warning, I guess."

"Let's see if it really works, boss," Van Doren said cheerfully.

"Why, Amos! I'm ashamed of you. It wouldn't be fair for Mungo to lose his head twice in a row, now would it?" McCade said sternly.

"As usual, I will ignore your jibes, rigid ones. Essentially you are correct. The little container dispenses chemicals which affect my metabolism and prevent me from changing appearance. A small gift from Sept Commander Reez. He thought forcing me to appear human on a permanent basis was quite amusing." The Treel shrugged. "It's all I deserved for trusting a rigid one."

"So why the falling out?" McCade asked, settling down again by Van Doren.

The Treel paused for a moment as though gathering its thoughts. There was pain in its eyes. "You were taken away. It was hot and uncomfortable in my native form, so I assumed the guise of an I1 Ronnian officer. I was escorted to the ship's recreational area and told to wait while they took Mungo's brain to a lab for pumping.

"After a while, I grew bored and decided to take a look around. There was a library just off the lounge. The auto-attendant ignored me, so I entered, hoping for a glimpse of my native planet. I selected the appropriate survey tape and plugged it into a holo player."

Watching Mungo's eyes, McCade saw the Treel's pain turn to despair.

"I turned it on. I looked, and looked again. There was nothing. Where my planet had once circled the 'Light of Yareel,' there was only the blackness of space."

The Treel looked at each of them in turn, his eyes searching their faces. Making sure they understood the significance of what he'd said. Looking for something. Compassion? Understanding? McCade couldn't tell.

"They destroyed it a year ago while I attended your Academy as Cadet Votava. They blew it up. My world, shattered into a new asteroid belt. Shattered too was the future of my race." With that his eyes fell and he began to chant in his native tongue. The chant had an eerie quality that sent a shiver up McCade's spine. It was filled with sadness and loneliness.

In spite of Cadet Votava, Laurie and all the others the Treel had killed, McCade felt sorry for the strange alien. In a way the Treel was as much a victim as those he'd killed. After a few minutes, the chanting stopped, to be replaced by an uncomfortable silence. McCade broke it with a single word.

"Why?"

The Treel looked up through Mungo's pain-filled eyes. "I asked their computer that very question. The answer was to quell a rebellion against Il Ronnian authority. As I explained to you once before, the Il Ronn have long held our planet hostage against the good behavior of agents like myself."

A look of pride suffused Mungo's face. "But apparently my brethren at home were not as easily intimidated as I. They rose up and fought as only Treel can. Imagine fighting a race which can endlessly shift forms. One moment vicious carnivore, the next your commanding officer, and then perhaps you yourself. We have never been a large race, but nonetheless that Il Ronn lost every battle. Remember that they also had to fight the endless variety of dangerous life forms that populated my planet. In the end, they had to destroy the planet or lose face. Something they cannot stand. So now I and a few like me are all that's left."

Even Van Doren seemed touched. His voice was gentle as he said, "And they caught you?"

The Treel nodded Mungo's head. "I don't know how long I sat there staring at the print-out. It must have been a long time. When I looked up, Reez was standing in front of me with a sneer on his face." The Treel sighed.

"They paralyzed me. . . . Yes," he waved a hand in McCade's direction, "it can be done if you know what to use. Some rather pointless negotiations ensued, during which Reez attempted to secure my continued services. I refused, of course. I have some self-respect. Then I was forced to assume this form. The chemlock was inserted to make sure I would remain this way. I was then sent down in a shuttle. Actually it was your ship if I'm not mistaken," the Treel said, nodding toward McCade. "And here I am. Selling me into slavery as a human amused Commander Reez greatly."

"The bastard," Van Doren said, imagining what he'd do to the Il Ronnian officer if he had the chance.

"You know," Phil said thoughtfully, "if I had some lab facilities, I think I could disarm and remove that chemlock."

"An interesting offer," McCade replied. "However I'm not sure it would be a good idea. Our friend here tends to be a little undependable given too much freedom. Besides, I like the way he looks, don't you, Amos?"

Van Doren grunted in the affirmative.

"I have a feeling my fellow homosaps are being less than forthright," Phil said gently as he examined a gleaming durasteel claw. "Perhaps you should tell me how all this began."

McCade thought about it for a moment and concluded there was little point in keeping Phil in the dark. Plus there was always the possibility that he might help. So he briefly outlined the events leading up to their present predicament.

When he was finished, Phil gave a low whistle. "So now the Il Ronn know where the War World is and you don't."

"True, I'm afraid," McCade confessed.

Suddenly the Treel sat up and spoke. "Yes, rigid ones, suddenly I understand. The great Yareel has truly blessed me! I shall be the instrument of his revenge! I shall bring down destruction upon the Il Ronn! And you shall be my allies. Together we will destroy the infidel!"

The three humans looked at each other in amazement. From the depths of despair, the Treel had somehow been transformed into a religious zealot, and an arrogant one at that. McCade's thoughts were interrupted by the rasp of un-oiled metal as someone unlatched the door to their cell.

A huge Lakorian foot kicked it open.

"Out," was all its owner said.

They obeyed; there seemed no advantage in doing anything else. One by one they emerged from the dim cell to stand blinking in the Lakorian daylight.

"Move."

The order was accompanied by a powerful shove from be-hind, and McCade found himself propelled toward the wooden platform which dominated the center of the com-pound. Now it was surrounded by a milling crowd of shout-ing, gesticulating buyers. The slave auction had begun.

McCade was surprised. For some reason he had expected more time to pass between their arrival and subsequent sale. He felt he should have developed some sort of plan. A means to escape. Something. But for the life of him he couldn't imagine what. As they moved toward the platform, he searched for some sign of Sara. There wasn't any and his spirits sank even lower. The crowd parted to let them through. Around him McCade heard snatches of conversation. He could understand most of it since it was in Standard, which functioned as a sort of universal trading language. As the humans made their way through the crowd, their merits were enthusiastically debated.

"Look at the big one, Forn. . . . If we were careful with him, he might last a whole year."

"Mebbe, mebbe, but how 'bout the furry one. . . . I say he'd do right well."

"Get serious, Forn. He'd be fine on an iceworld, but he wouldn't last a week on Lava."

"Up."

Another shove boosted McCade up the first two steps. As he gained the top he saw what might have been a Cellite being escorted off the other end of the platform. He couldn't be sure.

They were lined up without ceremony and told to strip. As McCade complied, he noted with interest that the auctioneer was an android. A General Electric Model Twenty, if he wasn't mistaken. Its makers had granted it a vaguely human appearance, though without much attention to detail. Some of its metal parts had begun to rust in the humid climate of Lakor, and it had taken some heavy-duty dents. However, in spite of the cosmetic flaws, the droid proved to be a skilled auctioneer. Evidently it had its own built-in amplifier, because when it spoke its voice boomed out across the compound with sufficient volume that even the most distant buyer could hear with ease.

"Gentlebeings . . . your attention, please. Before you is lot three on your print-out. Four human males, all in good health, all capable of running simple machinery. I direct your attention to item four. You will notice this item is an Iceworld Variant and a skilled biologist. You may wish to consider him for specialized activity. As usual we will take bids for the entire lot first. If we have no acceptable bids for the lot, we will then auction off each item separately. Bidding for lot three can now begin."

Bidding began at four thousand credits offered by a nasty-looking human dressed in worn body armor and using a nerve lash for a swagger stick. He was immediately outbid by a female Zord who, having no vocal apparatus, signaled her bids in universal sign language by use of her tentacles. Then the bidding grew hot and heavy, moving too quickly for McCade to track. The price had reached sixteen thousand credits when suddenly a booming voice cut through the cacophony as though it wasn't there.

"Twenty thousand credits, sport, and let's have done with it!"

With sudden hope, McCade searched the crowd and sure enough, standing like an island in the sea of bodies, was Rico. An enormous grin split his bearded face and tiny eyes twinkled merrily.

"Not that they're worth even half that," he added, laughing uproariously.

There were no further bids. "Sold to the human for twenty thousand credits," the android said. "Pay the slave master and collect your property."

McCade barely managed to snatch up his clothes before a Lakorian guard shoved him toward the other end of the platform with a grunted, "Off."

He was still struggling into them when a massive slap on the back threatened to drop him into the mud. "Good to see ya, ol' sport! Course I wasn't plannin' on seein' all of ya like that!" Once again the big man broke into gales of laughter.

McCade grinned and shook Rico's hand. "Go ahead, Rico, have your fun, I was never so glad to see something so ugly in my whole life! I thought we'd lost you back at the Rock!"

Just then Van Doren arrived. He and Rico proceeded to dance around each other, trading blows. When they stopped to shake hands, there was a moment of silence as muscles knotted and sweat broke out on their foreheads.

"Are they always like this?" Phil inquired as they watched the two men straining to best each other.

McCade nodded. "Worse, if anything. Maybe you'd like to join in." He looked Phil up and down. "I suspect you could take them both."

The huge Variant shook his head. "No thanks, given a choice I'm more the cerebral type."

With grunts of expelled air, Rico and Van Doren broke off their contest. Their happy grins indicated another draw.

"Well now that you've got that out of your systems, maybe we can get on with other things," McCade said in mock annoyance.

"What was that, slave?" Rico asked with a grin. "I paid good money to take this? Come to think of it, how am I gonna explain the twenty thousand credits to the Council? They're already complainin' about my expense account."

McCade laughed and then said worriedly, "Speaking of the Council, Sara is around here somewhere and we've got to buy her out too."

Rico's expression darkened to one of concern. "'Fraid I've got some bad news for ya. Sara's gone. She was sold a few hours ago . . . before I got here . . . and the buyer's long gone, with her in tow."

"Damn!" McCade exclaimed in frustration. "Off-planet?"

Rico shook his shaggy head. "Nope. They headed for the interior." He gestured toward the jungle, which crowded one end of the stockade.

"The guy who bought her is some kind of Lakorian noble-man. Calls himself 'King,' but I understand there's some who dispute that."

"Well what are we waiting for?" McCade asked grimly. "Let's go see the King."

Rico didn't move. He just smiled bemusedly and raised an eyebrow. "No offense, but what happened to the War World? Last time I heard it was top priority. If it's really as important as ya said, Sara'd want us ta deal with that first."

"And it is important, Rico," McCade said sheepishly. "I guess where Sara is concerned I've developed tunnel vision. Besides, for the moment we've hit a dead end where finding the War World is concerned."

Rico grinned ear to ear. "So it's like that, is it. . . . Well I'm glad to hear it. Just remember, ya treat her right or you'll answer ta Rico!" The big man slapped McCade on the back. "So what're we waitin' for? Let's go see the King!"

As they walked toward the gate, the other three fell in behind.

"By the way, who're those two?" Rico asked, gesturing over his shoulder with a thumb. "The only reason I bought 'em was ta keep it simple. Somebody might have run up the bidding on you or Amos. What're we gonna do with the hairy one?"

"Hell, Rico," McCade replied with a grin, "he isn't that much hairier than you are!" As they walked McCade filled the other man in on Phil's background and Mungo's true identity.

When McCade had finished, Rico glanced in the direction of the Treel and said, "That one'll bear watching. I don't like the look in his eye."

McCade nodded in agreement.

As they passed through the gate, Van Doren and Phil offered the Lakorian guards a parting gesture older than universal sign language. They were stoically ignored.

"Now what about you, Rico?" McCade asked. "How in the world did you manage to end up here at the perfect moment?"

"Well . . . first off, it wasn't perfect. If it had been, we wouldn't be goin' after Sara. Anyway it wasn't all that hard. I waited off the Rock just like we agreed. Had a coupla tense moments with a pirate destroyer but managed ta convince 'em I was relining a bare spot in the port tube. Then all hell broke loose and I wasted a lot of time picking you outta the mess. Finally I managed ta pick up the minibeacon Sara was wearin'," Rico said.

"Wait a minute," McCade interrupted. "What minibeacon? I don't remember any minibeacon."

Rico looked embarrassed. "Well ol' sport, Professor Wendel's people worked it up. It's specially shielded and undetectable. She's wearing it right under the skin near her left shoulder blade. Seemed like a good time to try it out." Rico shrugged and grinned. "Let's just say they wanted some insurance.

"Anyhow I sorted ya outta the herd usin' the beacon. I saw ya waste those two pirates—nice piece o' work by the way—and busted my buns tryin' ta catch up. Just as I was gettin' close, the biggest Il Ronnian ship I've ever seen came outta hyperspace and locked on ta ya." Rico gestured eloquently. "After that I just followed ya here. Fortunately there's lotsa slavers comin' and goin' so nobody asked me any questions. Then I lost some time sellin' *Lady Alice* or I woulda been here sooner."

"You sold *Alice* . . ."

"'Fraid so. They wouldn't let me buy ya with my good looks, ya know."

"I'm sorry, Rico. I know what the *Lady* meant to you. I'll make it up to you somehow."

"Not to worry. Feast your eyes on my new transport. Handsome, ain't she?"

McCade stopped in amazement. The vehicle to which Rico referred so proudly was a monument to the determination of durasteel molecules to remain in close proximity to each other. Its dents had dents. It was leaking fuel and lubricant from a dozen points. Entire treads were missing from the giant tracks. Rust had eaten deeply into its huge hull. And it *was* huge. It stood at least fifty feet high and twice that in length. The front end consisted of a circular energy projector the diameter of the vehicle itself. The center of the projector was hollow for some distance back, eventually narrowing down to a hole about five feet across. In operating, the energy projector could cut a circular hole through solid rock. Then the loosened material could be funneled back to be pulverized and superheated. After treatment with various additives, the liquid soil and rock would then be spun out behind the machine to form a perfect tunnel. If ore was located, the shaft thus created could be used to mine it.

"I bought her used," Rico said proudly.

"Thank God," McCade muttered, inspecting the vehicle's scarred plating. "I'd hate to ride in anything that looked that bad new."

McCade's comments were lost on Rico. He had already started to extoll the vehicle's virtues. "They brought 'er dirt-side ta do a mineralogical survey. Guess they hoped they'd find somethin' worth minin', but no such luck. Guess that's why slavin's so important here'bouts. Anyway everything ya could possibly want's built right in. Food, supplies, sleepin' quarters, even showers. She's got 'em all. Plus a few surprises. Come on."

A control box of some kind suddenly appeared in Rico's hand. He pressed a button and a door slid aside. Then a set of pneumatic stairs unfolded with a hiss of escaping air to touch the mud. McCade and the others followed Rico aboard.

The vehicle's interior was in marked contrast to its exterior. Everything showed signs of wear, but appeared to be well maintained, and was reasonably clean. Originally designed for crew of ten, it provided more than enough space for their small group. Besides the creature comforts, the vehicle boasted considerable armament, including auto-slug throwers, energy weapons, and a single battery of multipurpose missiles.

"Nice, Rico," McCade said, peering into the sighting scope of an energy weapon. "But is all this necessary?"

"'Fraid so, ol' sport," Rico said, handing McCade one of his imported cigars. "There ain't no public transportation where we're goin'. The King likes it that way. Plus I hear there's some real nasty critters waitin' out there. Not to mention the King, who ain't likely to welcome us with open arms."

McCade nodded agreement as he remembered the trip to the stockade. The armament would probably come in handy.

"How about air travel though?"

Rico shook his head as he blew out a stream of blue smoke. "Nice thought, but the King don't allow no atmospheric stuff ... 'cept his o' course. Sorry, but that's how it is."

"Thanks, Rico," McCade said. "You've done a fantastic job. How soon can we get under way?"

"Right now. Just give me a few minutes to crank 'er up."

While Rico ran through an operations list, McCade wandered back to check on the rest of the group. Van Doren had made himself busy checking out various weapons systems, the Treel sat lost in meditation, and Phil was halfway through an enormous sandwich in the galley. McCade realized it had been a long time since his last meal. He plopped down at the mess table and began building himself a sandwich.

"Rico's up forward, cranking her up, Phil," McCade said. "We're going after Sara Bridger. Frankly we could use your help, but you don't owe us anything. If you'd like to bail out, now's the time to do it. Rico's probably got enough credits to get you off-planet. How about it?"

Phil chewed a gigantic mouthful of sandwich thoughtfully for a moment before speaking. "Well I've been thinking, Sam. Like I told you, my partner's dead and chances are the company thinks I'm dead too. Why tell 'em otherwise? I've got another seven years to run on my indenture, assuming of course I survive that long. Well, maybe I could spend those seven years my way. From what you said, Rico's planet would be just right for a Variant like myself. So if they'd take me I'd like to sign up."

"United Biomed's loss would seem to be Alice's gain," McCade replied cheerfully. "I can't speak for Alice, but Rico sits on the Council. Let's ask him."

A few minutes later Rico was pumping the paw of Alice's newest citizen by executive decree. "If those bozos from Biomed ever show up on Alice, we'll arrest 'em for something and ship 'em out. By the way," Rico said, looking the big Variant up and down, "remind me ta talk with you 'bout a reserve commission in the militia."

As the huge vehicle's engines thundered into life, McCade entered a small stim shower. He was a free man again and he wanted to look like one.

Fourteen

BIG FAT RAINDROPS splattered against the windshield and made a drumming sound on the roof of the giant crawler as it fought its way through thick undergrowth. A steady wind bent the vegetation toward them, adding considerably to the strain on the howling engines. Inside the cab it was warm and dry, but far from comfortable. Every few seconds the violent motion of the machine threatened to throw McCade out of his seat. His shoulders were already sore from countless encounters with the harness holding him in place. In the driver's seat next to him, Rico frowned in concentration. They had tried the autopilot but found it couldn't deal with the irregular terrain. And deal they must to reach the glowing green dot representing Sara's minibeacon some two hundred miles ahead. At least she was still alive.

Rico's tiny eyes flitted from one instrument to the next while his large, hairy hands played over the controls with surprising dexterity. So far Rico's skill had taken them over sixty-degree slopes of loose rock, through a labyrinth of giant trees, and on one occasion, across a lake, underwater, an activity which didn't bother the machine, but scared the hell out of McCade.

In spite of all that, McCade felt better. He had slept for twelve hours, eaten an enormous breakfast, and then donned a one-piece black coverall which Rico assured him also functioned as light body armor. Welcome too was the new slug gun resting low on his right thigh, and the plentiful supply of cigars which filled the breast pockets of his jump suit. Rico had thought of everything.

As the crawler lurched along, McCade tried to plan for what lay ahead. It wasn't easy. For one thing they knew very little about what they might face. What Rico had been able to learn was a jumbled amalgamation of fact and fiction. The challenge lay in figuring out which was which. Sara's beacon had remained stationary for more than twenty hours, suggesting that she had arrived somewhere. Presumably King Zorta's castle. Nobody knew for sure because, with the exception of Zorta's most trusted advisors, those who went to the castle never came back. In fact it was rumored that the King's desire for privacy was so strong that those employed to build the castle were buried under it.

Without doubt, the King had good reasons to protect himself. For one thing there was a considerable number of other Lakorian nobles who felt that killing the former King didn't necessarily entitle you to his throne. They did, however, feel that it was a good place to start. As a result there had been numerous, though so far unsuccessful, attempts on Zorta's life.

Also counting against him, in McCade's estimation, the King had systematically encouraged the population to turn from their traditional pursuits of farming, fishing and light manufacture to an economy dominated by the slave trade. At first the population enjoyed the foreign exchange thus generated, but gradually their enjoyment began to wane as rumors began to circulate—rumors about slave raids on remote Lakorian villages. Then too, taxes had begun to rise dramatically. As a result, tax evasion had become a popular hobby. To counter this trend Zorta introduced a policy of not only executing tax evaders, but their families as well. As a result of these and similar policies, the King's popularity was decidedly limited. Nonetheless, due to an effective army and air force, he continued to rule. And it seemed would continue to do so indefinitely.

All they really knew was that Sara was probably being held in the King's castle. McCade forced his thoughts away from any consideration of why she had been taken there or what might happen to her. He forced himself to concentrate on how to get her out. In spite of the machine's violent motion, he found himself drifting into a light sleep, during which he imagined an endless procession of fantastic schemes by which the castle walls could be breached. Unfortunately something always seemed to go wrong at the last moment. His reverie came to an abrupt halt, along with the crawler itself.

"Damn! I'm afraid we've got trouble, ol' sport," Rico said, releasing his harness and sliding out of his seat. "'Cordin' ta the diagnostics, we've got some kinda problem with the port engine. Not too surprisin' considerin' the kinda country we've been going through. Anyway I'm goin' below for a look-see. Stay here and keep an eye on those sensors. Keep in mind that without the port engine we ain't got enough juice ta power the defensive screens."

On that cheerful note he was gone.

McCade flicked the detectors from low to high intensity. The driving rain rendered the high mag video cameras useless beyond a few yards. The metal detectors showed trace elements in the soil and surrounding vegetation, as did the radiation screens. Infrared indicated a variety of life forms in the area. They ranged in size from very large to very small. As far as McCade could tell, there were about the same number they'd been seeing all along. He sat back, lit a new cigar and kicked his feet up. As he smoked, he scanned the monitors occasionally, watching for changes.

The intercom chimed and Rico's voice boomed forth. "It appears we lost a bearing. Looks like a three-hour job. Say, send Amos down ta help, would ya? I need someone with more brawn than brains!"

At that point Van Doren broke in with, "The truth is he hasn't got a clue on how to change a bearing! Guess I'll go down and save his ass like always."

McCade laughed as the intercom went dead. Glancing up at the monitors he thought at first glance that they all looked the same. Then something about the infrared monitor made him take another look. Then he realized that the number of red blobs on the screen had doubled. Not only that, they were slowly moving to surround the crawler.

His eyes stayed glued to the infrared monitor as he reached for the intercom button.

"Phil . . . I think we've got company. I'm not sure *what* they are, but they're a lot of them, and they're slowly surrounding us. I'm delegating control of both waist turrets to 'local.' I suggest you pick one and stand-by. And while you're at it see if old Softie will come out of meditation long enough to kill a few infidels. If there's trouble we could use him in the other turret."

Phil's voice came back, calmly efficient. "You've got it, Sam. . . . We'll be on line in a minute."

As he watched the red blobs continue to surround them, McCade noticed that even more were slowly drifting into the screen's range. One by one he activated the crawler's weapons systems until all the indicators glowed green. All the while, the blobs continued their encirclement. Was it random movement of a herd of animals that just happened to be feeding in the area? Or were they guided by some intelligence? There was no way to tell. And until full power was restored, there wasn't much they could do. If the red blobs were hostile, limping at them on one engine wouldn't help much.

Conditions remained static for more than an hour. The gradual gathering of red blobs had peaked at about two hundred. Occasionally smaller groups of four or five would break away and disappear off screen. However their absence was balanced out as other small groupings and individuals drifted in.

McCade stubbed out his latest cigar and sipped a little cold coffee, trying to wash the raw taste out of his mouth. His left cheek twitched and his eyes hurt from staring at the monitors. He leaned back in his seat, consciously forcing his muscles to relax. Looking up he noticed with interest that the rain seemed to be slacking off. As a result the high mag video cameras had begun to clear. Without warning the rain stopped completely and McCade found himself looking at a scene of barbaric splendor.

His first impression was of vibrant shimmering color which ebbed and flowed with the movement of animals and riders.

The huge, six-legged reptillian animals wore trappings of bright blue. Each carried three Lakorian riders decked out in bright orange with dark brown trim. The lead rider of each animal carried a wicked-looking lance from which a long, green pennant flew. Behind him his two companions were armed with efficient-looking energy weapons of a design unfamiliar to McCade. And behind them, each mount carried a large set of saddle bags, filled no doubt with food for the riders and power paks for the weapons. It was an impressive and intimidating sight which, McCade reflected, was probably the whole idea.

The intercom chimed, followed by Phil's awed voice. "Holy Sol, would you look at that! What do you think, Sam . . . friend or foe?"

"Beats me, Phil," McCade replied. "But let's stay ready for anything."

It was hard to guess the intentions of the Lakorians because of the constant movement. Evidently their reptillian mounts didn't like to stand still. However the riders were obviously experienced and, while their animals remained in motion, they themselves managed to stay in the same position relative to all the other mounts.

As the warm sunshine came into contact with the wet earth, a ground fog began to form, making it seem as though the Lakorians were floating. As McCade watched, a single animal separated itself from the rest and began to move toward the crawler. Unlike the other mounts, this particular animal carried a single rider. The lance he bore carried a flag on which some complicated device had been embroidered. McCade also noticed a long whip antenna extending up from the back of the saddle to sway in the light breeze. Whoever he was he had a powerful radio at his disposal and that implied friends somewhere. Something to keep in mind.

A hundred yards from the crawler the reptillian mount stopped momentarily as its rider dismounted. The Lakorian planted his lance in the ground with something of a flourish and then assumed a position closely resembling parade rest. His animal began to pace back and forth behind him.

As McCade released his harness he hit the intercom once more. "Rico, Amos, you've been tracking all this?"

"Yeah, boss. . . . We've been watching with one eye. Looks

188

like a convention of pleasure dome pimps to me."

"Thank God you chose the marines and not the diplomatic corps," McCade said, getting up. "How long till full power?"

"Well, ol' sport," Rico answered, "we've been takin' a few short cuts, but even so it's gonna be another hour for sure."

"Okay," McCade replied. "It appears their leader's ready for a little talk, so I'm going outside."

"Wonder why he don't just call us on that radio," Amos wondered out loud.

"No way to tell, Amos," McCade said. "But I suspect there's some kind of ritual or formality involved."

"Or maybe they just want to waste you," Phil said suspiciously. "You're gonna be awfully exposed out there."

"True," McCade replied, checking the load in his slug gun. "But chances are he just wants to talk. If so there's the possibility of getting some help. Frankly, gentlemen, from what I've seen so far, I think we need it."

"In that case, talk his arm off," Phil replied with a chuckle. "We'll cover you. Won't we, Softie?"

The Treel's voice sounded distant and bored over the intercom. "Of course. Let's get on with it."

"Grab your pocket-com on your way out," Phil said. "We might as well listen in."

McCade agreed and stopped long enough to pick up one of the small devices, activate it and slip it into his breast pocket. As the hatch opened and the stairs unfolded to touch the ground, McCade took a deep breath of the fresh clean air. In a few hours the smell of rotting vegetation would once again dominate, but for the moment the rain had washed everything clean. His boots sank into the soft, spongy ground as he walked. Each one made a sucking sound as he pulled it free and each grew heavier with accumulated mud the farther he went. Ahead the Lakorian still stood where McCade had last seen him. He waited patiently for McCade to approach while the giant steed paced back and forth behind him. As McCade got closer he saw that the Lakorian was handsome, by the standards of his race. He had a high forehead, two wide-set, intelligent eyes, broad cheekbones, a short, rounded snout having three nostrils, and a wide thick-lipped mouth. He was slender by Lakorian standards too, though still heavier than any human, and he stood a good foot shorter than McCade.

McCade stopped a respectful distance from the Lakorian and, unsure of proper etiquette, bowed formally, a widely accepted sign of courteous greeting.

The Lakorian responded in kind. When he spoke it was in the High Standard favored by the Empire's nobility. His accent was atrocious. "Who have I the honor to address, and be you noble or vassal? I am Baron Lif."

Glancing down at his plain black jump suit and then up at the Baron's bright ceremonial garb, he understood the Lakorian's confusion. "My apologies, Baron, for not greeting you in more suitable garb, but I'm afraid my companions and I have foresworn normal dress due to a period of religious pennance. I am Sam McCade, Knight of the Round Table and trusted defender of King Arthur's court." He prayed Lif did not share his boyhood fascination with ancient legend. Especially Earth legend. He'd purposely chosen a rank below Lif's, having found through past dealings with aristocracy that this was less threatening, and placed them in a more amenable frame of mind.

The Baron nodded understandingly. "I too weary of the priesthood's restrictions, good Knight. I sometimes wonder if they have aught to do but think up new ones!"

McCade laughed appreciatively at the nobleman's joke and waited to see what direction the conversation would take next.

With the formalities taken care of, the Baron seemed disposed to get down to business. "I wish to bid you welcome to my poor barony and its meager resources. As you can see I ventured out this morning for a hunt, accompanied only by my personal bodyguard. I could not help but notice that your crawler seems somewhat incapacitated. How may I and my men be of help?"

McCade wasn't fooled for a moment. He was well aware that in spite of the Baron's polite phraseology, Lif had just informed him that he was trespassing, that the troops present were only part of the force at his disposal, that they knew the crawler was undergoing repairs, that the Baron therefore had the upper hand, and that McCade had better produce a good explanation of his activities and very quickly indeed.

Operating partly from intuition, and partly from shrewd guesswork, McCade assumed a slightly conspiratorial demeanor. "Well Baron, I appreciate your kindness. As it happens my men will soon have the crawler repaired and we'll be able to resume our journey. I hope we haven't inconvenienced your hunt."

"Not at all," Lif said with a negligent wave of the hand. "Where are you bound? This is not easy country. Perhaps I could offer you a guide?"

A spy is more like it, McCade thought as he smiled his thanks, but I have no intention of letting you off that easy. "Once again the Baron is too kind. But to answer your question, my mission is one of the utmost delicacy. Involved is a lady of noble birth who now finds herself in compromising circumstances. Now I must beg the Baron's indulgence, for I have said too much."

"Not so, good Knight! Though we be of different races, surely we are bound by the common threads of nobility. Your difficulties are mine. I insist that you allow me to help," Baron Lif said earnestly.

McCade shook his head doubtfully. "I dare not impose further on your good graces, Baron. And in all truth the matter may be better left unspoken of, lest I unknowingly compromise one or both of us. After all I am a stranger in a strange land and know not what alliances and conventions I might unintentionally violate."

With considerable satisfaction, McCade saw from Lif's expression that the Lakorian nobleman was deeply and completely hooked.

"I assure you, noble Knight, that whatever you say shall remain a secret between us and shall not be the cause of offense on my part. Pray tell me more of this matter, that I might assist."

Haltingly at first, as though unsure of himself and searching for words, McCade spun a tale made of both fact and fiction. The way he told it, Sara was the irresponsible daughter of a doting King Arthur. Ignoring her father's urgings, once too often she had taken off in her speedster, alone, unescorted, to visit her married sister on the fourth planet of their system. En route she had been chased and captured by pirates, who sold her into slavery. McCade and his men had managed to track her down by following the shielded signal broadcast by a minibeacon each member of the royal family wore. Now they were following that signal to her location, the castle of a certain King Zorta, whoever he might be. There McCade hoped to buy her freedom and restore her to the arms of her loving father. As McCade completed his tale, he watched Baron Lif's eyes light up as the significance of the beacon sank in. No doubt about it, the Baron bought the story hook, line and sinker. Nonetheless the Lakorian nobleman was nobody's fool and hid his interest well.

Lif shook his head sadly. "Yes, a sad tale indeed. The young ones never listen. I fear it is a condition common to all races. But don't give up hope, my friend. I feel certain that the gods ordained our meeting, for I see common ground upon which we might meet and aid each other."

"Nothing would please me more," McCade answered enthusiastically. "In all truth I have worried greatly about our ability to make our way through the wilderness to King Zorta's castle. The plant and animal life on your planet are so . . . er . . . vigorous."

The Baron laughed, a deep and genuine guffawing sound that made his mount shy away. "Sir Knight, your tact does you credit. We shall get along well, you and I. But enough of this. Our plans should be completed over a good meal, with Vak to wash it down."

As McCade began to protest, Lif held up a gauntleted hand. "No, I won't hear of it. My hunting lodge is nearby. As soon as your machine is repaired, we shall escort you there."

Much as a jailer escorts a prisoners, McCade thought. The Baron rattled off a radio frequency on which McCade could contact him, vaulted into the saddle, and sent his steed galloping off.

McCade heaved a sigh of relief, turned, and made his way back to the crawler. Once safely inside he was greeted by hoots of laughter over the intercom.

"Boss, you could sell vacuum to asteroid miners," Van Doren chuckled.

"Yeah, ya sucked 'im in real good," Rico agreed. "Only now that ya got 'im, what're ya goin' ta do with him?"

"Finish reeling him in, of course," McCade responded. "And then put him to work."

A few hours later the crawler followed the leading elements of Lif's bodyguard out of the thick vegetation and into a large clearing. A sprawling wooden building dominated the clearing's center. It was quite large, and seemed even bigger because it had been built on ten-foot pilings. As Rico guided the crawler up to the lodge, Lif's household troops began to picket their mounts under the structure, between the massive pilings.

Over McCade's head a speaker crackled into life. "Welcome to Treehome. As soon as the demands of your machine are satisfied, Sir Knight, please join me for dinner. Your squires are welcome also."

McCade left the Treel to watch the crawler, and Phil to watch the Treel. He was also concerned about Phil's reception within the lodge. There was no way to predict Lif's reaction to the Variant.

Together, McCade, Rico and Amos picked their way through the mud to the lodge under the watchful gaze of a small honor guard. With the emphasis on "guard," McCade thought with amusement. Together they mounted a flight of stairs leading up to intricately carved double doors where they were met by a uniformed major domo. The Baron certainly likes to do things with style, McCade reflected as they were shown into a large hall with vaulted ceilings. A log fire blazed at the far end of the huge room, its flickering light dancing across tapestry-hung walls. However the room's even temperature hinted at central heating. It seemed a comfortable marriage of old and new.

As they approached, Baron Lif rose to greet them. He had been seated at a long table of highly polished wood.

"Welcome! Please be seated here at my right hand, good Knight. Welcome, gentlebeings. Sit wherever you like." Lif clapped his enormous hands. "Bring food! Vak for my guests!"

During the polite conversaton preceeding dinner, McCade tried, without success, to get comfortable in the oversized chair. Then a seemingly endless procession of food and drink began. All was native Lakorian fare in which meat and vegetables played equal parts, often in the form of stews and casseroles. Most of it was quite good, although a couple of dishes were hardly to McCade's taste . . . particularly the white grubs served live with hot sauce.

Throughout the meal their Lakorian-sized mugs were never empty of the alcoholic Vak. It packed a real whallop and it was soon clear the Baron intended to drink them under the table. He would have succeeded, too, if the humans hadn't anticipated such a move and taken inhibitors prior to dinner. But, in spite of that precaution, McCade's head was buzzing by the time the dishes had been cleared away and serious conversation began.

Baron Lif opened the negotiations politely. "Earlier, my friend, you indicated some concern about your ability to carry out your mission, given the natural impediments native to my planet."

"Absolutely true, Baron," McCade said somberly, slurring his words ever so slightly. "I'm afraid that even with the crawler we may not make it, or if we do, it may be too late."

"Too late?" the Baron asked with open curiosity.

"Yes," McCade answered sadly. "The Princess has been conditioned to commit suicide rather than suffer the indignity of slavery. Of course it would break the King's heart. But there's no helping it. Can't have a princess as a hostage or a slave. On top of that, without the beacon we won't even be able to find her body and give it decent burial." McCade belched, excused himself, and swayed slightly in his chair.

"Quite, quite," Lif said, nodding in agreement. "You say if she dies the beacon is extinguished also?" he asked sharply.

"It's powered by her nervous system," McCade explained blandly, waving a hand and almost knocking over a full mug of Vak.

"Yes . . . I see," the Baron replied thoughtfully. "It would appear we must act quickly."

Now you're getting the idea, McCade thought, trying to suppress the buzzing in his ears.

The Baron regarded McCade with a shrewd look. "Perhaps, my friend, we can serve each other, and in so doing accomplish much. I am going to confide something in you and your men, which if it were known, could mean my death." Lif paused dramatically, looking at each man in turn.

Both Rico and Van Doren struggled to look both serious and impressed. But since both were more than a little drunk, neither was very convincing. Fortunately the Baron was no expert on the nuances of human facial expressions and appeared satisfied.

"Your secret is safe with us," McCade said reassuringly,

barely managing to disguise an enormous belch as a cough.

"I and certain other Lakorian nobles have long sought to overthrow the King," Lif said importantly, glancing around as though the King himself might be lurking behind a tapestry.

"No!"

"Surely you jest!"

"Really? Well . . . I'm sure you must have compelling reasons."

Each of the humans sought to outdo the others with expressions of incredulity.

Apparently satisfied with the impact of his revelation, Baron Lif proceeded to document in boring detail the many transgressions and crimes for which the King should be made to pay. McCade noted with amusement that mistreatment of the commoners and slavery were not on Lif's list of complaints.

Finally having reached the end of his lengthy indictment, the nobleman said, "Now pay close attention, gentlemen, for this is where our interests meet. For years my friends and I have been unable to topple this tyrant king because we couldn't find him. The location of his castle is a closely held secret. We've tried everything to find it. Our spies never return. Atmospheric craft are shot down. In short all our attempts have been frustrated."

"Why not just assassinate him and have done with it?" Van Doren asked respectfully. "Surely he appears in public occasionally."

Lif nodded. "Believe me it's been tried, good Squire. More than once. But Zorta's bodyguard has always proved effective. And we must not only crush the man, but we must also seize his base of power."

And his money, McCade thought cynically as he took another sip of Vak.

The Baron leaned back as a satisfied smile touched his lips. "But finally the King has made a fatal mistake. He bought a poor innocent girl as a slave. Unknown to him, the girl is a princess. And hidden in her body is a beacon. A beacon which can be tracked."

Lif paused, allowing the silence to add significance to his words.

"And tracked it is. Tracked by a loyal knight bent on rescuing this fair maiden. Tracked too by the knight's loyal friend and ally, Baron Lif. Tracked to the very doorstep of the King's castle, soon to be pulled down around his very ears!"

With a roar of approval, McCade, Rico and Van Doren banged their mugs on the table and then lifted them to drink the Baron's health.

Fifteen

EACH TIME THE crawler lurched, McCade thought he was going to die. He had the worst hangover he'd ever experienced. Sitting next to him, Rico was cheerful enough as he conned the huge machine over, around and through the frequent obstacles. Outside somewhere Baron Lif rode with his troops. And if his constant chatter on the radio was any guide, the Lakorian noble was in fine fettle. McCade consoled himself by reflecting on their excellent progress. With Lif's scouts ranging far ahead and warning them of the worst hazards, their speed had picked up considerably. Meanwhile the green dot still glowed steadily on the nav screen. But it was close now and with each passing hour it grew slightly larger. McCade wondered if he'd live to get there . . . or if it really mattered. He massaged his throbbing temples and yawned. Elaborately informing Rico that a nap was in order, he headed for a bunk, unaware of Rico's knowing smile or his unsympathetic chuckle.

A full rotation later, McCade felt better. In fact he felt very much better. Not only had he fully recovered from the residual effects of too much Vak, but he found they were at least halfway to their destination. Outside the crawler, a downpour obscured the video cameras as usual, but the infrared sensors showed another kind of progress as well.

Thousands of red blobs now moved along in company with the crawler. Included were not only Baron Lif's troops, but those of many other nobles as well. Hardly an hour passed without a baron, count or duke joining their informal army. Although Lif was outranked by more than half the nobility present he had still managed to retain overall control through his special relationship with the humans, and his own political skill. Not an easy feat since many present had more experience in fighting against Zorta. McCade remembered vividly the night attack on the slave tractor. No doubt about it, there were some very tough folks out there.

Nonetheless by tactfully referring to himself as "Military Coordinator," the Baron had nudged, maneuvered, wheedled and cajoled the disparate forces into a semblance of military order. McCade couldn't help but admire Lif's organizational skill.

Rico just shook his head and said, "He'd fit right in on the Council, ol' sport. Likes ta talk, that one does."

By evening of the second day, Lif had suggested a halt to rest the troops and prepare for battle. The other nobles quickly agreed, most being unused to a full day in the saddle. They also agreed to a council of war, each seeing it as an opportunity to express his valuable opinions on strategy . . . and to get rip-roaring drunk.

As darkness fell, the nobles made their way to a large tent which had been erected near the crawler. McCade went too, with Van Doren at his side. Lif had suggested that, religious vows allowing, they dress formally. He wanted them to make an impression on the assembled nobility and McCade promised to do his best. So as McCade and Van Doren entered the tent, the huge marine was dressed in full black body armor, and was wearing every kind of weapon they could strap on him. A helmet with a mirrored visor completed the effect. He hovered by McCade's shoulder . . . the very image of death incarnate.

Lacking any uniform or other ceremonial garb, McCade

had chosen stark simplicity. From the supplies he'd put aboard the crawler, Rico produced a new set of gray leathers in McCade's size. These, combined with shiny knee-high boots, produced a military aspect. Phil had contributed a pin in the shape of a sunburst, which he normally used to fasten his kilt. It now shone brightly on McCade's chest, either a medal or a badge of rank, whichever the observer chose to make it. Trying his best to appear both aloof and confident, McCade took his place next to Baron Lif at the circular table, which almost filled the tent's interior. The table had been his own idea, solving as it did the endless problems of rank and precedence created by such a gathering. It had amused him to borrow yet another aspect of King Arthur's legendary court.

Once all the nobles were present, and the obligatory ceremonial toasts had been drunk, Baron Lif called the meeting to order.

"Thank you for your attendance, noble friends. We are gathered on the eve of a great victory. For years the tyrant Zorta has escaped his just reward and now he shall have it. Death!"

A resounding cheer went up, interspersed with, "Hear! Hear!" Once the cheering and applause had died down, Lif stood and turned toward McCade.

"With us tonight is a great warrior from a distant kingdom. His is a mission which would credit any knight, the rescue of a fair maiden."

There was another cheer and more applause, which Lif waved into silence.

"Through his efforts, we now stand at the threshold of victory. Friends, I ask you to honor Sir Sam McCade."

With a roar of approval the Lakorians stood and drank McCade's health. As they sat down they looked expectantly in McCade's direction.

McCade stood, and allowed his eyes to roam the circumference of the table while the silence built. Then when every eye was upon him he spoke. "My Lords, I greet you in the name of my liege, King Arthur. Though he dwells on a distant world, I assure you his heart and hopes are with us tonight. Though we are of different races, nobleblood flows through all our veins, and will soon merge and mingle to bathe the soil of your beautiful planet. Soon we will fight and perhaps die, side by side." Here McCade paused and allowed a smile to touch his lips. "But friends, it comforts me to know that if I fall and take that final march toward either heaven or hell, I shall do so in the very best of company!"

The applause was deafening and lasted for three or four minutes. When it finally died away, Baron Lif stood and said, "Well said, my friend. Now let us discuss our plan of attack."

For two hours Lif allowed the debate to ebb and flow. Proposals, strategies and plans of all kinds were raised, discussed and rejected by those favoring their own approaches. Throughout all of it Lif listened attentively, maintaining an uncharacteristic silence.

Meanwhile McCade had begun to wonder if Rico had dozed off or something. He was just about to send Van Doren to find out when he heard a tremendous commotion outside the tent. Shouted commands were heard, along with the screech of reptillian mounts and the clash of loose gear. All eyes were on the tent flap as it was suddenly thrown aside. With perfect timing Rico strode through the entrance with a squad of Lif's elite scouts following behind. He was dressed exactly like Van Doren and in company with the colorful Lakorians made quite a sight. Looking neither right nor left, he marched to where McCade and Lif sat. Bending down between them he whispered in their ears.

"Looked pretty impressive, didn't we, Baron? How're ya doin', sport. . . . Hope everything's goin' good. Well that oughta do it. . . . See ya later." With that Rico snapped to attention, delivered a salute worthy of the Imperial Honor Guard, did an about-face, and marched out of the tent with the scouts following behind.

His features now etched in lines of concern, Baron Lif slowly stood to address the gathering. Rico's performance had accomplished its purpose. The debate had ended and the audience had been delivered back into Baron Lif's hands.

"Friends, critical information has just come to my attention. As you know we are within a half day's march of Zorta's castle. Therefore it seemed prudent to send out scouts to locate and probe his defenses. As you have just witnessed, a squad of my elite rangers under the command of Sir Sam's squire have just returned. The intelligence they have gathered on their daring mission behind Zorta's lines is astounding."

Lif couldn't resist letting them sit and stew for a moment before taking them off the hook. "Penetrating the very heart of the area indicated by the beacon's signal, they found nothing. Ground defenses and troops . . . yes. Hundreds in fact. But where Zorta's castle should stand, where the beacon says it does stand, there is nothing."

Expressions of confusion and consternation filled the tent as everyone tried to talk at once. McCade shifted uncomfortably in his oversize chair, wishing Lif would get on with it. From the start he'd understood the value of some drama, and the necessity of some verbal sleight-of-hand, but the Baron was overdoing it.

Twelve hours before, Van Doren and two of Lif's scouts had penetrated the King's defenses in broad daylight. The big marine had found it surprisingly easy to do. In fact Amos could tell that the defenders were completely unaware of the approaching army. Having never been challenged here, Zorta's forces were more than a little sloppy. Once behind the King's lines, Van Doren had expected to run into a castle, complete with battlements, flags, weapons emplacements, the whole ball of wax. Instead he found nothing. Zero. Zilch.

Suspecting more than met the eye, Van Doren had set up and used a small but sophisticated detector pak he'd brought with him. The truth practically jumped out at him. Or up at him, as the case might be . . . since every reading on the detector indicated he was standing on top of an immense underground complex.

Van Doren and the scouts slipped back through the lines to notify McCade. McCade informed Lif, and together they had planned the evening's charade. McCade's thoughts were interurpted as Lif delivered the punch line.

"Finally, my friends, our brave lads have laid bare Zorta's secret. For years our spies and secret aircraft have searched for his castle without success. Now we know why. The beacon does not lie. Zorta's castle is before us. But not above ground as we have always assumed! No. The cowardly cur has made his home underground like the lowly animal he is. Let's bury him in it!"

When the predictable reaction had died down, the nobles were ready to listen to the plan that Lif and McCade had carefully constructed. Heaving a sigh of relief, McCade pulled out a cigar and added another source of pollution to the already foul air.

The next day dawned brightly clear. There wasn't a cloud in the sky and nothing could have been worse. They had counted on the usual downpour to cover their attack. Fighting in rain and mud was no problem for the Lakorian troops and their mounts. They were used to it. In fact they preferred it. The more superstitious of them saw the sunny day as a bad omen, causing Baron Lif to become concerned about morale. However they all agreed the attack should go on as planned. If not they would soon be discovered and annihilated by Zorta's air force. Besides, their rather unorthodox plan of attack should offer some protection.

So Rico and McCade sat, side by side, waiting for the signal to attack. Lif and Van Doren had just finished a final strategy meeting. Bit by bit, Lif had come to seek more and more advice from the marine, who was after all an expert at ground warfare.

Now Lif was with his troops attending to a few last-minute details. Van Doren was manning the crawler's missile battery, while the Treel and Phil were strapped into the waist turrets. McCade would control the bow weapons and Rico would have his hands full operating the crawler.

The speaker over McCade's head crackled to life as Baron Lif gave the uncharacteristically short order: "Go." Rico revved the crawler's powerful engines, shifted into gear, and they lurched into motion.

They traveled as they had before, turning and twisting over and around the many obstacles. For a long time there was only radio silence. Then the forward elements of Lif's force came into contact with Zorta's outer defenses. At first the King's unprepared troops fell back in total confusion. Before long however they rallied and began to put up stiff resistance. Then by prior arrangement Lif's troops backed off slightly, keeping Zorta's soldiers engaged, but minimizing casualties.

Meanwhile Lif was flooding the airwaves with bogus radio traffic that seemed to confirm a stalled assault.

Rico and McCade looked at each other and smiled.

"Well, let's give it a try, Rico."

The other man grinned, eyes twinkling. Stubby fingers stabbed a series of buttons, resulting in a loud, whining sound. The sound, plus an indicator light, were the only signs the energy projector had come into use. But McCade knew that a cone of force was being projected in front of them, and that anything it touched would be cut, pulverized, melted and spun out behind them. That's how it's designed to work, and it had better work if they were to succeed.

Rico pulled a lever and the crawler's nose dropped. As it did, the cutting beam made contact with the wet ground. A tremendous cloud of steam rose to hide the crawler from Lif's amazed troops. The huge machine began to vibrate as earth and rock were cut and pulverized to feed its mechanical maw. Gradually the vibration grew more and more intense until McCade wondered if the crawler would come apart. Beads of sweat formed on Rico's brow until they got large enough to run down his face and glisten in his beard. His bright little eyes saw only the controls before him as he fought the big machine.

Moments later they were underground. As McCade watched, the forward and side video cameras went black behind armored hatches, leaving only the stern monitor. On it McCade saw a short tunnel with glowing red walls slanting up to a bright blue sky. They were on their way to Zorta's underground refuge. McCade knew that as soon as the tunnel cooled sufficiently, a horde of Lakorian troops would enter and follow the crawler downward until it breached the walls of the underground complex. Then things would really get interesting.

But until then, success or failure rested on Rico's brawny shoulders and on the machine he fought to control. Designed for short, exploratory tunnels, the crawler was being pushed to its limits. There wasn't a thing McCade could do but hang on and pray. Pray that the plan worked, and pray that if it did Sara would still be alive when they got there. As the crawler ground its way down, the sensors began to go crazy. From all indications there was a major heat source, a high concentration of radioactivity, and massive amounts of metal, all up ahead.

Then somewhere deep in the guts of the crawler something broke with a resounding clang. Fear struck the pit of McCade's stomach. His left cheek twitched uncontrollably as he looked at Rico.

Through gritted teeth Rico said, "Port engine again . . . just couldn't take it. Same bearing."

"Can we keep going?" McCade asked as a terrible groaning noise began.

"For a while," Rico said, fighting to correct a sudden skew to the left, "until she burns up. Then we walk. Or should I say dig?" Rico grinned before turning back to his controls.

McCade fought to control the combination of fear, impatience and frustration he felt. He knew Rico was doing all that could be done. Still it was hard to just sit. Glancing up at the sensors he saw that they were much closer. "Just a little bit farther," he chanted under his breath. "Just a little bit farther."

The stern monitor showed a much longer tunnel now, with only a small circle of daylight still showing at the far end. As McCade watched, dark shapes began to obstruct the light as Lakorian troops began to pour in behind them. Then they were gone . . . obscured by clouds of steam as they sprayed water on hot spots. Pretty soon all the troops would be committed. Then, if the crawler broke down, Zorta would be able to trap Lif's entire force by putting a single section at the tunnel's entrance. They'd roll a few charges down the passageway and that would be the end of it. For months Zorta would think about the army that buried itself, and laugh.

Forcing such thoughts aside, McCade resumed his chant. "Come on, baby . . . just a little bit farther."

Acrid smoke began to seep into the control room from the engine compartment. The grinding noise was now punctuated by a regular thump, and the overall vibration had grown much worse. Next to him Rico was bathed in sweat. His eyes were locked on the sensors and his lips moved in silent prayer. They were close. Very close. Then as though in answer to their prayers they were through. The front end of the crawler dropped twenty feet with a sickening crunch that left McCade's stomach somewhere on the overhead. All the external video cams came back on, along with a host of warning buzzers and trouble lights.

McCade hit the quick release on his harness as he checked the monitors. They had broken through the durocrete walls into some kind of warehouse. Stacks of crates stretched off into the distance in orderly rows. As far as McCade could tell there wasn't anybody around at the moment. He had a feeling that this wouldn't last long.

Hitting the intercom he said, "Amos, Phil, grab Softie and let's bail out. Do your best to set up some kind of a defensive perimeter until we get some troops out of the tunnel."

"Right, boss," Van Doren's voice came back. "Tell Rico this is the worst parking job I've ever seen."

Rico grinned as he picked up an energy weapon and back-pack from behind his seat. "Typical back seat driver. Ya just can't please everybody, ol' sport."

McCade laughed with relief as he grabbed his knapsack and auto-slug thrower. "Well, let's ruin Zorta's day!"

Moments later they were outside the crawler, spreading out to take up defensive positions. Behind them the crawler loomed like a beached whale. Its bow was smashed into the warehouse floor and its stern still rested in the tunnel some thirty feet up. There would just barely be room for the Lakorian troops to squeeze by the crawler and out the tunnel. While the others set up interlocking fields of fire, McCade climbed onto some of the crates.

They had been lucky to break into an unpopulated area of the complex. But they were going to need some transportation soon. Once the leading elements of the troops left the tunnel, they would have to move quickly, before Zorta could organize his forces and respond. Otherwise they would be bottled up in the warehouse area and might never break out. From the top of the crates McCade had an excellent view of the surrounding area. It took only a moment to spot a wheeled vehicle hooked to a train of power pallets loaded with cargo. Quickly scrambling down he started to work his way through the stacks of material and toward the vehicle. Then he heard a shouted Lakorian command and the sizzle of an energy weapon. The battle had begun.

Peering around a corner McCade spotted Zorta's troops. Only a half section or so, thank God. They had taken cover behind some duct work and were under fire from Rico and the others.

Turning his attention back to the vehicle, he took a deep breath, got set, and dashed across the open space between the crates and the small tractor. He knew he was in full view of the Lakorians and expected to feel the impact of a hit any second. He reached the vehicle and ducked around to the other side, surprised they hadn't spotted him, but damned glad.

In the driver's seat he found himself facing strange controls. Fortunately the answer was absurdly simple. In place of an ignition code there was a simple "on-off" switch. Flicking the switch to "on," he tapped the accelerator experimentally and then the brake. They worked perfectly.

Glancing over his shoulder he saw that two Lakorians were down and the others weren't looking his way. No time like the present, he decided, and put his foot to the floor. It was wasted effort. The little electric motor wasn't geared for fast getaways and was woefully underpowered to boot. Very gradually the little tractor eased into motion with its loaded train of power pallets following dutifully along behind.

McCade turned the handle bars and felt the vehicle's sluggish response as it headed sedately across the open floor toward the distant protection of the crates. From his left he heard a Lakorian shout and knew he'd been spotted. Gritting his teeth and gripping the handle bars until his knuckles turned white, he continued to hold the accelerator to the floor as the tractor gradually built up speed.

The flash of an energy beam cut across in front of him, leaving a black line on the durocrete floor. Swerving left and right he did his best to ruin their aim, but there was an impact as the rearmost power pallet was cut in two. Deprived of power, the front half of the pallet fell to the floor and was dragged along with a terrible screeching sound. It cut the tractor's speed in half. His eyes desperately searched the controls until he found a pictograph of the train. He touched the last car in line and then the button with the universal "disconnect" symbol on it. To his tremendous relief he felt the surge of speed as the wreckage fell away. Seconds later he was safely hidden behind some crates and weaving in and out toward the wrecked crawler.

Rounding a final stack of boxes, he saw the leading elements of Lif's troops making their way out of the tunnel and down to the warehouse floor. Swinging in front of them, he saw the Baron and waved. Lif immediately understood the need for transportation and ordered his troops to jump aboard.

Rico, Van Doren, Phil and the Treel hopped aboard too as McCade headed the tractor up a wide ramp. Glancing in his rear view mirror he saw that Rico and Van Doren had the troops hard at work taking cargo from the center of each pallet and throwing it overboard, thereby creating a hollow space in which they could take cover. It wouldn't protect them from energy weapons, but it would provide some defense against slug throwers. The ramp continued to lead upward in a gentle curve. McCade kept expecting to run into an organized defense, but they didn't. Later he would learn that Zorta had placed most of his available troops on the upper levels of his complex, assuming Lif would try to break in from above. When they tunneled in from below, the King should have moved his troops down to meet the invaders. Unfortunately for him, Zorta refused to believe the early reports of a subterranean breakthrough, and by the time he did, it was much too late.

However not all of Zorta's troops were on the upper levels. Some were engaged in routine chores on the lower levels, and some were off duty. These were more than sufficient to cause the invaders problems and quickly did so. Listening to the garbled reports of an underground invasion that flooded his belt radio, one corporal used his head. Quickly drafting every private in sight, he used them to erect a barricade across the main ramp leading up from the lower levels. At his direction the troops used anything that was handy, including office furniture, packing crates, and a wealth of odds and ends.

As soon as it came into sight, the tractor came under fire. The corporal had placed his men well and they knew their business. All McCade could do was keep going. If they left the protection of the train there was no cover at all. If he tried to turn around, he'd expose the length of the train to raking fire. He gritted his teeth and ducked, as did Baron Lif. A second later an energy beam sliced through the tractor's cab about head high, leaving behind the smell of hot metal and burned plastic.

Meanwhile, led by Van Doren and the others, Lif's troops opened an ineffectual fire on the barricade. Their efforts were hampered by the tractor and pallets in front of them, and their aim wasn't improved any when McCade began to swerve from side to side in an attempt at evasive action.

However Rico did manage to intimidate Zorta's troops with an automatic grenade launcher he'd picked up somewhere. As he targeted a line of explosions across the top of the barricade, the defenders were forced down and back.

The Treel did his part as well, yelling "Die, Infidel," as he systematically picked off enemy troopers.

McCade held the tractor's accelerator to the floor, but as before he found he couldn't make any real speed. The tractor took its own sweet time to cover the remaining yards and finally crash into the barricade.

McCade squeezed between a huge packing crate and a filing cabinet only to find himself the target of a wicked, foot-long bayonet in the fist of a charging Lakorian regular. McCade's slug gun bucked three times, stitching big black holes across the soldier's chest and spraying gore out behind him. The alien's inertia carried him past to crash into the barricade before sliding to the floor.

Around him similar encounters were taking place as McCade jumped on top of a desk. "Take prisoners! We need prisoners!" he shouted.

His reward for exposing himself was a searing line of pain across the top of his shoulder. He spun around, searching for the source and found it. The slug gun roared twice and the impact of the huge slugs blew one side of the Lakorian's head off before spinning him around like a top.

Then, as quickly as it had begun, the battle was over.

"Over here, boss!" Van Doren shouted. "We've got a live one!"

McCade arrived to find there were four live ones. And as luck would have it, one of them was the same corporal who had ordered the defense.

"So far he's not talking, boss," Van Doren said crossly. "Shall I knock him around a little?"

"First allow me to test my powers of persuasion, good Squire." Baron Lif smoothly inserted himself between Van Doren and the corporal. "We have a saying. The wise man trades words before blows." With that he began talking to the soldier in low, urgent tones.

As the Baron interrogated the corporal, a second contingent of his troops arrived from the tunnel and formed up to advance upon command.

At a gesture from Lif, McCade moved over to join him. To McCade's surprise the corporal was smiling as he ripped Zorta's insignia from his own uniform. His three remaining subordinants were doing likewise.

"I would like to introduce you to Staff Sergeant Poka, good Knight. The sergeant and his men have decided to ally themselves with the side of freedom and justice."

And the side that's winning, McCade thought. "Welcome aboard, Sergeant," McCade said. "You and your men put up a valiant defense."

Poka inclined his head respectfully. "Thank you, sire. How may my men and I serve you?"

"First as guides, I suspect," Lif answered, looking at McCade for confirmation. "I assume that was why you called for prisoners, my friend."

"Exactly, my lord," McCade bowed slightly. "I suggest you and your men strike out for Zorta's quarters under the sergeant's guidance. Once Zorta is in your hands, his troops will cave in rather quickly, I think. Meanwhile, if one of the sergeant's men could be spared, we will search for the Princess."

"Of course, good Knight, it shall be as you say." The Baron regarded McCade silently for a moment before speaking again. "You and your men have forged links of friendship not easily broken, my friend."

Lif was saying good-bye. Somehow he knew McCade didn't intend to be around for the victory celebration—or defeat—whichever might occur. As he gripped the Baron's hand, McCade saw genuine regret in the Lakorian's eyes. To his own surprise he realized he too felt regret. Lif was a crafty bastard, but a good bastard all the same.

Sergeant Poka detailed a Private Ven as McCade's guide. Ven was undersized, by Lakorian standards, and had a shifty look about him. McCade had a hunch their new guide would be about as dependable as a Linthian Rath snake during the mating season. With that in mind, he called Phil over.

"Phil, I'd like you to meet Private Ven. He's going to take us to the slave quarters, aren't you, Ven?"

The Lakorian nodded eagerly, eyes shifting nervously back and forth between the human and the Variant.

"Make sure that nothing happens to Ven, Phil," said McCade meaningfully.

"Gotcha, Sam," Phil replied with a grin that revealed rows of durasteel teeth. "Ven and I are going to be real close friends, aren't we, Ven?"

The Lakorian didn't reply, seemingly unable to tear his

eyes away from those gleaming teeth.

Lif's troops meanwhile had begun their advance up the ramp in search of King Zorta.

After a short huddle with Ven, Phil said, "According to my good buddy here, the slave quarters are directly above us. Evidently the lower levels of the complex are considered the least desirable. We broke in on the lowest or utility level. Above us are the slave quarters, kitchens and mess hall. The troops are quartered on the level above that, and then comes a floor dedicated to Zorta's private quarters and guest suites. The very topmost level is all for defense and features an air strip and a small spaceport."

He looked at McCade with a raised eyebrow. McCade nodded his understanding. It was something they had to think about. With the tractor gone and their crawler out of action, they needed a way out. If they could find Sara and then reach the top level, maybe they could steal a plane. Time would tell.

"All right, let's get moving," McCade said, reloading his slug gun. He'd lost the auto-slug thrower somewhere, but decided not to look for it.

Using an electronic key, Ven opened one of the hatches spaced at regular intervals along the ramp's wall. Once open, the hatch revealed a vertical ladder, evidently provided for maintenance purposes. Without hesitation Ven started climbing upward and Phil followed. McCade was next. As he climbed, he found the spacing of the rungs more suited to shorter Lakorian legs than his own. Below him Rico, Van Doren and the Treel followed. Cold air blew down against his face. Evidently the shaft also served as part of the air conditioning system. By the time they reached the next landing, McCade was out of breath and damned cold to boot. With Phil and Ven, he waited on the landing, catching his breath as Rico, Van Doren and the Treel climbed up to join them.

Ven opened another hatch and peeked out. A moment later he slipped through the opening, motioning to the rest to follow. They emerged into a side corridor which was, for the moment, empty. As they followed Ven down the hallway, McCade could hear the distant sounds of an alarm gong and fighting. Lif's forces had evidently made contact with Zorta's troops.

"Stop!"

The order came from behind them and was answered with a bolt from Van Doren's energy weapon. A soldier wearing half a cook's outfit and half a uniform crumpled to the floor, his weapon falling from dead fingers. They were off and running after that. Ven led them from one corridor to the next with remarkable speed. Of course the fact that Phil was right behind him probably helped.

As they ran they traded occasional shots with barely glimpsed troops who also seemed to be running somewhere. But they managed to avoid prolonged firefights. Until Ven whipped around one corner too many without looking first. They rounded the corner and ran full tilt into a whole section of Lakorian troops. Fortunately the soldiers were facing the other way with their weapons trained on a large steel door. In a flash McCade guessed why. The slaves were taking advantage of Lif's attack and were trying to escape. The searing white light of the energy beam cutting its way around the lock from the other side confirmed his guess.

Unfortunately Ven's inertia proved to be so great he was unable to stop and crashed full speed into the rearmost trooper, who took several others down with him as he fell. Taking advantage of the confusion thus created, McCade and the others hit the deck and opened fire. Caught between hostile fire and a steel door, it didn't take the noncoms long to decide that discretion was indeed the better part of valor and try for a hasty retreat down a side corridor. Their orderly withdrawal was turned into a rout when Rico brought his grenade launcher into play.

Approaching the steel door, McCade felt a wave of heat and smelled a mixture of smoke and Lakorian body odor. He noticed that the cutting beam had almost circled the lock. He stepped back and went to kneel beside Ven's body. At McCade's touch the Lakorian's eyes flew open and flitted about, shrewdly evaluating the situation. Satisfied the danger had past, Ven quickly regained his feet, evidently untouched, and confirming McCade's estimate of the Lakorian's potential for duplicity.

"Well, sire," Ven said blandly as he dusted hinself off, "I guess we showed them!"

With a loud clang, a six-inch thick circular slab of metal hit the floor. Slowly, against the resistance of its normal mechanical system, the huge door was rolled aside to reveal a mob of angry slaves. They were waving weapons of all kinds, from chair legs to captured energy weapons. As the door slid out of the way, they charged, and then jerked to a sudden halt at a sign from their helmeted leader.

The leader took two paces forward before lifting the helmet's visor. "Well, Sam," Sara said, "what took you so long?"

Sixteen

THEN SHE WAS in his arms, covering his face with kisses, laughing and crying at the same time. She filled not only his arms, but his heart and mind as well. For the first time in years, he felt really happy, and he didn't want to let go of either Sara or the feeling.

Nonetheless Rico managed to get his attention with a none too discreet cough. "Turn 'er loose there, sport, and give someone else a shot. Always hoggin' all the pretty women."

"Rico!" With a shout of glee Sara was lifted and spun around like a little girl. Laughing, she said, "Put me down, Rico! This is no way for Council members to act. It's not dignified."

"Not dignified, huh," Rico said as he put her on her feet. "How about that outfit. Since when did Council members go around wearin' nothin' but two scraps o' cloth and a helmet?"

Looking down, Sara blushed. McCade saw that Rico was right. Sara had made her escape in a wispy two-piece costume that left very little to the imagination.

"Well I like it," McCade said.

Sara made a face and turned to Van Doren. "Well Amos, at least you're always nice to me." Standing on tiptoe she kissed him on the cheek. Much to McCade's amusement, the big marine turned bright red with embarrassment and didn't say a word.

Then Sara caught sight of Mungo and stepped back, bringing up her energy weapon.

Moving quickly to her side McCade said, "No Sara, it's not Mungo. It's the Treel again. For the moment, he's on our side. Believe me it's a long story."

"The rigid one speaks truly," the Treel said. "We are fellow warriors in the service of the great Yareel! Death to the infidels!"

"Like I said, it's a long story," McCade said, seeing her amazement.

"And time is what we don't have, Sam," Phil interjected. "Those troopers will probably be back with friends for company."

"I'm sorry," McCade said. "Sara, meet Phil. By the way, he's now one of your constituents."

If Sara was surprised by Phil's appearance, she gave no sign of it.

"I'm pleased to meet you, Phil," she said.

McCade watched in astonishment as the big Variant bowed gracefully to gently kiss her hand. "The pleasure is all mine, beautiful lady."

Turning to McCade, Sara said, "Is he always like this?"

"No, thank God," McCade replied with a smile. "He hasn't tried to kiss any of us. Anyway he's right about getting out of here. Say good-bye to your friends over there and let's get going."

"Good-bye?" she said. "I can't just leave them here. They followed me. What if some of Zorta's troops come back? They wouldn't have a chance. No," she said firmly, "they'll just have to come along." Her face was set and determined. McCade had seen that expression before and knew trying to change her mind would be a waste of time.

For their part, the slaves stood patiently awaiting Sara's orders. There were about thirty of them representing perhaps a dozen races. As far as McCade could tell, they were all females, which made sense. No doubt Zorta kept his male and female slaves separated.

"All right," he said. "Tell them to follow us. Ven, what's the fastest and safest way to reach the air strip?"

After a moment's hesitation, the Lakorian replied, "There is a way, sire. It won't be comfortable, but I believe it will be safe."

As he followed Ven down the corridor, McCade had complete confidence in the alien's choice. After all, his greenish hide was on the line too. They turned into a hallway lined with metal carts.

"These are food and laundry carts, Sire," Ven explained. "They are sent from one level to another in these vertical conveyor shafts."

By way of demonstration he lifted a sliding door to reveal a shaft only slightly larger than the carts. Inset in the wall of the shaft were endless belts mounting metal arms climbing up and out of sight in eternal progression. Grabbing a nearby cart, Ven shoved it through the open door and into the shaft. It was smoothly engaged by the next set of rising metal arms and lifted out of sight.

Turning back to McCade, Ven said, "Your opinion, sire?"

"You were right, Sergeant. It isn't going to be comfortable, but it looks like a good idea."

McCade would have sworn Ven looked pleased in a sly sort of way.

Quickly they organized the rest. McCade, Phil, Sara and Ven would go first, then the slaves, followed by Rico, Van Doren and the Treel. Ven opened a small access panel and set the controls for the uppermost level.

Climbing onto the top of the cart, McCade felt awkward and damned silly as Ven pushed it into the shaft. Rico's huge grin confirmed his suspicions. The metal arms engaged the cart with a slight jerk and he started smoothly upward. It wasn't too bad for him, but it would be a tight fit for Rico and Phil. As the cart moved upward and past the next two levels, McCade heard the sounds of battle, but they were faint and some distance away. But as the cart approached the next level, the one which housed Zorta himself, the sounds grew louder. Much louder. Craning his neck to look up, McCade saw why.

The next access door up was open. Light, smoke and noise

flooded through to fill the shaft. Pulling his slug gun, McCade inched around to face the door. Seconds later, as his cart drew level with the open door, McCade had an excellent view of the battle raging in the corridor outside. Almost in front of the door a brightly garbed Lakorian officer wrestled with two of Zorta's bodyguards. It took McCade a second to realize the officer was Lif, and another to shoot one of his adversaries in the leg. Then they were gone as the cart carried him up and away.

Bracing himself McCade got ready for the next and last level. As the cart reached it, automatic machinery opened the door, ejecting both McCade and the cart. Together they rolled out of the shaft and into a milling mass of Zorta's troops. Surprise was all that saved him. The slug gun roared five times and five troopers fell. Leaping off the cart he landed in a forward roll. Behind him the cart was melted to slag as a dozen energy weapons were brought to bear on it.

McCade pulled the trigger three more times and two more died. Now it was his turn. His gun was empty and there was nowhere to run. Then he was blind-sided by a huge noncom wielding a wrench. He went down hard and stayed down. He was conscious, but just barely, and no matter how he tried, his body just wouldn't get up. Nonetheless he could watch what went on in a distant sort of way. Just as the troopers began to move his way with every intention of finishing him off, Phil emerged from the shaft.

He didn't have the advantage of surprise, and as it turned out he didn't need it. Had Zorta's troops nailed Phil as he emerged from the shaft, they would have won. Instead part of their attention was still on McCade and their first shots went wild. They didn't get a second chance. McCade had never seen anything like it. Phil had gone into full augmentation.

Implants fed chemicals into his brain, nervous system and muscles. His response time was amplified. His strength doubled and then tripled. His movements became a blur of continuous motion. Without hesitation, Phil moved in among the Lakorian troops. His motions became dancelike as he whirled, leaped and executed the intricate movements of death. Around him Zorta's soldiers died by the dozen, cut down not only by Phil's weapons, teeth and claws, but by their own comrades as they fired in panic trying to hit the augmented Variant.

Sara and Ven emerged from the shaft, adding their fire to Phil's efforts. As the shaft ejected the slaves, they fell to the floor and took advantage of the shelter the carts provided. By the time Rico, Van Doren and the Treel arrived, the fight was over. The few remaining soldiers had fled, leaving behind a scene of unbelievable carnage.

As Van Doren helped McCade to his feet, Rico surveyed the damage and said, "Wait till ol' Larkin gets a load o' this one! Phil's a one-man army!" Shaking his head with amazement, Rico went over to help the shaggy Variant patch up the wounded.

The motion involved in standing up had sent waves of pain pounding through McCade's head. Reaching up to touch its source, his fingers encountered a growing goose egg and came away red with his own blood. He obeyed Van Doren's command to sit down on a piece of broken cart, and Sara's gentle hands cleaned and closed the cut, using the contents of his own first aid kit. She also cleaned and disinfected the shallow wound across his shoulders. The disinfectant stung. Finally she hit him in the arm with a styrette. Moments later he felt the drug spreading through his system, pushing back the pain.

Sara nodded knowingly. "It feels good now, Sam, but you're going to pay the price later on, when it wears off."

"Thanks," he said, allowing her to help him up. "With any luck at all we'll be well clear of here by then."

He reloaded the slug gun while glancing around. They were standing in the middle of a large aircraft maintenance area. Aircraft in various stages of repair were parked in a series of bays filled with tools and test equipment. Beyond them other aircraft were visible, in a line stretching off into the distance. Hopefully some of those would be operational.

"All right," McCade yelled. "Let's go." With that he started jogging toward the distant planes. Surprisingly he felt no pain, just a feeling of elation, which he knew was too good to be true. As he cleared the maintenance area, the view opened up to reveal something just beyond the farthest planes. Something familiar but impossible. His heart leaped and he broke into a full run, afraid his eyes had deceived him. They hadn't. *Pegasus* sat on a small pad, wisps of vapor curling up and around her warm tubes, a patch of blue sky visible overhead where a section of roof had been slid back. Then he noticed the ground crew. They were lounging around, apparently waiting for something or someone. Zorta. It had to be. He'd left himself a back door in the form of *Pegasus*. McCade ran even faster. Maybe he could slam that door, get his ship back and clear the planet all at the same time. A cry went up behind him as the others saw his intention and raced across the hangar toward the slender shape of the spacecraft.

"Spread out!" Van Doren shouted. "Spread out or you'll be cut down with a single beam!" Slowly they separated into a line abreast as they continued their charge.

On his right, Sara uttered a most unladylike war cry as her long white legs carried her toward the enemy. The scar across her face was a white slash and in her brief costume she looked like an avenging goddess of war. To McCade's left Phil loped along in huge, ground-eating strides, his rows of gleaming teeth making the weapon in his hands seem redundant.

McCade felt happy, even joyous, and completely without fear. A part of his mind told him to be careful, that the drugs were affecting his judgment. Another part of his mind replied, "Who cares?" Then they were within range. Energy beams rippled and flashed incandescent while slug throwers boomed out a staccato challenge. Two of the charging slaves fell, hit by an automatic weapon. Farther down the line another was burned in half by an energy beam, her severed legs still moving, pumping, until her lower torso toppled and fell.

Whether it was the returned fire, or the sight of the oncoming and apparently suicidal mob, McCade couldn't tell, but abruptly the ground crew folded and ran, leaving behind three or four unfortunate comrades.

Yelling to get Van Doren's attention, McCade said, "Throw a perimeter around her, Amos. I'm going aboard to check her out!"

"Right, boss!" Van Doren acknowledged with a wave of his hand.

As McCade headed toward the ship, the marine was already barking commands to the ex-slaves, all of whom were now armed with weapons taken from Zorta's troops.

As McCade entered the ship, Sara was right behind him. The first thing he noticed was the smell. The ship reeked of Lakorian body odor. The next thing he noticed was dozens of boxes of clothing and supplies Zorta had had put aboard just in case. They filled the tiny cabins and spilled out into the main corridor. The King certainly didn't travel light. The lounge contained more than just luggage. It had been transformed into a throne room, complete with a gilded, Lakorian-sized acceleration couch. Above it, Zorta had mounted a full-sized 3-D likeness of himself. Like most official portraits, it looked anything but natural. Zorta stood in a stylized pose, noble head lifted, eyes apparently focused on something not quite visible to mere mortals. McCade decided the King was definitely on the homely side, as Lakorians go.

Turning to Sara he said, "It appears Zorta has no intention of staying to share his well-deserved defeat with his loving subjects. I don't think that's very sporting, do you?"

"You're absolutely right, Sam. They just don't make Kings like they used to. I think we should help him meet his royal obligations, don't you? Of course Commander Reez will be disappointed . . . but that's life!"

"Disappointed?" McCade asked, suddenly serious. "Why will Reez be disappointed? For that matter, why is he still around? I assumed he would be on the War World by now, raising the Il Ronnian flag or something?"

Sara shook her head. "So did I. But while I was waiting for my turn to entertain some of Zorta's human guests"—She made an expression of distaste—"I kept my eyes and ears open. The grapevine around here is incredible. Since slaves never leave alive, everyone talks freely in front of them. Anyway it didn't take long to find out that Reez had been in and out of here for a long time. In fact he and Zorta have a deal. In return for various kinds of technology, Zorta agreed to loan Reez some troops. That's how Zorta wound up with *Pegasus*. Reez gave it to him as a present to seal the agreement."

McCade's heart went out to her as her face reflected briefly the fear and uncertainty she had felt, though there was no hint of either in her voice or words.

As though reading his mind she said, "I'm okay, Sam . . . thanks to you and the others."

"What I can't figure out is why," McCade said thoughtfully. "Reez has troops of his own."

Sara nodded. "Yes, but not enough to hold the War World if it comes to a fight. All he's got is the contingent aboard his ship. He's way too far from home to use a combeam, and he's afraid to go there for more troops because the Empire might discover the War World while he's gone. After all, he knows if we're looking, then there's probably plenty of others looking too. So he plans to land Lakorian troops to hold the War World until he can bring in more Il Ronnians. Plus if there's a fight, it's Lakorians who will die." She paused for a moment and then continued. "I think that's the real factor." Her lips curled derisively. "Because it reduces the potential magnitude of Reez's failure should things to wrong. He's acting on his own, after all . . . something Il Ronnians aren't noted for . . . and the defeat of his troops in an unauthorized conflict could end his career."

McCade frowned thoughtfully. He knew Sara was right. As far as the Empire's social scientists could learn, the Il Ronn operated from consensus, a fact which many felt had allowed the human empire to grow at a faster rate, thus making it possible for them to catch up with the more advanced Il Ronn. By nature humans were much more independent and willing to take risks.

"Zorta was going to meet Reez?" he asked.

Sara smiled. "Reez tricked him into heading up the expedition to the War World. They are to meet in orbit today. Zorta's troops lifted off yesterday."

That would account for Lif's relatively easy victory, McCade mused, for there was little doubt in his mind that Lif was winning, With a large contingent of Zorta's troops up in orbit, they had encountered lighter resistance . . . and that had made the difference.

McCade's eyes were drawn once more to Zorta's portrait. Suddenly he had an idea. It was beautiful! He started laughing and grabbed Sara, picking her up and planting a kiss on her lips. Looking up at him with curious eyes, she laughed too, and asked, "What are we laughing about?"

"That would be telling." He chortled. "Go get Phil and Softie. Tell them we've got an idea they'll like."

She made a face at him, but left as he started rummaging through Zorta's luggage. Before long he had assembled an outfit quite similar to the one the Lakorian king had worn for his official portrait. Picking up the rest of the luggage in the room, he crammed it into a storage compartment and managed to close the hatch.

Sara arrived with a curious Phil and indifferent Treel in tow.

"What's up, Sam?" Phil asked, looking around the lounge, his eyes coming to rest on the golden throne. "Kind of gaudy, isn't it, Sam? Frankly I thought you'd have better taste."

"It's Zorta's taste, not mine, I assure you," McCade laughed. Quickly he filled the Variant and alien in on what Sara had found out.

"So," he concluded, "since Reez is expecting Zorta this morning, I thought we should oblige." He looked up at the portrait and then over to the Treel. "If you get my drift."

Phil burst out laughing, along with Sara.

The Treel looked thoughtful for a momet and then said, "Actually not a bad plan, rigid one. In the guise of Zorta I could gain entry to the Il Ronnian ship, and then devise the means to eradicate those who offend the eyes of Yareel." His eyes took on a dreamy, wishful look. "Unfortunately, however, I am limited to my present form by the device implanted behind my ear." He reached up to touch it.

"That's where Phil comes in, I hope," McCade replied. "How about it, Phil? You said you might be able to remove the chemlock."

"Yeah, with the proper facilities, I said," the Variant answered, glancing around. "And frankly this isn't what I had in mind. How good is the sick bay on this space-going bordello anyway?"

"Now you watch your mouth," McCade grinned appreciatively. "With the exception of the throne, this is my bordello you're talking about, and my sick bay is pretty good."

"Okay, let's have a look," Phil replied. "Just remember two things. First I've got to disarm the chemlock's explosive device. If I screw it up you won't be able to find enough of me or Softie to say prayers over, plus you won't be going anywhere in what's left of this ship. Secondly we're gonna have to work fast. In an hour or two at the most, I'm gonna fall apart for a while. It's the price I pay for using full augmentation. It really burns up energy and afterward I come down hard. So if we're gonna do it, we'd better hurry up."

McCade nodded his agreement, wishing they could delay the operation and do it in space. But with Phil about to crash, and the need to show Zorta to the Il Ronn after lift-off, there didn't seem to be much choice. So he led them to the galley.

Through clever design the galley was easily converted to a small but efficient surgical suite. Phil pronounced it adequate and hurried to prepare the Treel. Over McCade's objections, Sara insisted on acting as Phil's assistant.

"It's got to be done, Sam, and I'm the best one to do it." Her mouth was set in a hard, determined line. "Besides," she added, "if the real Zorta shows up, they're going to need you outside."

Accepting the inevitable, McCade went back through the main entry port to confer with Van Doren and Rico.

The two humans had organized the former slaves into a respectable defensive zone around the ship. Lighting a cigar with careful movements, McCade could feel the medication starting to lose its effect. Like Phil, before long he wasn't going to be worth much.

"How 'bout the ship's guns, ol' sport?" Rico asked after McCade had explained his plan. "If Zorta shows up with some of his troops we may need somethin' a little heavier than pop guns."

McCade agreed and it wasn't long before he was glad he had provided weapons all around. They heard the engines first.

The roaring noise was magnified by the walls of the hangar. The noise was soon followed by a flying column of armored vehicles which were headed directly for the spacecraft. As soon as they came into range, Rico opened up with the ship's guns, immediately blowing two of the ground cars to bits.

Their advantage didn't last long. Someone in Zorta's command had some brains and knew how to use them. Maybe even Zorta himself. In any case the vehicles picked up speed and quickly closed, with *Pegasus*, sweeping around the ship to encircle it before screeching to a halt. When they stopped they were so close to Van Doren's defenses that Rico couldn't fire without hitting the defenders as well as the enemy.

Piling out and using their vehicles for cover, Zorta's troops opened fire. McCade noticed they were careful not to hit *Pegasus*. Zorta clearly didn't want to lose his way out. Van Doren took advantage of this fact by deploying his forces so that the ship was directly behind most of them, thereby increasing the odds of Zorta's troops hitting the spacecraft. As a result the column of incoming fire dropped off dramatically. Zorta's soldiers were ordered to take careful aim before each shot.

Not so constrained, McCade and Van Doren urged the former slaves to pour it on. They did so without hesitation. Knowing Zorta was out there somewhere, each hoped it would be her energy bolt or slug that cut him down.

McCade chose his targets with methodical care. Aim, squeeze off two shots, and then aim again. After nine shots reload. He felt a touch on his shoulder and turned to find Sara crouched by his side. There were tiny lines around her eyes, hinting at the strain she'd been under.

"Phil's done, Sam. You've got to see it to believe it. He did an incredible job."

McCade bent low, using what cover there was, and followed her to the main entry port. Once inside they made their way to the lounge. As he entered McCade found himself face to face with a perfect likeness of King Zorta. Even though he'd seen the Treel's abilities demonstrated before, it was still astonishing. The Treel was sitting right below the Lakorian king's portrait and the likeness was exact. Phil had collapsed in the throne and was snoring softly.

"We're working on his speech," Sara said, indicating the Treel. "We found some recordings in his luggage of various speeches Zorta's given and our friend here will pattern on those."

"I assure you, rigid ones, given my enormous intellectual capacity, it will be child's play. Then I shall storm the very heart of the infidel stronghold!" the Treel said fervently in what McCade assumed was Zorta's voice.

"Good idea," McCade replied dryly. "However there's one little chore we'd like you to do first."

"You have been fair, rigid one," the Treel intoned gravely. "Ask me not to spare the infidels. All else within my power shall be yours."

"I'll not ask you to spare them," McCade said with equal seriousness. "Only to delay slightly that moment when the great Yareel shall cleanse them from this existence."

"Granted, rigid one," the Treel said. "Continue."

Turning to Sara, McCade said, "Tell Van Doren and Rico

to pull back into the ship. We're about to lift."

When she made no move to go he said, "The slaves too, of course. In fact they are an important part of the plan."

Sara smiled and disappeared into the corridor.

"Now," McCade continued, turning back to the Treel. "Here's the plan. We'll send three or four of the Lakorian slaves along with you, ostensibly as part of your harem. They'll be of considerable assistance when push comes to shove." And they'll have instructions to kill you if you make one wrong move, he thought to himself. Each would be equipped with an overdose of the substance obtained from the chemlock Phil had removed.

The Treel nodded.

"Once you're aboard Reez's ship, just sit back and relax," McCade continued. "Reez will head for the War World to off-load you and your troops. We'll follow. Once there, we'll have the coordinates."

"And then, rigid one? What would you have me do then?" the Treel asked.

McCade shrugged. "I guess that's up to you. But I suggest you insist on taking personal command of your troops. Reez will agree. I doubt he wants Zorta along when he goes home to collect his 'attaboys.' Once he's gone we'll whistle up some Imperial assistance, they'll return Zorta's troops to Lakor, and you'll probably be knighted. End of story."

"That sounds most satisfactory," the Treel replied, much to McCade's surprise. "It's a good plan, rigid one. I am sure it will work."

So am I, McCade thought as he found a half-smoked cigar and lit it. Then why am I so damned worried? he wondered.

Seventeen

McCADE WATCHED THE main entry port monitor as the last former slave dashed aboard and Van Doren closed the hatch behind her. Outside, a hail of slugs hammered the hull as energy beams probed and searched for a way in. Zorta had changed tactics. Seeing they were about to lift, he no longer cared if his troops hit the ship, and they were doing so with a vengeance.

McCade wasn't too worried, since the hand weapons they were using wouldn't even scratch the ship's paint job. Of course there was always the possibility of cumulative damage or of Zorta bringing up heavier weapons. With that in mind he opened the intercom and said, "Okay, let's hose 'em down, Rico. Try to move them back out of the blast area while you're at it. Otherwise they'll get cooked as we lift off."

"Nothin' to it, ol' sport." Rico sounded cheerful as he opened up with the ship's guns.

As the spacecraft's heavy weapons traversed the area, Zorta and his troops quickly pulled back. Once they were out of the way, Rico did his best not to hit them. Lif's troops would be along soon to mop them up. McCade smiled to himself as he imagined the meeting between the Baron and his former king. It would have been a pleasure to see.

"Sam! Look!"

Beside him Sara pointed at the bow screen which moments before had shown only sky. Now the blue rectangle was growing steadily smaller as powerful motors worked to close the camouflaged roof. Zorta hadn't given up. Within minutes they would be trapped under the roof and unable to lift off.

McCade's voice boomed throughout the ship as he shouted, "Stand by for emergency lift!" Turning to Sara he said grimly, "Let's hope everybody's strapped in. This is going to be rough."

Quickly running through the pre-flight checks, he noticed that Zorta's techs had given the ship a complete overhaul. How considerate, he thought as he reached up, grabbed the red knob, turned it to the right, and pushed. The ship shook as the engines built thrust, spewing flame and heat out in all directions. The vehicles left behind by Zorta and his troops exploded from the heat, throwing out a curtain of red hot shrapnel that clattered against the hull.

Straining against the acceleration, McCade released the ship's defenses from manual to automatic as a familiar female voice flooded the control room. "This ship is under attack by an unknown number of atmospheric craft. Please stand by for high-speed evasive action and high G forces. Due to the time elapsed under manual control, it is impossible to guarantee your safety. Although defensive missiles have been launched, this computer and the ship's manufacturer disclaim all responsibility for any subsequent damages to this spacecraft, its passengers, or contents, consistent with Article 47, subsection eight, paragraph three of Imperial Insurance Regulations."

McCade watched as the atmospheric fighters were snuffed out one after another. They were no match for the heavier armament of the spacecraft. They tumbled out of the sky in ones and twos, leaving dark smears of smoke against the blue sky to mark where they went down. As the ship's computer added even more acceleration, McCade felt himself pushed down into a wall of pain. The medication had completely worn off and his head felt as though it might explode. As the pain smashed into him, McCade searched for and found the welcoming darkness.

When he awoke it was to the realization that the pain was gone. Cautiously he moved this way and that, searching for the pain, and couldn't find it. With that in mind it seemed worthwhile opening his eyes. To his surprise McCade found himself stretched out on his bunk in the master stateroom. They must have moved him down from the control room after he'd passed out. Concern flooded his mind. The fighters . . . and Reez in orbit above them. What was going on?

With an effort he managed to sit up and swing his feet over the side of the berth. With the exception of a narrow path, pieces of Zorta's luggage still covered the deck. Using the bulkheads and boxes for support, he made his way into the lounge and collapsed into a seat. He still felt a bit weak. Sara and Van Doren were there and·looked up with surprise.

"Hey, boss, what are you doing up and around?" Van Doren asked with obvious concern.

"Trying to kill himself, that's what," Sara said, moving over to sit next to him.

"You two worry too much," McCade replied, patting his pockets for a cigar. "I laugh at pain. I'm bulletproof and will live a million years. What happened to the fighters anyway?"

"Long gone," Sara replied. "A few seconds after you passed out, we cleared the atmosphere."

"And now we're on our way to the War World, we hope," Van Doren added sourly. "Although you couldn't prove it by me. Reez is probably sucking us into some kind of trap." His big fingers tapped out a nervous rhythm on the seat beside him.

Sara shrugged. "Anything's possible, I guess. But personally I doubt it. I think Reez bought the whole thing. And why not? It all went just like he expected it to. We met him in orbit, instead of one of *us*, he saw Ven on the com screen, we matched velocities and locks, King Zorta went aboard with slaves, assured Reez that his troops were winning on the ground, and made one request."

"Which was?" McCade asked.

"That his yacht not be taken aboard," Sara replied. "Zorta insisted that his crew be allowed to follow on their own as a training exercise. At least that's what he was supposed to say." She shrugged. "It must have worked, because here we are."

"Yeah," Van Doren said. "Here we are, wherever that is."

"O ye of little faith," Rico said, squeezing his bulk into the crowded lounge. "Good ta see ta up and around. How ya feelin'?"

"Great," McCade lied with a smile.

"Well that's good," Rico replied, "'cause I got a feelin' things are about to get interestin' again. We just had a com call from some Il Ronnian sub-sept commander. He fed the computer coordinates for a hyperspace shift. Told Ven it's comin' up in about ten minutes." With a wave of a hairy hand he disappeared in the direction of the control room.

Rico was at least partly right. About ten minutes later McCade felt the slight nausea and momentary confusion characteristic of a hyperspace shift. But he was wrong about things getting interesting. Instead they got very boring. Two standard days passed without anything further happening to break the monotony. That, plus the fact that *Pegasus* was severely overcrowded, quickly began to wear on them.

Besides McCade, Sara, Van Doren, Rico and Phil, the little ship was also carrying Ven and about fifteen former slaves. Each dealt with the boredom and overcrowding in his or her own way. McCade slept and ate the first day away. Rico prowled the ship searching for routine maintenance chores to do. Van Doren exercised the ship's weapons, offering classes in gunnery. Some of the former slaves took him up on it. Meanwhile Phil just spent his time asleep, waking only briefly for meals and a little conversation before dozing off again.

At first Sara stayed busy organizing shifts for meals, sleep and exercise. But before long, things pretty well ran themselves. So for something to do she began an inventory of Zorta's considerable luggage. Although the Treel had taken a few changes of clothing along to the Il Ronnian battleship, he'd chosen to leave most of Zorta's belongings behind. Among them Sara discovered a suitcase full of computer tapes on Lakorian governmental affairs. She began scanning them, and before long was immersed in the endless detail of planetary affairs.

Toward the end of the second day, McCade felt both better and worse at the same time. Physically he was much better.

The combination of rest and medical treatment had done wonders. But emotionally he was tense and edgy, wishing desperately for something to do and unable to find it. Everyone else had found something to keep them occupied and had somehow disappeared inside it. For a while he tried reading, then holo games, and finally took to prowling the ship in search of somebody to talk to. But nobody wanted to talk. So, in deference to the already overloaded air scrubbers, he was sitting in the lounge chewing on an unlit cigar and fuming when Rico's voice came over the intercom.

"Well, folks, Ven just heard from our pointy-tailed friends and you'll be glad ta know we're comin' outta hyperspace in a few minutes . . . unless o' course you'd like to extend this luxury cruise."

Rico didn't need the intercom to hear the jeers and howls of outrage that followed. Grinning, he poked the intercom button again and said, "Sam, ol' sport, I think we could use ya here in the control room."

Happy to have something to do, McCade made his way to the control room. "What's up?"

"I ain't sure. But from the way they phrased it, I think Reez is plannin' ta cut it real close. First they told Ven ta prepare for a shift and fed us the coordinates. But here's the interestin' part. They also specified the orbit they want us to park in."

"So maybe we're going to come out right on top of the War World," McCade mused. "Reez is probably in a hurry to dump Zorta's troops and then run for reinforcements."

"Seems like it," Rico said, his tiny eyes twinkling. "And all we gotta do is sit back and wish him bon voyage."

"That's right," McCade replied with a grin. That's right, *I hope,* he thought to himself. For some reason he couldn't shake the feeling that it wouldn't be quite that simple. A few minutes later and they emerged from the hyperspace shift.

McCade watched with intense curiosity as the screen cleared. Where the computer had projected the War World as a featureless globe, lacking sufficient data to do anything else, the real thing now hung before them.

It was smaller than most planets yet larger than most moons. The scattered clouds covering it testified to an atmosphere. Bodies of blue water were visible but, unlike anything he had seen before, they were strangely geometrical, each forming a perfect circle of uniform size. There was green vegetation too. But it also had an unnatural appearance. It covered the worldlet in alternating squares, making it look like a checkered ball. The areas not covered by either water or vegetation were metallic gray. The gray squares displayed various textures, suggesting surface structures of some kind, but with one exception were too far away to identify. The exception was clearly visible due to its vast size. It was a spaceport. A huge spaceport, large enough to ground a fleet. And right in the middle of it McCade saw something that shouldn't have been there. Frowning in disbelief he punched the forward screens to high mag and then sat back in his seat as it became apparent that he'd been right. There she sat, looking foreign among the gantries and support equipment left by the long-dead race. An Imperial destroyer.

"What the hell?" McCade said in amazement. "How did they get here?"

"That ain't all, ol' sport," Rico said, pointing a stubby finger at the second screen. "Take a look at that."

As he spoke another ship emerged from behind the far side of the globe and orbited into full view. There was no mistaking her lines. An Imperial Class A Freighter. As they watched, a shuttle detached itself from the huge ship and started down toward the surface. Whether it departed in reaction to the arrival of the Il Ronnian battleship, or was simply unaware of it, McCade couldn't tell. It didn't get far. The little ship exploded and literally disappeared as the Il Ronnian warship opened fire.

"They didn't have a chance! That bastard!" McCade pounded his fist on the arm of his chair. As he spoke the freighter herself came under fire. Her defensive screens came up and flared through all the colors of the rainbow as the incoming fire grew more intense. Though the freighter had no offensive armament to speak of, it did have plenty of defensive capability and lots of power. Most of that power was now going to the defensive screens and, for the moment, they were holding. But McCade knew that in the long run the Il Ronnian battlewagon would beat the screens down and win.

He glanced at the first screen just in time to see a missile hit the grounded destroyer. It still seemed mostly intact, but now had a noticeable list to starboard. There wouldn't be much help from that quarter.

"I guess it's up to us," McCade said grimly as he reached for his harness and began to strap himself in. "Rico, tell 'em to stand by for combat and evasive action." As he reached over to activate the ship's weapons systems, he felt an iron grip on his wrist.

"Whoa ol' sport . . . not so fast," Rico said, his eyes serious. "This play-pretty ain't no match for a ship o' the line."

"Goddamnit, Rico, let go," McCade said, trying to pull his arm loose from the other man's viselike grip. "You saw what they did to the poor bastards in that shuttle. Maybe we can distract them a little, slow them down, buy a little time."

"Sure, ol' sport," Rico replied calmly, "like about thirty seconds, which is how long this little toy's gonna last. There's a better way."

For what seemed like an eternity but was only a fraction of a second, cold gray eyes locked with bright brown ones. Then McCade said, "Okay, Rico, say your piece, but make it damned quick."

Rico spoke earnestly as McCade listened. When the bearded man was through, McCade chuckled and said, "I'll probably be sorry, but that's just crazy enough to work. Let's give it a try. Rico, get Ven up here while I get ready."

A few minutes later he was wearing full armor and strapped into the harness of the sleek little Interceptor. He'd completely forgotten about it until Rico reminded him. It seemed like years since he'd asked Laurie to substitute it for the ship's boat, and been surprised when she'd agreed. Rico had stumbled across it during the hyperspace shift from Lakor. Looking for something to do, he'd decided to pull a maintenance check on the ship's lifeboat. Opening the lifeboat bay, he'd been surprised to find the deadly shape of a Navy Interceptor in place of the tubby little lifeboat he'd expected. McCade listened to the intercom channnel on his headset as Rico and Ven got ready. He used the time to run through the Interceptor's pre-flight program. Everything checked out, just as Rico said it would.

"All right, Sam, stand by," Rico said over the intercom.

"Remember, after Ven does his bit, we'll wait till the last second before givin' ya the go, so be ready, and don't waste any time."

"Yes, Mother," McCade said sweetly. He was answered with a snort of derision. Moments later the deception began as Ven called the Il Ronnian ship.

"This is Captain Ven commanding His Majesty's yacht, *Lakor Avenger*. Please respond." McCade almost laughed out loud at the name Zorta had bestowed on the small ship.

McCade couldn't see the video but could easily imagine the stern countenance of Commander Reez as he appeared on the com screen.

"Captain Ven, as you can see we are presently involved in an action with an Imperial Navy ship. What do you want?"

With a masterful blend of timidity and dogged determination, Ven replied: "With all due respect and my apologies for the inconvenience, sire, but His Majesty left very strict standing orders which I disobey at my peril. In the case of a naval engagement, it is His Majesty's wish to assume personal command of this ship that he might lend personal assistance to our noble allies, the Il Ronn."

McCade knew Reez wouldn't believe a word of it and he wasn't meant to. It was exactly the kind of order the real Zorta might have left to ensure his escape from potentially dangerous circumstances.

Commander Reez allowed himself an audible snort of disbelief as he replied, "I assure you, captain, that the King is in absolutely no danger. We have already destroyed one Imperial ship, disabled a second and the third will soon follow. However if you must, I suppose you must. Stand by."

McCade fidgeted in the small cockpit, checking his instruments for a third time.

"Uh-oh," Rico said.

"What's going on?" McCade demanded. He felt isolated. The muscle in his left cheek twitched.

"They just launched about ten of their Interceptors," Rico replied evenly, "which means we're in deep trouble."

"I'd say *they're* a bit shorthanded myself, boss," Van Doren's voice interjected. "All secondary weapons positions are closed up and ready."

"Royal yacht *Lakor Avenger*," came a different Il Ronnian

voice. "Permission to come alongside granted. Please dock at lock four just aft of our port solar panels. We are standing by."

So far so good, McCade thought. The plan was working. Reez had decided to be magnanimous. And why not? He was winning and could therefore afford to humor Zorta and his staff. Besides, he still needed the King and his troops to hold the War World while he went for reinforcements. Something that no doubt seemed even more important now that the Imperial Navy had also located the War World.

"Thank you, my lord," Ven replied humbly. "We are on our way."

"Understood," the Il Ronnian snapped and was gone.

McCade felt *Pegasus* bank and begin a smooth turn to intercept the Il Ronnian ship. "Stand by. . .," Rico said. "Hold, hold, hold . . . all right, he's let his screen down, we're inside, the screen's up behind us, hold, hold, all right go! Good luck, sport!"

With that the bay doors opened and the Interceptor was ejected into space and immediately left behind as *Pegasus* continued her arc toward the warship's lock.

McCade ignited his engine, felt it cut in, and banked down toward the bow of the Il Ronnian vessel. Suddenly a hard Il Ronnian voice flooded McCade's headset.

"Attention Royal yacht. Our sensors have detected an unauthorized launch of a power vessel now closing with our ship. It has five seconds to alter course or be destroyed."

"Uh-oh," Rico said. "Looks like they're on to ya, sport. We'll pull off as many as we can! Looks like there's five fighters comin' your way."

"Roger," McCade said grimly. "Here goes nothing!"

Below, the surface of the huge ship raced by. Like all of its kind, the Il Ronnian vessel had not been designed to pass through planetary atmospheres. Therefore no attempt had been made to streamline its hull. Vents, pipes, weapons platforms, turrets, launch tubes and much more formed a metal maze across the surface of the ship's hull, adding to the sense of speed as he raced toward the bow.

Ahead, five dots filled his target screen and as he watched they resolved into the form of Il Ronnian fighters. Without conscious thought, his fingers followed the deeply memprinted pattern learned years before, activating weapons systems and checking for system malfunctions. As the range closed, his hand tightened on the control stick and his thumb was poised over the trigger of his two energy cannon. The Il Ronnian fighters fired first, and quickly regretted doing so, as their heat-seeking missiles sorted out the closest and most intense heat source around, and went for it. Unfortunately for them, the closest intense heat source was their mother ship. A series of explosions along the surface of the huge vessel marked where their missiles hit.

The Il Ronnian pilots were aghast at what they had done. In a way, their mistake was quite natural. They had been trained to fight outside the mother ship's defensive screens, where a misdirected missile could explode harmlessly against the powerful defensive fields that surrounded the vessel during battle.

While their attention was still on the destruction created by their own missiles, McCade opened fire. Two of the fighters exploded, while the third, still shocked by what he'd done, and scared by the sudden destruction of the other two, dodged into a bank of cooling fins and blew up. That left two Il Ronnian fighters still out there, and unfortunately they showed every sign of being very very good. Unlike their brethren, they had realized the potential problems missiles might cause, and like McCade, were relying on energy cannon. Fortunately they missed on the first pass. One moment they were there, growing large in his target screen, and then they flashed by and were gone.

Instinctively McCade dove his Interceptor down until it was just barely skimming over the surface of the large ship. His muscles were tight and his eyes narrowed in concentration as he searched for and found his target. He knew he had only seconds before the two fighters, and maybe more, would be on his tail again, and this time they might not miss. It was just ahead. A raised area, just behind the bow, crowned with a thicket of sensors and other gear. In the center of the area was an open platform on which the Il Ronnians could land the skeletal maintenance craft used to perform repairs on the ship. That was where he planned to land. If he succeeded, he'd be sitting right on top of the control room, which contained the ship's computer, navigational instruments, and of course Reez himself.

"Watch out behind you, sport! There's two of them on your tail!"

Rico's warning was punctuated by bursts of blue light as the two Il Ronnian fighters tried to nail him. Doing his best to ignore them, McCade brought the little ship into line with the landing platform, waited as long as he dared, and then killed power. He'd waited too long. The Interceptor was moving too fast. He was overshooting the platform. Desperately he hit both his retros and the tractor beams. The beams were very light, but they made the difference. As the beams locked on to the larger vessel, he felt himself jerked down to meet it.

He hit with a crash and the screech of tortured metal, carving a violent path through the forest of sensors and antennas as he did so. As the noise died away, he glanced around, surprised to be alive and unhurt. The Interceptor had come to rest half on and half off the platform. Not one of his better landings, he decided, but what the hell, you can't win 'em all.

Swiveling his head, he looked up through the cracked canopy searching for signs of the two fighters. One after another they flashed by before swooping off to return and fly by once more. McCade slumped back into his seat with a satisfied grin. Not a damn thing they could do. If they shot at him they'd hit their own ship's control center too. As he chinned the transmit switch in his helmet, he noticed the cockpit pressure had fallen to zero. Evidently the Interceptor had been holed in the crash. His suit tanks were good for two hours. Hopefully that would be enough.

"Okay, Rico. I'm in position."

"Glad to hear it," Rico said with a chuckle. "For a minute there it looked like you were gonna land *in* the control room instead of *on* it."

McCade responded with a rude noise. Rico laughed, and then adopted a more serious tone as he said, "This is Fredrico Jose Romero, Council member of the Independent World Alice, and presently in command of the ship you know as the *Lakor Avenger*. I call upon Commander Reez to surrender his ship and all personnel aboard. Failure ta do so will result in the immediate destruction o' your ship. Before you reply, Commander . . . remember there's an Imperial Interceptor armed with two nuclear torpedoes sittin' over your head. The pilot is prepared ta activate a timer which will allow him time ta escape before the torpedoes completely destroy your ship. Ya have one minute to respond."

McCade waited nervously for the Il Ronnian response. He was all too aware that there was no timer which would allow him to escape before the torpedoes detonated. The only way he could use them was to program them to explode on contact, and then fire them the ten or twelve feet that separated his launch tubes from the Il Ronnian hull. He'd win, but he wouldn't be around for the victory party. He wondered if he could do it. Finally, Commander Reez broke the silence.

"This is Star Sept Commander Reez. My officers and I accept your offer of surrender, rigid ones. We will power down and await further orders. Out."

Eighteen

As McCade stepped down onto the surface of the War World, it felt strange. He wasn't sure why. Everything seemed normal enough. A light breeze brushed his cheek, carrying with it the sweet scent of distant flowers. The warm dry air tasted good after the fetid atmosphere of the ship. But a pervasive silence cloaked everything. There were no birds chirping or insects buzzing, and as far as the eye could see, there was no movement, and aside from the destroyer slumped some distance away, no sign of life. He jumped at the sudden pinging noise as the ship's tubes started to cool. Feeling foolish, he turned to see the last of the slaves disembark under Phil's watchful eye and mill around looking curiously at their surroundings.

"Well, Phil, if we aren't back in an hour or so, you and the girls capture that destroyer and hold it against our safe return."

Phil laughed and waved a hairy paw in reply.

If the navy ensign was amused, he gave no sign of it. Ensign Peller was from the destroyer. They had grounded on the taciturn orders of the destroyer's captain, who sent them the chubby young officer as a guide, probably on the theory that Peller was the most expendable man aboard. After all, with a crippled ship to repair, the captain wasn't going to send anyone useful. And Peller certainly wasn't useful, at least to them. So far all of McCade's questions had been answered with "I don't have that information, sir," or, "I'm sorry, sir, I really wouldn't know."

As far as McCade could tell, the young officer's mind was as blank as his face.

"This way, sir," Peller said with carefully modulated politeness, and led them toward a distant structure.

McCade was struck again by the unreality of their surroundings. The unnatural symmetry of the landscape, the ensign's featureless face, and the timelessness that seemed to be part of the very air they breathed.

"It just ain't right, boss," Van Doren whispered from behind.

McCade understood the marine's reluctance to raise his voice. The silence was oppressive. He felt Sara's hand slip into his. As they walked hand in hand across the slick surface of the huge spaceport, they were awed by their own visions of what it had once been like. From its size, hundreds of ships must have grounded at once. The planet's name suggested huge war fleets, yet their surroundings held none of the grim oppressiveness common to the military installations they knew.

Come to think of it, where were the weapons emplacements, fortifications, and other military paraphernalia which should be all over the place? Why call it the "War World" if it had nothing to do with war? The silent gantries and clusters of support equipment lining the edge of the spaceport gave no answers.

"Where're we headed?" Rico asked with forced casualness.

McCade turned and shrugged. "Your guess is as good as mine, Rico. Mr. Peller here says our presence has been requested. He didn't say by who."

If the young officer heard McCade's comment he gave no sign. Eventually they approached a massive arch of shiny red stone. Centered under the arch, a high wide door stood open in silent invitation, the darkness beyond it providing no hint of what might lie in wait, but its huge size suggesting a heavy

flow of traffic. As they neared it, McCade saw it was flanked
by metal plates set into the stone.

Each was covered with writing in a language he hadn't
seen before. Or had he? He stopped and dredged his memory
for a connection. Then it came. Bridger's plate. The one he
called the "Directory." The plate in front of him and the in-
scriptions which covered it looked exactly like the one Bridger
had found on his artifact world.

The rest of the group had followed Peller through the door
and were waiting inside for McCade to catch up. As he hurried toward them, he considered the implications of what he'd
just discovered. In retrospect, Bridger's discovery was truly
amazing. He'd been right all along. His metal tablet *had* been
a directory.

A directory to various artifact worlds, complete with coordinates. A simple road map for a long-vanished race. Driven
by his hatred and deepening insanity, Bridger had picked the
one that seemed to meet his need. The War World. Joining the
others, McCade shook his head to Sara's silent question. He
didn't want to share his thoughts with Ensign Peller. The
game was not over and he couldn't tell yet where the advantage lay.

They followed Peller down a short hall which suddenly
widened into a huge chamber that once could have been a
lobby. Rows of parked ground cars, tractors and power pallets
of Imperial manufacture filled most of it. McCade found that
intriguing, since it suggested the navy had been in residence
for some time. Long enough to need ground transportation and
to have had it shipped in. He was reminded of the freighter
still in orbit above.

After climbing into an open staff car, they rode in silence
through the enormous corridors and halls, all of which shared
the same dim, artificial light. It had a warm glow, suggesting
a preference for orange or red light. Occasionally they passed
giant halls filled with seats never intended to accommodate a
human body. McCade noticed they were narrower than human
equivalents, with higher backs and longer seats, suggesting
tall, thin beings with long, spindly legs.

There were hundreds of side rooms, both large and small.
From glimpses of these chambers, McCade saw that while a
few were filled with unidentifiable objects, most were bare,

though it appeared they hadn't always been that way. Empty pedestals, display cases, and shelves spoke of things no longer there.

The ground car turned a corner to enter a large, circular room. In it a huge, three-dimensional star map dominated all else, suspended somehow in midair, glittering as billions of miniature stars and planets wheeled through intricate paths, acting out a dance as old as time itself. While probably intended to merely reflect the natural movements of suns and planets, it managed to be much more, a work of art, a living sculpture. Circular seating surrounded it and reached up into darkness on every side.

As they climbed out of the car, their eyes were drawn to the map and its stately movements. Where had they gone, those who conceived and created this? What had happened to a race capable of such learning, architects of an entire planet, creators of such beauty?

"Beautiful, isn't it?" Swanson-Pierce said, stepping out of the shadows, into the light. His eyes too were locked on the beauty that swirled above. "I thought you'd like to see this." Tearing his eyes away from the map and turning to McCade and his people, Swanson-Pierce said, "Well, Sam, I see you've managed to indulge your weakness for dramatic violence once again."

"Lucky for you I did, Walt," McCade replied, hiding his surprise behind a cigar. "Otherwise you would have wound up as the best-dressed specimen in some Il Ronnian exobiology lab."

"I must admit we weren't expecting company, at least not so soon," the naval officer replied, strolling toward them. "But I will take this opportunity to thank both you and your companions. Hello, Section Leader Van Doren. Good to see you. Council Member Romero. You've played a critical role in all this. Thank you. And this must be none other than Sara Bridger. We were introduced many years ago, Council Member, but I doubt you remember that. I was pleased to learn of your survival."

Sara extended her hand. "Of course I remember. You've done well, Captain. I remember my father saying you were a very promising young officer."

Taking her hand, Swanson-Pierce executed a formal half-bow. "You are too kind, madam. I had great respect for your father and his death saddened me."

"Thank you," Sara said simply, "but it had to be."

"Yes," Swanson-Pierce replied. "It had to be. Come, you may find the seating none too comfortable, but it's all we have. I'm sorry I can't at the moment offer refreshments."

"Which brings us to a very interesting question," McCade said, shifting in his seat and examining a cigar with care. "How did you find out her father *was* dead? Or that she was alive for that matter?"

"Quite simply, actually," Swanson-Pierce answered. "Major Van Doren told me. Under the cover of weapons practice, he's been sending off message torps on a regular basis."

McCade swore, turning toward Van Doren. The big marine shrugged sheepishly. "Sorry, Sam. . . . For whatever it's worth, they were good reports."

Turning back to Swanson-Pierce, McCade said, "Congratulations, Walt. I should have known. I figured Laurie was your watchdog, while actually there were two."

"And a good thing too," the naval officer said, smoothing an imaginary wrinkle from his right sleeve. "Lieutenant Lowe's true loyalties were something of a surprise, and I'm sure, in retrospect, you'll agree that Major Van Doren came in handy from time to time."

"Granted," McCade replied. "But why, Walt? I mean why go through this whole charade? It's obvious you already knew where the War World was."

Swanson-Pierce was silent for a moment as he perched on the armrest of an alien chair. He looked at each one of them before he answered.

"Time, Sam. The answer is time. This 'charade' as you call it bought us some time. To understand why that's important, you must realize that, in most respects, I told you the truth from the very start." The naval officer held up his hand to still McCade's unuttered objections.

"Yes, yes, I'll admit I didn't tell you everything we knew, however; the fact remains that what I did tell you was mostly the truth. As you know by now, Captain Bridger finally managed to decode his so-called 'Directory,' and came up with a list of artifact worlds plus coordinates for each. On that list he found one called the 'War World.' We kept an eye on him, but frankly we didn't think he could manage to get away. By the time we realized our mistake, it was too late."

Swanson-Pierce looked at Sara and shrugged apologetically. "By then of course he was no longer sane. He became fixated on the War World as a weapon of vengeance. He imagined it to be a world dedicated to war, an arsenal which he could use to destroy the enemy which had robbed him of his wife, his daughter, and his career. With it he could destroy the pirates. If doing so meant giving that arsenal, plus his expertise, to the Il Ronn, then so be it, for he saw the pirates as the greater threat."

The naval officer gestured at their surroundings. "As you can see, his vision of the War World was not entirely correct."

"But not entirely wrong either," McCade said.

The other man nodded.

"It was a museum, wasn't it?" McCade asked.

Swanson-Pierce smiled. "Good for you, Sam. I'm glad to see there's a cultured side to your personality. Yes, this whole planet is what we would consider a museum. A museum dedicated to war. The funny thing is, we can't figure out if it was built to glorify war, or to warn against it. The displays we found here could be interpreted either way. Which you see depends on your own attitude.

"In any case our experts say it was probably just part of a network of such planets, each dedicated to a particular subject, or area of interest, although most were probably natural, rather than artificial like this one. There's even the possibility that this entire worldlet is a converted battleship."

McCade tried to imagine a battleship the size of a small world. The very idea was mind boggling.

"So now you're stripping it of whatever knowledge and power you can." Sara's voice was icy.

"True enough," Swanson-Pierce replied calmly. "Although in truth the process is almost complete. It will be, as soon as we finish loading the freighter you were kind enough to save. And, for what it's worth, we've learned a great deal. Like most military museums, this one contained endless displays of what the curators considered to be antique weapons and other related gear. Needless to say much of it was quite new to us, and I might add, quite useful. Little items like the original design for a hyperdrive, for example." The naval officer smiled sardonically, enjoying the impact of his words.

"Hyperdrive?" McCade said in amazement. "I thought it was invented back during the civil war." He knew that in the hands of the man who would later declare himself "Emperor," it had proved the key to winning the war, and had later become the foundation of the Empire.

"As a student of naval history," Swanson-Pierce replied, "you'll remember an admiral named Finley."

McCade thought back to his Academy days. "Finley? The one they call the Father of the Navy?"

"The same," Swanson-Pierce agreed. "As it happens Finley's rise to that lofty rank was fueled more by luck than brave determination and brilliant service. It seems that as junior lieutenant, Finley commanded a small scout assigned as part of the escort for a supply convoy. The convoy and its escort were ambushed and nearly wiped out. With his two-man crew dead, and badly wounded himself, Finley tried to head for the nearest friendly planet. He never got there. Instead he stumbled onto this planet. It was pure blind luck. But luck that served the human race well."

"Served the Empire well, is more like it," Sara snorted.

Swanson-Pierce shrugged and smiled disarmingly. "I understand the way you feel. However, keep in mind that we're talking about something as fundamental to our present existence as hyperdrive. You'll recall that when Finley landed here, we didn't have one. And all the evidence suggests that the Il Ronn, who shortly thereafter made their existence known to us, did. In fact most experts agree they were substantially ahead of us in all areas of technology, at first contact."

Swanson-Pierce examined his immaculate fingernails critically, and then looked up meaningfully.

"So," he continued, "if Finley hadn't managed to patch up his ship, and limp back with the coordinates of this planet, I think it's fair to say that instead of our present standoff with the Il Ronn, we would now be their slaves, a circumstance none of us would enjoy. I might also add that it was hyperdrive, after all, which made possible the colonization of planets like Alice. So while the knowledge gained here did help establish the empire you despise, it also made possible the rather chilly freedom you relish on Alice."

Sara was silent as McCade dropped his cigar on the floor and crushed it out with his boot.

"So," McCade said, "the Empire's been systematically looting this place for years. How many of the Empire's so-called 'scientific discoveries' were really found right here?"

"Some," the naval officer replied distastefully as he watched McCade smear the remains of the cigar under his toe. "But by no means all. Although I'll admit some have been spin-offs of the artifacts found here. But, as you saw on your way in, that's pretty much over now. Oh we've got lots of stuff to study, and no doubt we'll make more discoveries, but time's running out. You asked if there's a point to all this. Well there is. By using the knowledge found here, by keeping the source of that knowledge secret, by pitting the pirates against the Il Ronn, we've managed to buy some time. Time to achieve parity with the Il Ronn."

"What about the other worlds listed on my father's Directory?" Sara asked suspiciously. "Are you looting those too?"

"Unfortunately the answer is no," Swanson-Pierce answered patiently. "We've investigated hundreds of them without finding anything like this," he said, gesturing to their surroundings. "Many of the planets listed turned out to be among those already discovered by accident. Others were new to us, but no more productive than the other artifact worlds already known. This world was evidently a fluke. Because it's artificial and self-repairing it has been able to defy the effects of time. Again, we aren't sure if it was built for this purpose, or converted from another use. In any case, we haven't found anything else like it."

Swanson-Pierce smiled. "I'd say that's more up to you, and those like you, than it is to us. Anyone who really thinks it through soon realizes the future lies with planets like yours, rather than with the fat, complacent inner worlds. Already you have secret governments and are starting to form loose interplanetary ties."

Sara started to object, but Swanson-Pierce held up a restraining hand. "Don't bother to deny it. Give our intelligence people a little credit. As I was saying, you've started to organize. Who knows what final form that organization will take? Another confederation? An Empire? Something new? It's hard to say . . . but, whatever it is, it will replace the present order."

"Has anyone notified the Emperor of all this?" McCade asked with a raised eyebrow. "He'll probably want to update his résumé."

"Oh I think his job's safe for quite a few years yet," Swanson-Pierce replied, tugging on a cuff. "As is mine. Keep in mind I'm talking about the long run. But if the Emperor were here, I think he'd agree with what I've said. He's not a stupid man. Of course there are stupid men and women, many employed by the Empire, all of whom would not agree. Those who benefit most from a system don't like to envision its destruction."

For a moment there was silence all around. McCade finally broke it. "So what about us? There's a shipload of Il Ronnian prisoners in orbit up there." He gestured toward the ceiling.

Swanson-Pierce regarded him with pretended surprise.

"Prisoners? You must be mistaken, Sam. Prisoners imply armed conflict, which in turn suggests war. And we aren't at war with the Il Ronn. If we were, we might very well lose. No, I'm afraid there's been a terrible mistake. We'll apologize, they'll apologize, we'll remove the radio control unit you put on those torpedoes, and everyone goes home happy."

"Except the crew of the shuttle they destroyed," McCade said.

"And except for the pilots of those fighters you blew out of existence," the other man countered dryly. "Plus any personnel lost when their own missiles hit. No, I think it's about even. With that in mind, Council Member Romero, perhaps you'd be so kind as to contact their commanding officer, what's his name, Reez? Explain that there's been a terrible mistake. He'll understand. I'd do it myself, but I'd rather stay in the background, if you don't mind."

Rico nodded his agreement.

"Well I guess that about wraps it up then, Walt," McCade said. "I can't say it's been a pleasure, but that's life. I assume you'll clear my title to *Pegasus?*"

The naval officer nodded. "Who knows, Sam, we might even throw in a bonus. Where do we send it?"

McCade looked at Sara. She smiled and he saw the future reflected in her eyes.

"Send it to Alice, Walt. . . . From what you said, that's where the action's going to be."

As Swanson-Pierce extended his hand, McCade saw something come and go in his eyes. Something that just might have been envy.

They left him there, hands folded behind his back, staring up at the map of a long-forgotten empire, dreaming of what had been, and what was yet to be.

On the surface again, McCade stopped and turned to face Van Doren. Try as he would, he couldn't find any anger at the other man's deception. "Thanks for everything, Amos."

The marine's huge fist tightened around his own. Amos smiled from beneath bushy brows. "Anytime, Sam. You take care out there. Save me a place. Who knows . . . I can retire in a few years, if I live that long."

"You'd better!" Sara said fiercely, hugging Van Doren's huge frame.

"That's right, sport," Rico said, coming up behind them. "We're always short o' bozos with more muscle than brains!"

As the two men gripped hands in one last trial of strength, McCade looked up toward there the Il Ronnian ship orbited high above. In a few minutes Rico would place the com call to Commander Reez. After a brief diplomatic ballet, Lif's Lakorian troops would be off-loaded onto the surface of the War World to await transportation home, and the armorers from the destroyer would go up to disarm the torpedoes which still stood guard over the Il Ronnian battleship's control room.

To the Il Ronnian's surprise, King Zorta would not be found aboard their ship. Perhaps he was killed when the missiles struck. Or maybe he attempted to reach his yacht in space armor, and being inexperienced, failed. In any case they wouldn't spend much time worrying about it now that Zorta's usefulness had come to an end.

The Lakorian troops would return home to find King Lif on the throne, the relieved populace telling of Zorta's death or imprisonment. They might for a while tell confusing stories of an imposter who fooled everyone and then disappeared without a trace. But who would care?

That, however, wouldn't help the Il Ronnians, who might never learn that their commanding officer was really a Treel. After all he'd been through, it had taken McCade awhile to figure it out. But something about the Il Ronnian surrender had bothered him from the first. It had come too easily, too quickly, but it was more than that. Then it hit. Reez had said,

"My officers and I accept your offer of surrender, rigid ones!"

Only the Treel talked like that. Somehow the strange little alien had killed Reez, gotten rid of his body, and taken his place. He knew Walt wouldn't approve . . . but so what? McCade wondered what the Treel would do. Would he destroy the ship, and himself with it? Or would he be satisfied with killing Reez, and continue to impersonate him, perhaps for years, waiting for a time and place in which to more fully avenge the extinction of his race.

There was no way to know. But over the years, McCade would often think of old Softie, and chuckle to himself.